7 SONS

OF SIN

Tammy Teigland

Other titles by

Tammy Teigland

Stranger in the Night series:

A Stranger in the Night

Taken

Coming 2013

Zephyr's Kiss

To contact Tammy Teigland, or to be placed on a mailing list to receive updates about new releases, visit her website:

www.tammyteigland.com

Published May, 2012

I want to thank all those who took the time to confer with me for certain aspects of this book.

My thanks and appreciation go out to those men and women who work diligently everyday to keep our communities safe. For the Gurnee Police Department, your graciousness and accessibility has been instrumental. To Martin Deperte and Carlos Hevia, you have revived my enthusiasm and have given me a renewed outlook on police work.

Thank you, J.C. Smith! You are incredibly creative and talented; you have done it again! I love the cover.

I want to thank Dave Schad for lending some humor, and allowing me to use your story and run with it. You have been a great sport.

Mary Sutherland, with your combined research and support, you've helped to create a strong interest in this story. Thank you for everything!

To my confidants and other partners in crime...Eva Bair, Becky Bair, Greg Garofalo, Steve Kramer, Linda Teigland and Susan Seefeld (a.k.a. Mom) I am eternally grateful for all the time you've spent being my sounding boards, editors and for keeping me on track. I know it was not easy!

Once again, I find myself blessed with wonderful friends and family who support me and encourage me to write.

For my husband, Mike, you allow me to entertain my adventurous endeavors, thank you!

Enjoy!

1

"It all started 3 years ago. I had graduated from college and was doing my second internship with Paul Richter, the architect I am working with now. My boyfriend at the time was extremely jealous of Paul and all the time we were spending working together."

"I quit early one night to surprise Derrick at the bar he frequented. That's when I saw him with *her*. He had been cheating on me. I was so hurt and angry. I didn't confront him then; instead, I had turned to my best friend, Pete, and told him all about it."

"A few days later I saw a picture in the newspaper of the woman he had been with. It said she had been found raped and murdered. I told Pete I was going to confront Derrick about it, but he told me not to. He told me to wait until he could go with me, but of course I didn't listen. I was too angry, and I guess I was naive to think I could question Derrick about it on my own - although I didn't think he had anything to do with her rape or murder, I just thought...I don't know what I thought. I was too hurt."

"I was so wrong about Derrick! He did rape and kill that woman, and when I confronted him about it...he snapped."

Katie was numb, remembering back to that horrific day hurt just as much now as it did then. Some how she learned to distance herself enough to retell it. She turned her gaze out the window to the snow majestically falling in soft fluffy flakes.

She continued to tell her story, "Derrick almost killed me that day. He beat me and...forced himself..." She swallowed hard, "Derrick *raped* me after I was so broken, I couldn't fight back." Katie took pause in her story and took a deep breath.

"I was lucky that day. I was lucky because Pete showed up. He came in just after Derrick was finished with me. As he was choking the life from me, Pete chased Derrick out. He saved me that day. If it weren't for Pete...I *know* Derrick would have killed me." Katie quietly reflected, consuming the still raw pain of it all.

"After my body had healed, I just could not take it anymore. I couldn't get past the fact that someone I thought I loved had betrayed me like that. People were starting to talk, and I needed to leave. I had to get away, so I could start over...I needed a fresh start. I left my job, my old life and moved to Burlington. I found a quaint little old farmhouse, and got a job as a cocktail waitress at the Brick Yard, a popular bar in town. It was my fresh start. Well, except for my friend BJ, well her name's Billie Jo, but we call her BJ; she knew what had happened to me. She and I have been friends since high school. BJ was already out this way, so I got her a job at the bar, too. We would have each other's backs, ya know?"

Katie allowed herself to smile, "That's when I met Cal, a detective with the Burlington PD. There was just something about him. We hit it off, and things were going well, *really* well." Katie looked down at her hands folded in her lap, and then stared back out the window to watch the falling snow.

"Except, things started to happen to me; I thought I was losing my mind! A man by the name of Scott Warren was breaking into my house. He had lived there previously and kept a stash of drugs and cash in the attic. We found out he had come back in the middle of the night to get whatever it was - out of the attic."

"Then the new bouncer, Eddie Landers, started stalking me. He had even drugged me before I left work, so he could break into my house and do God knows what!"

Katie started to wring her hands, as she continued, "He later admitted he killed Scott to keep him away from me.

Because of all these things, I hadn't confided in Cal like I should have. Instead, once again I turned to Pete, and he came to stay with me. Eddie of course tried to kill him, too. Thank God, Pete is okay."

"At first, I had pushed Cal away, but I soon realized I loved him, and if I was ever going to find any real happiness, I needed to tell him *everything*. I was not sure if my secret would scare him away or not, but I took the chance anyway. Let's face it...that is some pretty messed up baggage to share."

Katie's eyes welled up as a smile spread across her face, "He didn't run. Cal stayed by my side." She gave herself a moment thinking back to that night. "He's actually the one who caught Eddie, and put him away." A single salty tear ran down Katie's cheek, "Cal had recently proposed to me, and I've since moved in with him at his place."

Doctor Reynolds interrupted, "How did you feel about leaving what would be considered *your* place, *your* sanctuary and moving into Cal's?"

Katie threw up an almost angry brow, "Cal has been wonderful. He never says it's *his* house! He always calls the Victorian *ours*! And that's how I look at it, it's *our* home. I feel very comfortable there with Cal."

Katie's expression suddenly became somber, "We were happy until Eddie escaped from Waupon Prison, and came after me again."

Katie had felt the anger building from deep down and in the next breath there was no controlling it. "That bastard had the balls to wait for Cal to leave for work and then took me, from *our* home! He took me to some shack out in the middle of the woods up in Wautoma, Wisconsin. It was obvious he had planned this entire thing before Cal put him away!" Her green eyes showed a flash of fury as she continued. "He had the place stocked with all the things I used. Did you know that *bastard* chained me to the bed? He thought he was going to *keep* me! Like I was his for the taking!"

Katie got quiet, "I had gotten very sick, very fast while he had me. He must have cared for me in his own sick, twisted, and sadistic way."

Once again Doctor Reynolds interrupted, "I'm curious; you said he 'cared for you', in what way do you mean?"

Katie was getting frustrated with Doctor Reynolds. It was hard enough for her to retell her experience, but this lady kept interrupting. Katie tampered down her temper, and gave a long sigh, but almost came out as a growl. "*Look*, it means what it means. I was sick, and even though he knew the authorities were looking for him *and* me, he still ventured out to steal some medicine in town to try to help me. What would *you* call it?"

This time, the doc backed off, "Fair enough...continue, please."

Looking back down at her hands, Katie fidgeted with her fingers. She tried to regain some composure, and then said in a low soft tone, "Once again I was very lucky. Cal found me." Even though she fought it, Katie's eyes watered and the tears gently rolled down her cheeks. She had to take a moment, "I had no idea the police had the shack surrounded."

She quickly met her counselor's gaze, "Oh, I forgot to tell you about Duane Jackson, the rapist who escaped with Eddie. Eddie actually protected me from being raped by him. He snapped Duane's neck, killing him just like that!" She said as she snapped her fingers. "That's when I ran. I had no idea where I was or where I was going. I only knew I had to get out of there and get as far from him as I could. It all happened so fast, with the fighting and the snow, and wind, it was all too surreal."

Glancing to Dr. Reynolds and then back down to her fidgeting hands, "I didn't *see* anything or *hear* anything, until out of no where I was knocked to the ground with such force, my face hit the snow." Katie became quiet again.

Her tears flowed a little faster, "I didn't know what happened. I just remember hearing gunfire and then a scream. Apparently, the scream was mine. There was someone holding me down, and blood. I remember the blood."

Katie dabbed at her tears with a tissue. "Pete was there. I heard him talking to me, and another man, Officer Randy O'Brien, was there too. He and Pete were..." Katie gave a heartbreaking pause. "It was Cal. Cal saved my life, but he was the one who got shot. Eddie was shooting at *me*!"

Taking a moment, Katie collected her thoughts before she continued, while it was still fresh in her mind. Her heart raced thinking about it.

The counselor asked, "What happened to Eddie?"

"Eddie? Eddie is dead. He won't be coming after me anymore."

Then the counselor asked, "What happened to Cal?"

"Cal took the bullet for me, but he's doing well." Katie's face lit up. "He's doing really well."

*

Katie ended another session with her counselor. Cal had insisted on it. With everything she had been through she needed to talk to someone.

Cal had been waiting for her in the lobby and beamed when she came down. To everyone, she was Katie, or Red, even lovingly known as Freckles, but to Cal she would be forever, his Kate. He greeted her with a one-armed hug. "How'd it go?"

"Good, I guess."

"Thank you, Honey." Cal said as he kissed her on the forehead.

"For what?"

"For agreeing to talk to someone."

It had snowed quite a bit while she was in her session. A fresh blanket of fluffy white covered the ground, giving a blank canvas for a new day. Katie thought how beautiful it was to cover up the ugliness in the world.

Katie's determination not to sit around and feel sorry for herself drove her to be more...to do more. Refusing to wear the label of a victim on her sleeve, Katie was anxious to throw herself back into the research project with Paul.

There was no way she was going to dwell on her horrific experiences. She had a very positive attitude, and one that would reflect upon everyone around her.

On the outside she was strong and confident, but she still struggled with inner fears that she kept from Cal. She felt blessed to have Cal in her life. He was her savior in body and soul. He was good for her and whether she knew it or not, she was good for him, too.

2

Cory Walker worked for a local tile-roofing company with his friends, Jim, and Joe Reid. Unlike Cory, the Reid brothers were not living with their father; they had to pay their own bills. Cory was feeling a bit lazy, and decided it was too cold to work out in the snow, so while they went to work, he hung back to play hooky.

The large docile 19-year-old kid plopped himself down in an old tattered beanbag chair to eat Cheetos and play Tetrus on the large flat screen TV he stole from the Pioneer's Inn back in December.

Washing down the cheesy puffed snacks with a 2-liter bottle of Mountain Dew, Cory was completely shocked when the door flung open, and three of the meanest bikers he had ever seen stepped in.

"What the hell, man!" Cory yelled.

"You - Cory?" Inquired Adam Knox, the 7 Sons of Sin's road captain and enforcer.

"Why?"

With that, Luke Michaels, the other enforcer for the gang grabbed Cory by the arm, and forcibly stood him up out of his beanbag chair.

Cory was confused. In his panic he rapidly spewed questions, "What's happening? What did I do? What's going on?" He was a big guy; however, these bikers scared him. There was no way he was going to fight them.

The most daunting of the three bikers, was Brock Miller, the sergeant at arms for the gang. His dark presence stood quietly by the door as Luke and Adam vehemently escorted Cory out of Nick Bolen's crash pad.

Brock unlocked the trunk to his spotless red 1976 Cadillac Fleetwood. He raised the heavy trunk's lid, and barked at Cory, "Get in!" with a cold indifferent expression.

Wearing only a concert T-shirt and jeans, Cory stood in the bitter cold, fearfully gazing into the large empty void.

Cory realized there was no use fighting back, especially after Brock flashed him his gun. Fearing for his life he reluctantly crawled into the trunk of the Caddy. "But why?" he pleaded. "Why are you doing this? I don't even know you. I didn't do anything!"

Brock took one last look at the beseeching over grown adolescent. "Kid, you did somethin' to somebody or we wouldn't be here!" With that he slammed the trunk shut.

As a rule, Brock had no qualms about cleaning up after his brothers. The guys he disposed of were bad men, dreads on society; no one would miss the scum he killed. This was different...this did not feel right. This was just a kid hanging with the wrong crowd - a kid who was in the wrong place, at the wrong time.

They drove him out to the Puss 'n Boots strip club just outside of town. Alison, an exotic dancer at the club was just leaving the dressing room when she saw Brock, Adam and Luke coming up the hallway. She quickly turned back and closed the dressing room door so they would not see her.

Waiting for them to enter Manny's office, Alison slipped off her high-heeled shoes before sneaking back out into the hallway. She cautiously made her way to Manny's office door and quietly listened just outside.

Richie was seated on the couch leaning forward, resting his forearms on his knees, playing with his old Zippo lighter; weaving it in and out between his fingers. Flipping it open and slamming it shut, repeatedly. "Did you find the Walker kid?"

"Yeah, he's in the trunk. He honestly has no clue about the *ice*. What do you want to do with him?" Brock asked in a cold tone, for once hoping Richie only wanted to scare the crap out of the kid.

He slammed the Zippo closed, "I want you to play Tiddly Winks with him - what do you think I want you to do with him? If he doesn't know where the packages are, then he needs to be made an example of. I want it made clear, you don't steal from us and get away with it!" The expression on Richie's face was one of indifference. He could have been ordering a tap beer, instead of a hit on a 19-year-old kid.

Luke being a little slow on the up take, asked, "So - you want us to kill him?"

Brock slapped Luke upside the head.

Adam furrowed his brow as he shook his head in disgust at Luke.

"What the fuck, man? I'm just making sure I understood what he's asking us to do!"

Alison heard every word. It made her sick knowing the emanate death sentence that was so easily decided. Her heart rate quickened; she had to tell somebody. Alice was scared to death, but the only one she knew she could trust was her old friend's father, Sgt. Jim Nelsen. He would believe her. She hurriedly made her way back to the dressing room before the men left Manny's office.

3

Based on Kate's traumatic experience of being abducted by Eddie, Cal anticipated her to have some difficulties readjusting. He was just so pleased to have her back home, safe. As much as he wanted to take her in his arms and make love to her, Cal knew she needed to take things slow. Kate needed to be the one to come to him. Cal loved her deeply and did his best to be the one she could turn to for whatever she needed.

Cal's shoulder would heal in a couple months, and he would be fine. However, it was Kate he was concerned with. It had already been a couple of weeks since she had come home from the hospital, and although she kept telling Cal she was fine, he knew differently.

To lie next to Kate, listening to her painful whimpers as she slept was difficult for him. Cal's heart ached. Tonight, those muted cries had turned into a night-terror.

With an increasing apprehensive moan, she cried out in pain as she fought an invisible foe.

Startling Cal, he just about jumped out of his skin. Even Hondo, their 6-month-old German shepherd leaped up, and raced to their bed-side to investigate.

Cal felt her anguish. As he gently tried to wake her, to console her, she lashed out striking him. He desperately tried to reach her, calmly speaking her name, and stroking her hair.

She felt his touch, but in her heightened state of fear, it was Eddie who was with her, not Cal. As she shot-up out of her sleep and in a panicked scream, *"DON'T!"* escaped from her lips, ringing out into the night.

Now awake and in a cold sweat, Katie was breathless even panic stricken. She looked around at her surroundings trying to get her bearings when she looked to Cal and the distress on his face; she quickly realized it was only a bad dream.

Softly he implored, "Kate?" He sat-up beside her in bed as he placed a tender arm around her.

Katie's ridged body softened with Cal's touch. She allowed herself to relax into him, and quietly sobbed.

He held her close, allowing her to let it all out.

The love she felt for Cal was what had gotten her through the kidnapping. Between her sobs, she was finally able to let go of everything she had been holding in. "I can't get rid of this feeling that I lost you that day."

"You didn't lose me, Kate. I'm right here." He tenderly kissed the top of her head.

"These dreams feel so real. I can *feel* everything. I don't mean to keep putting you through this!"

Cal swallowed hard, and clenched his jaw. As he held Kate in his arms, he rocked her back and forth in a slow rhythmic motion. "You're home, Kate. You're here with me, and that's all that matters."

"I don't know what I would do without you?"

Cal just held Kate close. He listened to not only her words but her touch.

Katie lightly stroked the caressing arm which held her. She nuzzled her face into the nape of Cal's neck. She loved his warm natural scent; bringing back pleasant thoughts of their love making in Scotland. The feel of his touch was engrained in her very essence.

She tipped her face up to meet his. Their eyes locked, searching each other's shadowed expressions, in the quiet tension of the night.

A glint of light reflected in Katie's green eyes.

Cal placed a gentle finger under Kate's chin to guide her soft lips to his. His kiss sent an electric current through to her core. Radiating from her soul, a sinuous warmth gave Kate a renewed glow.

"Cal, you know I love you...with all my heart."

"I know you do." Cal's tone was tender and loving. "And, you mean *everything* to me, Kate."

It felt good to have her back. The light easy way they had with each other was incredible. Ignoring the nagging pain in his right shoulder, Cal managed to snuggle with Kate. Her soft curves nestled into his firm toned body as they lay together.

In hushed voices they spoke only as lovers do. Intimately discussing their future together, the life they hoped to have.

"Are you sure you're ready to go back to work? I don't want you to rush into anything. Bob and Paul, both told you to take your time."

"As much as I appreciate everyone's concern, sitting around the house is driving me mad. If it weren't for Hondo keeping me busy..."

Hondo heard his name and raised his head.

Kate rested her head against Cal's bare chest, listening to the sound of his heartbeat while tracing his well-defined abs with the delicate touch of her finger.

Cal gently stroked Kate's arm and shoulder enjoying the feel of her smooth skin and caressed her supple curves. Their conversation died down as they just enjoyed each other's touch. Cal never again wanted to feel the emptiness he felt when she had disappeared.

In Cal's arms Katie felt safe. It was not long before he felt her body give in to sleep. "Sweet dreams, my Love!" He whispered, as he leaned in to softly kiss her cheek.

Her light sent was heavenly. Admiring the beautiful woman he held, he carefully brushed away the tendril of hair that had fallen across her lovely face. He glanced back to the clock beside the bed. It was already 3 a.m., and he was wide awake.

He thought about all they had been through in their short relationship. Every time they had a moment of bliss, life seemed to rear its ugly head and pull the rug out from under them, testing how much more they could endure.

Remembering once again, the dark emptiness he felt when Kate was taken from him. In truth Cal wanted to know every little detail and yet nothing at the same time. He knew all he needed to. He read the reports, he spoke to the doctor, but he never asked Kate what happened, and never would.

It did not matter. She was in his arms and here to stay.

4

It was the nights that were difficult for Katie. She had trouble sleeping and when she did, she had vivid nightmares. Her cries in the middle of the night haunted Cal; they were a painful reminder of what she had been through.

Although the last few nights had been the roughest for both Katie and Cal; something changed last night. She had a reoccurring dream about the 480 Milwaukee building. Although her dream had felt solid, she had slept well, almost peaceful.

This morning when she awoke, she remembered her dream with such detail. There was depth, and vitality to it. Twice she dreamt she had walked down a long dark hallway aligned with boarded up doors. This was not just any hallway; it seemed to be made of brick. Her attention was always drawn to the end of that hall. She would almost reach the last boarded up door when she would hear a woman crying. Katie always turned toward that sound to find one door in particular, would have an eerie glow leaking out from behind it.

Katie had been consumed by this brick building with its chipped white paint. Something was drawing her back to the abandoned building she had been researching before she was taken. Whether it was curiosity or obsession, it did not much matter. Katie was determined to discover everything there was to know about this building.

Paul Richter, Katie's boss, and mentor, was very supportive of her. After her kidnapping ordeal, he fully understood she needed time. Paul told her there was no rush and to come back when she was ready. Only, Katie felt a strong need to get back to work.

*

Cal watched Kate from across the kitchen table. A ray of sun painted vibrant streaks of glistening amber in her auburn hair. Hoping for that brilliant smile of hers to flash him a "good morning" perk; however, Cal knew she was deep in thought by the way she held her coffee mug, rolling it back and forth in both hands. Her gaze fixed on the rich dark liquid it held.

Cal took a sip of his coffee and then asked, "Is everything okay, Kate?"

Shifting her gaze to Cal, "Yeah, everything is good."

"You want to talk about it?"   He was a quick study and had learned how to read Kate.

Kate's eyes softened as her lips formed the beautiful warm smile he was hoping for.

"Really, I'm good! Just thinking about that building I'm researching."

"How so?"

It was good to see that smile of hers.

"Doesn't it seem odd to you, that someone would only maintain the exterior of a building, and never do anything to its interior since the 1930's? I mean, it's just too odd that someone would pay taxes on an empty building all these years!"

"How can *that* be?"

She had now even piqued Cal's curiosity.

"*That's* what I'm going to find out. Billie and I found an entrance to the basement that had been paneled over. That's the other question, why would anyone want to conceal the basement?"

Cal smiled, knowing how driven Kate was to dive right back into this research project. "Sounds like you have a mystery to solve!" He gave her a little wink, and kissed her as he got up to leave for work. He looked down into her brilliant yet mischievous green eyes, framed her lovely face with his hands and said, "I love you."

Placing her hands over his, "I love you, too!"

He kissed her again with wanting lips. She returned his kiss with matched enthusiasm, locking her arms around Cal's neck as she wound her fingers through his hair. He so desired her, and if he was not already running late for work, he could have easily been talked into a morning tryst.

One last loving yet firm kiss good–bye, "I want you to be careful, and try not to find trouble today", he said with a smile and turned to rushed out.

"And *you* play nice!" She quipped back in kind.

Hondo was used to Cal racing off to work. She looked down at her dog as he lay on the floor next to Katie's chair basking in the sunlight coming in through the large window. "Are you sure you're not part cat?"

For now, things were going well, Katie was happy. They were not quite back to where they were before Eddie took her, but they were working on it, together.

Katie's cell rang, on her way out the door interrupting ambitious thoughts of her investigation. The caller ID told her it was Pete.

Pete had been her best friend since the 5th grade. They were extremely close; he was more like a big brother, and had an uncanny knack for knowing when she was in distress and needed him the most.

She answered with an up beat, "Good morning, Pete!"

"G'morning, *Sunshine*!" He had always called her that. "How are you doing?"

"I'm good." She said without meaning to sound distant

"What's wrong?"

"Nothing's wrong…I'm just not sleeping all that well."

"Nightmares again?"

"You could say that."

"Have you told Cal?"

"Cal knows, and he worries. I see it in his eyes."

"Hun, that's because he loves you and probably doesn't know what to do for you. Have you been keeping your appointments? You *need* to talk about it."

"I know - I am."

"*But?*"

"What makes you think there's a *but*?"

"How long have I known you? There's always - a *but*!"

"It's not just the dreams about Eddie. I think I've discovered something about that building I'm researching. There is more to it some how."

"How so?"

Katie hesitated.

"*Kate?*"

"I'm not quite sure, there is just this feeling I have that there is so much more to this building…I can't put my finger on it, yet. I want to learn as much about it as I can before I say anything."

Pete got the same unsettling feeling as he did 8-months ago when Katie had a stalker breaking into her house. "This can't be good!"

"Why do you always assume …?"

He quickly interrupted, "Because, I *know* you! You have this way of finding trouble."

"*Fine*, point taken! I'll tell you this much, we found a hidden entrance to the basement in that building, and the past few nights I've had some bizarre dreams about this building. Today, we are going to open up all the doors that have been sealed shut to find out what the hell has been hidden all these years!"

"Whoa – whoa – whoa! *We*?"

"Yeah, BJ is helping me."

"Billie Jo? You and Billie are snooping around an abandoned building that has a hidden basement and breaking open doors to rooms that have been sealed up for years? Yeah – that doesn't sound like trouble at all!"

"I caught the sarcasm, Pete! There isn't anything in the basement, just wine racks. But - there is something about those closed-up rooms that must be wearing on my subconscious. Otherwise, why would I be dreaming about them?"

"I don't like it, Kate! I *know* you - and *you* already sound obsessed with this building. You should tell Cal what you've found? Don't treat this as some nuclear secret. I would feel a lot better if you shared what you found with Cal."

"Pete - I already told Cal about the basement. But, if I promise to keep Cal informed, on all future findings, will you be satisfied?"

Pete let out a long growl, and then sighed. He knew Katie all too well. "Hun, just do me a favor? Be careful!"

Katie let out a little chuckle, "I will – I promise!" she said as she rolled her eyes. That was twice this morning she was told 'to be careful'.

"I don't exactly believe you, but okay, I better get back to work. Love ya, Sis!"

"Love you, too!" She sarcastically replied, and then snapped her phone shut as she pulled into the back lot of the chipped white brick building.

*

Cal was in his office going over the Robert's case with Sgt. Nelsen when he looked up to find his mother and a very distraught woman knocking on his door.

He waved them in. "Mother?"

"Calvin, this is Mary Walker, and she needs your help."

Jim got up offering Mrs. Walker his seat in front of Cal's desk. She gladly took it. Constance remained standing, gently consoling her friend by placing her hand on Mary's shoulder and handing Mary another tissue for her tears.

"Mrs. Walker, how can we help you?"

Between sobs, Mary explained to Cal that her son, Cory, was missing. "No matter what, he'd always call me to let me know if he wasn't coming home. He had promised he'd be home for supper. That was two days ago."

Before Cal could say anything, his mother gave him the 'look'. "Calvin," she said in a strong yet tender voice. "She fears Cory has gotten himself involved with something bad." Then she stressed, "Very bad."

Cal turned his attention back to Mary Walker. "Ma'am, what makes you believe something bad has happened to Cory, and he's not just off with his friends; he *is* over 18?"

"Because, he's never *not* come home; he'd always call me to make sure I don't worry. He's a good boy. This is not like Cory. He wouldn't let me worry like this." The tears started to flow again. "A mother knows things. She feels things. Something has happened and he's not coming home, I feel it."

"Mrs. Walker, was Cory into drugs?"

"If he was, he kept it from me. But those Reid boys...those boys are trouble! I told him to stay away from them. I told him they were not really his friends. I tried to warn him about them, I really did. Whatever happened to my Cory, I bet *they* know. They know *something*!"

Cal shared a look with Jim. Instinct told Jim that whatever happened to Cory was connected to Courtney's murder as well as the break-in at Pioneer's Inn. He left the office to get things in motion.

Cal wrote out a missing persons report for Mary's son. He felt remorseful for the woman. If Cory's disappearance had anything to do with the Courtney Robert's case, she was probably correct; he was not coming home. He was already dead, but they would eventually find him.

Constance put her arm around her grieving friend. Being a military wife, Constance knew from experience that feeling one gets when a child or husband isn't returning home is usually correct. She knew Mary should not be left alone right now; and was going to need all the support she could get. As they solemnly left Cal's office, Constance turned back to give Cal an expressive heartbroken glance.

Cal had the same dreadful feeling, but hoped he was wrong.

On his way back in, Jim closed the door behind him. His expression was one of deep concern. "Do you think this has anything to do with the December break-in at Pioneer's Inn?"

"Assuming the worst...you don't kill a kid for stealing steaks. With the extra bit of info Jack dropped in our laps, obviously there was more taken than what was reported."

"We don't know that he is dead, Cal. Right now, he's only missing."

Cal shot Jim a look. "Aren't you Mr. Optimistic? Have you been paying attention to the body count? We questioned Cory on the break-in, Courtney's demise and now he's gone! Those boys are involved in something way over their heads in trouble, and too stupid to come clean about it!"

"Look, Cal...for Mary's sake I hope we find him alive, but I know the odds of that aren't very good, considering Charlie Nix and Richie Collins could be involved."

"We need to go back."

Nelsen furrowed his brow, "Back where?"

"Back over everything we know and their connection to each other. The answer to Cory's disappearance and Courtney's murder are here. And if Jack is right, it's all tied into the drugs the 7 Sons of Sin are running." Cal placed his hand on some manila case files lying in front of him.

Sgt. Nelsen blew out a long breath, "I'll round up all the usual shitheads!"

"While we're at it we should check the social networking sites. These nitwits can't stay off Facebook. Maybe we'll get lucky, and they've posted something that can help us."

*

Katie parked along side Billie, put her Jeep in neutral and set the brake. She looked up at the buildings boarded up windows, and from this angle she could see the scars from where a fire escape had once been, along with the boarded up opening for a door which had led out to the absent fire escape.

Billie impatiently tapped on Katie's window. "Are you comin' or what?"

Katie hopped out and moved to the back of her Jeep to open the back end. She pulled out a large heavy canvas bag, and headed for the white brick building with purpose.

Billie gave Katie a puzzled look as she followed her to the building.

Instead of accessing the hidden basement like Billie thought they were going to do, Katie trod up the well-worn steps. Billie marched up behind her, listening to the curious heavy clanking sounds coming from the canvas bag.

Once on the second floor, Katie turned to Billie with a mischievous gleam in her eyes and smiled.

In a cautionary tone, Billie asked, "What are we doing?"

Katie simply reached into the canvas bag she carried, pulled out a pry bar and handed it to her bewildered friend.

"Are we breaking in?" Billie asked with a quick hushed tone.

"No - we're not breaking in. I've been hired to investigate and research this building, remember? It's called field work."

Billie raised a questioning brow to Katie; she was not so sure about what they were about to do.

"Billie, how are we going to know what's behind these doors if we don't open them?"

"*Okay...?*" Billie sounded more cautious than usual.

"All we're going to do is open up these rooms, and document everything we find. Did you bring your camera?"

"Yeah, it's in here." She said as she patted the black bag that hung from her shoulder.

"Great!"

"What about the basement?"

"We'll get to it - but first I have lots of questions which need some answers, and I think we're going to find some of those answers in these rooms. If the basement was concealed, what do you think could be behind these doors?" Katie said enthusiastically.

Katie pulled out a pry bar for herself along with a hammer. She jammed the flat end in between the plywood and door jam. Then with some force she tried to pry up. When she did not get the results, she wanted she took the hammer and gave a hard 'whack' to the bent end of the bar. The nail squeaked in protest from the force of being loosened, the rest soon followed. Billie helped her remove the old sheet of plywood and set it aside.

They stood in front of a cream-colored wooden door with its antique hardware. Katie's anticipation grew as she reached out, gave the knob a turn and then pushed the door open.

Old musty air filtered out of the room.

Katie felt cheated. The room was empty.

Billie put a hand on Katie's shoulder, "Just because it doesn't look like anything is here, doesn't mean there isn't."

Katie's hopes had been dashed, but Billie was right. "Let's plug in some lights and take a look."

Billie already had the length of extension cord run with the female end in hand. Katie moved the lights into the room and then plugged them in.

Dingy, but once beautiful antique wallpaper covered the walls. The wooden floors were handsome where furniture previously stood. There was a well-worn pattern from the door to where the bed must have been. The walls held nails where pictures at one time had hung, and they could make out a darkened silhouette from the frame that had been there. The deep baseboards from an era long ago were covered in a thick layer of dust. The windows were boarded up although a faint light pierced its way in through warped gaps in the plywood that covered them; while particles of dust danced in the light beams. Billie took pictures, while Katie made notations in her notebook along with the measurements for that room. Later, Katie would draw a floor-plan from these measurements for each floor of this building.

They did not find anything interesting or unusual in this first room, so they moved on to the next room. By the time they opened the third room they had their routine down.

Each room was bare; the wallpaper for better or worse was the same, the floorboards were all the same, even the holes or marks on the walls reflected the previous room. Katie's enthusiasm was crashing quickly.

Billie could sense the let down in Katie's spirit. "Katie, do you want to break for lunch? I'm getting kind of tired, besides I'm famished!"

Katie knew this was Billie's way of offering a reprieve. "Absolutely! I think I need a break. All this dust is bothering my eyes. What do you feel like?"

"How about something hot and greasy!"

"Doug's?"

"Sounds good to me!"

*

As disappointing as Katie's first day back at the 480 Milwaukee building had been, it felt good to concentrate on something other than the four walls that had threatened to suffocate her.

This was also Katie's first night back at the Brick Yard. Although Billie had managed to handle the tables by herself, she was definitely happy to have Katie back at the bar.

The March evening air was cold and damp. Winter still had its grip and was reluctant to let go. The freezing rain brought Katie's thoughts back to that fateful day in February. As hard as she tried to push those memories from her mind, something always seemed to trigger the raw feelings attached. She shook off a chill, closed her eyes and took a deep breath before stepping into the warmth of the bar.

Erik, the doorman, as always, was the invariable overgrown teddy bear, even though it was only Katie who saw him as that. He greeted her with a large friendly hug, "We missed you, kiddo!"

"Thanks, Erik! I missed you, too." In truth she really needed that hug.

Steve happily shouted out from behind the bar, "Hey, Freckles, welcome back!"

Tanya was in a hushed private conversation with a patron and barely glanced up to see why everyone was so joyful.

"Everybody is downstairs, they'll be happy to see you, kiddo." Erik said in a jovial tone.

"Thanks, Erik! It's good to be back." Katie said with a smile as she turned to follow Billie down to the lower level.

TJ had just stepped out of the back room from changing out a keg, when he spotted Katie with Billie. He beamed, "Well - look what the cat dragged in!" His boisterous welcome brought attention to the girls.

Bob was sitting at the bar conversing with Jack and Jessica. On TJ's cue, Bob spun his stool around, "Hey, Darlin'! It's good to see *your* smiling face around here again."

"Thanks, it's good to be back!"

"Are you sure you're feeling up to it?"

"Most definitely!" Katie flashed Bob one of her honestly happy smiles.

"Good...I'm glad." Then, Bob got serious, "Now, that being said...I want you to let TJ know if *anyone* makes you feel uncomfortable - got it?"

"I got it." Kate answered with a quick glance to TJ standing at the end of the bar.

"That goes for you, too, BJ. No one...and I mean no one needs to put up with drunken assholes! I won't have it."

Billie gave a shy grin, and shared a look with Jack. She had a feeling she had been the topic of discussion at some point.

Bob was one of the nicest bosses either of them had had. He genuinely cared what happened to his employees. And for that reason, Katie wasn't quite ready to quit. She liked working for Bob. The money was good, and it was a fun place to work, usually. They had some great regular customers, too. It was going to be hard for Katie to walk away from that. These people had become like family. The research, the architecture, creating new designs all motivated her to be more than just a waitress. Working for Paul again was what she desired. Ultimately, she also knew with everything that had happened and the danger some of the patrons had brought into the Brick Yard, Cal would be more at ease if she were not working there anymore.

5

Alison Chambers, was a beautiful, long legged, curvy blonde with big blue eyes, a cute turned up button nose and full luscious lips. She also was the most popular dancer at Puss 'n Boots. She was well known for her "Alice in Wonderland" costume and the Queen of Hearts tattooed on the back of her neck.

Alice never wanted this kind of life. She aspired to go to college and make something of her life. However, just before she graduated from high school her mother had a stroke, which left her unable to care for herself. Alice did what she could to help, but it became too much for an eighteen-year-old to manage on her own. She had to put her mother in the assisted living facility, Green Gables. The only way she was able to support her mother was to sell the family home and get a job stripping. It was great money, but came with dangerous strings attached.

Puss 'n Boots, was managed by Manny Cruise, the Vice President for the 7 Sons of Sin. It was easy to run the gang's drugs through there, with the added bonus of prostitution.

Three years ago, just before the motorcycle gang's President, Richie Collins, went to jail, Richie "claimed" Alice for his own. Everyone knew that meant "hands off". Alice could not be put out for sale unless Richie wanted it. Now that Richie was out, he expected her to be "his girl". Never being told "no", Richie was determined to have her. One night, he took what he wanted from Alison, right in Manny's office. She was too scared to fight back, which probably saved her life.

After that night she hated herself, hated her life and wanted out more than anything. Her mother's care was the only thing that kept her there. Only now that she knew about

Richie's book with the mayor's name in it, she was resolute on taking it to the cops hoping that would be her ticket out. One cop in particular she would trust with her life, her old friend's father, Sgt. Jim Nelsen.

*

Puss 'n Boots was not your typical dive strip club. It was actually on the clean side if you can imagine a motorcycle gang owning such a classy joint. Even their strippers were mostly attractive young women. Women you would not think would be working in such a club, prostituting themselves or moving drugs. That was the point. Richie was smart. He did not want trash selling his product. They all feared Richie Collins, and that kept those working for him in line. When Richie was not happy - someone usually got hurt or disappeared. For the most part, these girls were owned by Richie, with no hope of ever leaving.

Tonight, was one of those nights. It did not take long before he realized Alison had gone A-WOL. Not only was she gone, but Richie found his ledger listing particular clients and their business with him, missing as well. Naturally assuming Alice took it, Richie was beyond enraged.

Charlie Nix, a.k.a. drug dealing chef from the Pioneer's Inn, was called to Manny's office at Puss 'n Boots. It was never good when he had to meet there. Manny, was a nasty piece of work. His mean mug had an ugly jagged scar running across his left eye and down his cheek. Some say his wife did it; others say it was a rival gang member. His wife had disappeared 6-years ago, and nobody seemed to know her whereabouts. He kept their daughter, Jocelyn who was now 16, close and under his overly protective supervision. She was an attractive young lady and he kept her away from the gang. Anyone associated with Manny knew to stay clear of her, or else.

Everyone knew Charlie's vicious reputation for beating the girls he was with. Although, Manny was sure he'd killed one of his girls, Courtney Roberts, Richie wouldn't let him do anything about it, just yet. Charlie screwed up and knew the hammer could fall at any moment. He had two options; run or try to work things out with the 7 Sons of Sin.

Reluctantly Charlie showed up at the strip club just in the nick of time. Two of Richie's crew were waiting at the bar to escort him back to the office. The tension was thick, so Charlie knew it was serious.

"Shut the door." Manny ground out from behind his desk. His tone was cool and direct.

The hairs on the back of Charlie's fat neck stood at attention sensing he was the fly who just got caught up in the spider's web. Before he could do what was asked of him, the door quickly slammed shut behind him making Charlie jump.

Instantly, Richie spewed an angry verbal assault directly at Charlie.

Charlie not wanting to show his obvious fear for the man, stood still, keeping eye contact with Manny.

"You owe us Charlie! It's time to pay up, you fat bastard!" Richie paused, getting in Charlie's face to take a long look into his cowardly murderous eyes.

Charlie swallowed hard, not meaning to show any reaction. He knew all too well what these guys were capable of. Since the break-in at the Pioneer's Inn, he needed to pay them for the drugs that were stolen or get the drugs back. On top of that, now Manny was holding him responsible for Courtney's death. Therefore, he knew in the end he would have to get Manny before Manny got him. Charlie turned his attention to Richie, while keeping a cautious eye on Manny's scarred face. "What do you want me to do?"

"You are going to do a little job for me. I had something taken from me and *you* are going to get it back. *You* are going to find Alice, and bring me back *my book*!"

Richie glared back at Charlie; his pugnacious demeanor flared. "And this time, you – stupid – fat - fuck" Richie gritted his teeth, "you *better not* fail!"

"Where do I start? What if I can't find her?"

"Her mother lives at Green Gables, you can start there. Understand that this book is worth more than your miserable life...ya feel me?" Richie's black soul seeped through his glaring eyes and bore down into Charlie, which left him feeling violated and cold. "Just find her, find the book and bring them *both* back here!"

Charlie knew what was asked of him. He did not have a problem roughing up the girls, but he didn't like having his head on the chopping block knowing that if he failed, he would be a dead man. This just added to his stress. Not only did he have to find Alice and get the book back, he had to find the stolen drugs and pay Richie the money he owed. With a wave of hot and cold flashes his nerves fraying, Charlie started to perspire. "I'll take care of it."

"See that you do. I'd hate to have to sever our business arrangement." Richie always meant what he said. It kept the opposition from wondering where they stood with him. It kept things – simple.

Charlie left, understanding what was expected. Getting into his old Buick he closed its large heavy door, hard. He took one last look at the neon signs that lit up the front of the club as he turned the ignition. Charlie backed out of the parking space, and then pulled out onto Highway-36.

Green Gables was one of Mayor Dunn's "good will" projects. The papers had praised him on being a friend to the elderly and those in need. The propaganda certainly helped him to get into the mayor's seat. Truth be told, the Greens' land was a highly sought-after piece of property, when a mysterious fire took the Green farm. The mayor's wife, who just happened to be in real-estate, was able to pick it up for a song when the family could not afford to rebuild. The whispered rumor was it was not an accident. This was only one of the many skeletons hidden away in Dunn's closet.

Sitting outside Green Gables, Charlie waited for Alison to leave. He did not have to wait for long. He pulled his old Buick up along side her. As she unlocked her door to her little Volkswagen Bug, Charlie lowered the passenger side window and barked, "Get in the car, Alice!" His voice was void of any emotion.

She jumped, instinct told her to run, but before she could make that decision, he pulled his Glock .9mm pointing it at her. Her large blue eyes fixed upon the gun he held in his stubby hand.

Charlie growled, sounding even more fierce, *"Don't make me ask twice!"*

That sinking feeling that she had been caught washed over Alison; it was just too easy walking out with Richie's ledger. She got in quietly and shut the door. He said nothing more to her. They drove in silence for a few minutes before Charlie turned off into the industrial park.

At that moment, Alice came to the realization that she might not ever see her mother again. Her eyes watered and tears streamed down her cheeks. She ran a nervous hand through her long blonde hair. Even if she could run, he had a gun trained on her. He was too fat to chase her, but he would not have thought twice about shooting her. A glimmer of hope ran through her mind, *"Maybe he didn't know she took it. Maybe he only wanted what she wouldn't give him. She had been raped before."* But this time she knew if Richie found out what Charlie did, *he* would suffer horribly.

Charlie parked the old rusty Buick. As he got out, the car rocked with the release from his weight. She sat still, mind racing debating her limited options. She kept thinking she should have taken her chances back at Green Gables.

He opened her door, "Get out!" he snarled angrily.

His bitter bark made her cringe. She did what she was told, hoping things were not as bad as they seemed.

Charlie grabbed her roughly by the arm and forcefully jerked her into a building under construction. She quickly looked around the enormous dimly lit cold empty space. He kicked a chair that was sitting by a makeshift desk made from plywood and saw-horses. It made a loud noise as it skidded and flipped over. He quickly pushed her forward again.

Her eyes darted back and forth to the dark recesses of the large empty space desperately looking for a possible escape.

He then picked up the chair, setting it down hard with one hand and simultaneously slammed Alison into it.

She tried to fight him off to no avail as he grabbed a fist full of her hair, jerking her head back so he could get in her face, "Shut up, Bitch!" Spittle landed on her cheek.

"Let me go!" She yelled, trying to pull away from his grasp.

He reached out for her arm, grabbing her and then with the hand that held the Glock, he back-handed her hard across the face as he sat her back into the chair. The side of her face throbbed. A deep gash dripped blood into her eye that stung. She settled down enough for Charlie to violently tape her arms to her sides with Duct tape.

Reaching down for some courage she boldly warned him, "I would not do this if I were you. I promise I won't tell Richie if you let me go now."

Charlie's ugly mouth formed a sinister grin, "Babe, he already knows."

Still holding onto some bravery, she protested, "I don't believe you. If you do anything to me - I'm going to tell Richie, it was *you*. He *will* kill you!"

Charlie only laughed. "You took something that doesn't belong to you, girly."

Instantly she knew her first suspicions where correct. They knew she had taken Richie's ledger. Sudden doom filled her conscience.

"I need that book, Alice, and you're going to tell me where it is."

"I don't have it." She said as she started to cry.

"*Yes* - you do! Manny *knows* you took it – *Richie* knows you took it."

"But I *don't* have it!"

Charlie was tired of her little games. He casually took out a pack of cigarettes, tapped it and then pulled one out. He placed it between his puffy dark lips as he returned the pack to his pocket to pull out a lighter. Charlie's pock-marked face illuminated as he lit his cigarette, casting grotesque shadows making him look even more like the monster he was.

Alice cautiously watched him, as he took a long drag turning the end into a long, hot, red burning umber. Exhaling, he blew the smoke in her face as he flicked off the ash.

The smoke stung her eyes; she closed them as she turned her face away from him.

"You're going to tell me where that book is." He took her delicate face in his dirty stubby hand and squeezed hard, "*And* if you don't…I'm going to have some fun with you until you do." He then took his cigarette, holding it very close to her left eye, enjoying the look of terror she gave him.

She jerked and struggled trying to pull her face from his grip.

His face wore an evil grin as he burned her lovely soft cheek.

She screamed out in pain.

Charlie only laughed at her. "Scream all you want, Whore! Ain't no-body gonna hear you out here!"

She cried even harder.

Charlie wore a perverse grin when he burned her the second time, and again, this time on her neck just below her ear.

Her tender flesh sizzling; she screamed out in pain, again and again, each time he burned her.

Burning her repeatedly with his cigarette did no good. Frustrated he slapped her again, splitting her lip open. Bright red blood mixed with saliva shot from her mouth.

She cried out, "I told you; I don't have the book!" The burns caused her unbearable pain, but she feared for her life more than anything. She needed that ledger. It was what was going to get her away from Richie.

Her seemingly defiant attitude was pissing Charlie off. He placed the cigarette between his lips, closed his chubby fist and punched her with such force she tipped over in the chair.

Her head bounced off the concrete floor. Grimacing at the pain, her vision narrowed.

"You stupid – little *Bitch*! Just tell me where the fucking book is!" His anger turned to rage.

She felt his boot embed deep into her rib cage, and she heard a sickening *crack!* She tried taking a breath, but the pain was too much to bear.

Frustrated and angry, he kicked her repeatedly while she was down.

The pain that radiated through her body was more than she could endure. In excruciating pain and with difficulty she tried to take a full breath...she tried to tell him she would get the book, but he wasn't listening to her.

Not now.

He was taking some perverse pleasure out of pounding on her. A true sadist, Charlie was a sexual psychopath who hated women.

Alison cried out giving him the location of the book. She was a strong woman, but she was not totally stupid either. She wanted out of the life she was living, but she wanted to live too.

Unfortunately, Charlie had tuned out her pleading voice. He could not stop himself; he enjoyed hurting her too much. While she was lying on the cold concrete floor, his full weight compressed down on her while he continued striking her face and head, her jaw, nose, eyes, and temples; continually with both fists blazing, taking out all his frustrations on her.

Frothy blood bubbled from her mouth. The only sounds she made now were gurgled. It was not until she was completely unconscious, and barely breathing did his frenzy come to a halt. He sat there straddling her, covered in her blood. He had not killed her; she was still attempting to breathe. Realizing what he had done, he panicked. He scanned the area in search for a weapon. He then spotted a stack of 2 X 4's in the corner behind him. He took one that had already been cut, walked back over to Alice's broken body, looked down at the once beautiful girl's face, and swung. He felt the blow strike her, crushing in her left temple. Bright crimson blood flowed from her, pooling all around her head. Desperate he found a roll of plastic sheeting to wrap her body in. Charlie's bulk made it difficult to maneuver her lifeless body onto the plastic. It became slick with the wet pinky red sticky fluid leaking from her crushed skull. He managed to haul her out to his Buick and place her in the trunk, and then went back in to haphazardly clean up the blood. Only to realize he was making a bigger mess.

"Oh, fuck me!" His temper flared, "Fuck – fuck - fuck!"

While he was brutally killing Alison, it had begun to sleet. The freezing rain made driving difficult. Heading west on Highway-36 he negotiated the large curve leaving town and pulled over to the side. He figured this was as good of place as any. It was just after 9:00 p.m. and not a soul was around right now. He opened the trunk. Charlie struggled to lift the broken, bloodied, lifeless girl out, only to toss her down the steep embankment. The sleet made the snow-covered incline slippery, and being wrapped in plastic, she easily slipped away into the dark.

6

A young college kid was hurriedly making his way home from Geneva. In his rush, he carelessly took the curve a little too fast for the slick road conditions. A doe jumped out from the ditch, startling him. He swerved to miss her and lost control as his front-end spun out. In an instant, he was hydroplaning sideways then riding down the embankment backwards. When he came to a stop, he gave pause assessing what had just happened. He tried to compose himself, only to realize his headlights had illuminated something just in front of his car. He decided to brave the steady pelting of the frozen rain to check it out.

The young man approached cautiously, not quite sure what it was he saw. Training his flashlight on the object, its light barely shone through the thick semi-opaque plastic. To his horror, there was a distorted bloody face staring back at him. Completely disconcerted, the kid ran back to his car and locked the doors. His heart pounded hard in his chest as he called 911 keeping a horrified eye on the grotesque discovery before him.

The dispatcher answered, "911 – what's your emergency?"

He answered in a quick frantic tone, "Yes! I got into an accident, and there's a body!"

"Do you need an ambulance?"

"No – I'm pretty sure they're dead. I need the cops and a tow truck! I'm on Highway 36 at the curve just past Wilson's field."

*

Officer Randy O'Brien heard the call go out and made sure he was the first to arrive on scene. He was a pretty boy of sorts, with brown eyes of liquid chocolate and a boyish grin. The other officers nicknamed him "Hollywood", because he looked more like an underwear model than a cop. Although his good looks lead others to underestimate him, Randy was a young, ambitious, quick study who refused to play the Chief's games.

With his lights flashing he angled his squad parking in such a way to protect the shoulder just before the curve started. He got out, turned on his flashlight, walked over to take a look down the embankment to where the kid was. When he saw the kid getting out of his vehicle, O'Brien called out to him, "Just stay in your vehicle until we come for you!"

Randy did not want any more possible evidence being compromised. The freezing rain was going to make it difficult as it was. Carefully negotiating the slick slope, he made his way to the kid. He approached the plastic wrapped victim. Putting on a pair of rubber gloves, he crouched down beside the body to check for life. Sadly, there was none.

Not sure with whom or what they were dealing with - he got a quick statement. "What's your name kid?"

"Toby Anderson, sir."

"Okay Toby, after you came to a stop what did you do next?"

Toby said "I saw *that!*" as he pointed to the body wrapped in plastic. "I didn't know what I was seeing, so I checked it out. That's when I saw the bloody face looking at me. I ran back to my car and called 911."

"You didn't go back to the body?"

"No, sir!"

"Okay – good.

As O'Brien escorted Toby to be seated in the back of his squad, with lights flashing Rescue showed with both an ambulance and a truck.

Randy shut the kid in his car. Pleased with the fact he arrived on scene first, before the first responder guys could track-up his scene. He addressed a lieutenant, "I'm not a doctor, but I'm pretty sure she's dead. I'll take you down for confirmation."

The EMS confirmed the vic was deceased, "Well, there's no need for us!"

O'Brien radioed Sgt. Nelsen. "89, be advised. I'm blocking road at scene."

"10-4. I'll pull up to center before you and close the lane."

Nelsen called Chapman to the scene, "It's gonna be a long night!"

Randy stood topside in the sleet directing minor traffic when the road cops arrived along with Sergeant Nelsen.

Within minutes Chapman arrived from the east. Nelsen started giving his officers orders, "Hollywood, I need you to wait here for the County Evidence Techs. Cal, you and I will establish the crime scene."

Jim and Cal cautiously proceeded down to the kid's car, illuminating their path with flashlights. The snowy grass was slick and the 35-degree angle of the embankment made it difficult to navigate without slipping. They panned their lights back and forth searching for any clues along the way.

Cal's light panned across to the body. The sheen from the plastic caught his eye. If he did not already know it was a body, it would have been difficult to tell just what it was. Then he scanned back up the hill to the road with his light. From this angle Cal could easily see the hard slide marks in the snowy embankment.

The college kid's 911 call was the only thing they had to establish a time frame, right now. Cal and Jim went back topside; their flashlights were not enough. They waited until the county ETs (evidence technicians) got there with better lights. The only marks they found were from the kid's car, and the yawling on the shoulder.

The ETs drove in from the west. As Randy walked over to speak to them, he noticed a deep tire mark in the soft shoulder. Luckily the mark appeared to flash-freeze; however, he needed to retrieve a tarp to protect it so he broke a glow stick and set it down at that spot.

Jim and Cal were busy staking posts with red flags on the side of the road, as well as on the incline where the yawl marks were, marking the initial crime scene. They placed 2 by the body, 3' – 4' away and then marked where the car came to final rest. They ran a yellow police tape-line across.

The ME (medical examiner) had arrived with the County ET team. The scene quickly grew into a buzzing hub of activity. The team worked swiftly setting up lights that lit the area up like a ballpark.

Randy kept a log, and worked diligently diagramming the scene in detail. One of the county guys helped Randy triangulate how the body came to final rest while another was busy taking moulage castings of tracks.

The ME, Mitch Carter, joined Detective Chapman and Sgt. Nelsen at the body.

"Hey - Hollywood!" Jim called Randy over.

Before they could transport the body, they needed photos taken. The multi-tasking ET stopped what he was doing so he could take pictures. He preferred using the digital with O-ring light for crime scene photos, especially since the body was wrapped in heavy plastic. He took shots at numerous angles.

The body had been facing the car's headlights. Her eyes not quite swollen shut; looked out searching for help that never came. This filled Randy with an eerie sensation as he snapped the photos.

After a preliminary exam by Mitch at the scene, he authorized the removal of the body and plastic processed as evidence by the County ET team. The decision made by all parties present felt that an autopsy and forensic exam of everything should continue immediately.

The freezing rain let up to a miserable mist as Lois Towing arrived. Nelsen informed him to keep clear of the tire marks. He would have to maneuver his truck around to bring the kid's car out at an angle to keep from destroying any evidence. Dan Lois knew what to do; he worked accidents with the police all the time.

In wrapping things up, two of the County guys were to follow Randy and Mitch back to the morgue. The other half of the ET team transported evidence to county.

*

As they brought the body into the cold immaculate morgue, the quiet was interrupted by the buzz from the lights automatically coming to life. Once they set up in the morgue, Randy proceeded with note taking and snapped photos of the condition of the woman's crushed and beaten face, which would have made even the most veteran cop cringe.

Randy's usual 'happy go lucky' demeanor was dampened by the almost hypnotic grotesque image of the woman's bloody, bruised, and broken face. It was so bad that it did not appear to be real. More like a prop from a 'house of horrors'. She was unrecognizable.

When Randy finished, the ME got right to it, noting the extent of the traumatic injuries. Her blood kept its crimson color. It was not yet tainted and lavidity just started to progress. Mitch took her core temperature, giving her estimated time of death 2.5 – 3.5 hours ago. However, due to the weather it was merely an educated guess.

Mitch moved her head slightly to the right when O'Brien noticed there was a familiar tattoo on the back of her neck. The ME took his pen and carefully moved aside the tangled mess of bloody matted hair from the side of her neck, revealing a Queen of Hearts tattoo.

"Aw hell!" Randy spoke with recognition.

Mitch asked, "Do you know her?"

"No, but I have a pretty damn good idea who she is!"

Mitch thought it was best to call in a Forensic Odontologist due to the condition of her face. Although Randy recognized the tattoo on the back of her neck, the only way to truly ID this body was through dental records.

Mitch Carter told O'Brien along with the two from county, "Why don't you guys rest up. Be back here by 5 o'clock, that's when I'm starting the autopsy."

*

Randy phoned Jim, "Serge, I think the body might be Alison Chambers."

"Christ!" In hearing this, Nelsen's throat tightened as he swallowed hard. "Just keep me informed."

"Will do!" the voice on the other end answered.

Jim shared a look with Cal. "It might be Alison." He was to meet Alison at 9 o'clock. She had urgently wanted to meet with him, except she never showed.

Cal had known about their meeting. He radioed for a road cop to go to Alison's apartment. Then he called dispatch to run a Soundex for Alison Chamber's vehicle information and to put an APB on it.

Fifteen minutes later, Officer Gentry called Cal. "We have a second crime scene."

"What?"

"Her car isn't here, but Chamber's apartment has been tossed."

"Okay. I'm on my way." Cal left to join Gentry at the apartment.

"I want to know if you find *anything!*" Tonight, of all nights they were shorthanded. So, with troubled thoughts, Nelsen had to get back on the road.

When Detective Chapman arrived at the apartment on 117 N. Pine St., Officer Gentry had already started taking prints. Surveying the mess, it was obvious someone had been looking for something specific. This was no robbery. Her TV and stereo were still there. Her jewelry box on the dresser had not been touched. Gentry even found an envelope containing $1,280 lying on the bed amongst the contents of one of her dresser drawers. There was more to this homicide. Chapman and Gentry would spend hours collecting fingerprints and taking photos.

It was already 2 a.m. and Cal thought he had better call Kate.

Katie was startled awake by the ringing from her phone and quickly answered. "Hello?"

"I'm sorry to wake you, Darling; I just didn't want you to worry. We have a homicide, and I won't be coming home anytime soon."

Katie was relieved for the call. "Ok, Hun...be safe."

"I will."

"Love you!"

"I love you, too. Sweet dreams!" Then he snapped the phone shut. When he turned around, he found Gentry staring at him with a smirk on his face. "What the hell are you smiling at?"

"You!" Gentry just shook his head, "You're different somehow."

"Oh, is that right?"

"Yeah, I'd have to say so!" Then Gentry laughed.

"Laugh it up, Chuckles!" Cal said with smile.

*

Randy was prompt, even a bit early. Mitch appreciated O'Brien's work ethics. Like clock work Mitch started his autopsy and then the County guys appeared, five minutes later.

Randy kept very good notes making the initial report and asking questions as Mitch proceeded.

By 6 a.m. the dentist arrived. Terry Gerber, DDS had helped the police throughout the years in dental forensics; and had spent his entire career in Burlington. Just about everyone knew him. He was a hunched over smallish old man with dark puffy bags under his eyes. What little hair he had left was white fuzz. His large ears housed long straggly hairs. He wore thick, black-framed glasses, probably from the Eisenhower era. He set down his worn black leather case and then shuffled over to the stainless-steel table containing the woman's body.

Randy noticed how he straightened up as he put on his lab coat, knocking 20 years off his stature.

Dr. Gerber took his time, carefully examining the victim's mouth and teeth. Then compared the X-rays to the ones he had of Alison. He confirmed ID, "Without a doubt, its Alison Chambers. But you should note, not only are these teeth here fractured; take a look at her Central Incisor and Lateral Incisor on her upper left side. See how they are chipped? This is new!"

Mitch nodded in agreement, "Thank you for coming in Dr. Gerber. I appreciate your insight and I'll take the extra time to find possible trace evidence left behind on those teeth."

Mitch continued with the autopsy. The beating this woman received was one of the worst the ME had seen in his career. Courtney's murder was brutal enough, but this, this was pure evil. The autopsy was long and taxing.

Randy was a trooper, continuously taking notes and asking pertinent questions throughout the autopsy.

Carter finished up around 1 o'clock that afternoon. He took off his gloves stepped on the pedal to the stainless steal garbage can, which opened its lid as he discarded the used gloves inside. The lid made a hollow thud sound as it shut. "I'll give my secretary the recording of my findings and send typed copies over."

The county guys were relieved to finally go.

"Randy, you should go home and get some rest. We'll go over everything tomorrow."

Randy was chilled to the bone, mentally numb and dead on his feet, but probably would not be able to calm himself enough to really rest for hours.

When Randy returned to the station, Dotty, BPD's longtime dispatcher, was already in the middle of the day's hustle and bustle. She managed to give O'Brien an encouraging wink along with one of her warm friendly smiles.

He returned a warm but exhausted smile.

Relieved to find the locker room abandoned, he sat heavily on the bench in front of his blue locker. Randy had always wanted to be a police officer, but this part of the job sucked the life out of him. Not realizing how long he had been sitting there, Randy must have zoned out.

Deputy Chief Dogget was standing out in the hallway when Randy emerged. "O'Brien!" he called.

The Deputy Chief's bark stopped Randy in his tracks. He sighed to himself, *"Shit!"* as he walked over to find out what Dogget wanted. "Yes, Dan, what's up?" Randy answered the Deputy Chief with a little more attitude than he intended.

"The Chief wants to be filled in on what's going on with the Chambers case?"

"What - now?" Randy could not believe it. The chief obviously wanted as much early information as he could get to quickly spin this homicide in such a way that would keep Burlington unblemished.

"As soon as you can."

"When I know something – he will! I haven't slept in over 24 hours, and I'm going home! I will make a point to see him tomorrow."

The Deputy Chief was not thrilled with O'Brien's lack of enthusiasm regarding the chief. "Sounds like the substation is rubbing off on you!"

Randy ignored the Deputy Chief's antagonizing comment and just walked away.

*

Solemnly, Randy opened the door to his dark apartment, not quite remembering how he even got home. Robotically he locked the door behind him, and tossed his keys to the table. He retrieved a beer from the fridge, twisted the cap, and tossed it onto the counter. Taking a swig of the cold amber ale, which he usually enjoyed, today had no taste.

He plopped himself down in his comfy chair, took another swig, and set the bottle down next to him before reclining back. He looked around his seemingly quiet living room. Randy rested his head back to stare up at the stark white ceiling replaying the past 18 hours in his mind.

The brutality these two women suffered was horrific. The worst part of being a cop, was working these types of cases. What magnified and really hit Randy in the pit of his stomach was to witness the autopsy, to see what was once alive, opened up and taken apart piece by piece. It dehumanized them. Even if it was something - which legally had to be done, and which he, the investigator had the responsibility to witness, take notes and photograph. It left such a horrible remembrance in his mind. You never get used to it. Each one brought its own bad memories and horrors.

The horrors seen, the evil men do, and not bringing that home was impossible. Learning to separate work from home was the challenge. Randy was single, had no children and was not involved with anyone special. He was left to carry these known atrocities alone.

As exhausted as Randy was, his mind could not quiet down. He went back over each step in his mind, making sure he did everything right, he even began to rethink why he became a cop. There was really never another option for Randy. He was born into it. His grandfather was a cop, two of his uncles were cops and even Randy's father, Jon was a hard-nosed Irish detective from Chicago.

The summer Randy turned 16; his father was murdered during an investigation. The strongest man he knew, in his faith as well as his actions. He was Randy's hero but was taken away from him all too soon. Who was to teach and guide Randy to be a man? This would most certainly be the driving force behind Randy's decision to become a cop. But it was also because of his father that he kept his relationships at a distance. He knew how short a time with loved ones could be. Randy would not want to be the cause of someone's heartache. He saw what it did to his mother.

Even at 16, Randy had questions that went unanswered. The evidence in his father's murder was sketchy at best. In truth, Randy always suspected his father's partner of somehow taking part in Jon's death. As far as Randy was concerned, there was nothing worse than a dirty cop.

There was always this feeling of deceit when it came to Jon O'Brien's case. The man, who became the scapegoat, committed suicide in jail. All the loose ends seemed to be tied up, a little too neatly. After all, what was the motive? What reason could *this* particular man have to kill Jon?

That was it! Randy could not swallow Alison's brutal death without a motive. She did not seem to have any enemies. She was also protected by Richie Collins and the 7 Sons of Sin. No one was foolish enough to cross Richie, which left the obvious.

Alison told Sgt. Nelsen she had some information, and was going to meet him the day she was killed. What could she possibly have had on Richie to get herself murdered?

That is what they needed, to find what information she had. They were looking for *something*, her apartment was trashed, and they did not even bother to take an envelope full of cash that was there. *What did she take from them? It had to be pretty damn important to torture her for it.*

7

The next morning, Mitch Carter was busy looking over his own report when Chapman and O'Brien arrived to go over his findings.

"I hope you guys got plenty of rest." He said, not bothering to take his nose out of his notes to acknowledge them.

Cal had brought an extra coffee for the overtired ME. "Black, right?"

Mitch turned around, taking a quick observing glance at the two officers in his presence. Cal was a veteran at functioning with little or no sleep, but Randy looked a bit haggard. Carter said, "Yeah, thanks!" as he took the hot cup from Cal.

Mitch took a deep breath, and then blew it out as he vibrated his lips, making some sort of sound that resembled a horse. He furrowed his brow, and then got right to it. "Alison Chambers, 20 years of age. 5'9", 130 pounds. Noted markings: Queen of Hearts tattoo on back of neck, also a rabbit tattoo on her right hip."

His tone was strong and straight-forward as he continued, "Burn marks to face, neck and chest from a cigarette. Lacerations on face. Severe deep bruising on head, face, arms, and torso. Her more extensive injuries were to her face and head. Broken eye socket, nose, cheek, jaw," He started to list everything broken but decided to sum it up. "Basically, her entire face was broken, including some teeth. She had bleeding of the brain." He gave a slight pause, as his voice faltered, "Broken clavicle, 6th, 7th and 8th ribs, resulting in punctured left lung, internal ruptures and bleeding. She did not die right away. She suffered a great deal. This woman was tortured and beaten repeatedly...she died of blunt force trauma to the head. There were no signs of rape. This was extremely violent and personal. I found traces of concrete dust on her clothing and hair. I retrieved second party DNA; tissue, blood and sweat. Some skin cells were actually left on her teeth. Whoever did this will have broken skin on their knuckles. Her skull was crushed with a severe blow to her left temple leaving an angular mark along with wooden splinters. Pine to be exact."

Randy and Cal shared a questioning look.

"A 2 X 4?" Randy offered.

"Most likely, and with the concrete dust I'd say your murder took place at a construction site."

Cal added, "The plastic she was wrapped in was construction grade. There aren't many new construction sites in the area; it should be relatively easy to find out which one was used, there will be plenty of blood."

Cal kept in the back of his mind that she urgently needed to speak to Sgt. Nelsen. Jim did not know what she wanted, but she claimed it was really important. "Her place was tossed, and we know it wasn't a robbery. Let's start by questioning the people she worked with. Maybe there was a client that wanted more attention than she was willing to give. Then you can take a look at her car."

Mitch commented, "Don't forget about her mother, she lives over in Green Gables. Maybe she knows something?" Then Mitch offered. "By the way, County got a great print off the duct tape as well as DNA, so when you find this bastard, we'll nail his coffin shut!"

Randy turned to Cal as they walked out, "Cal, I've been thinking about this and you said it yourself...she had something to tell Nelsen. What if she had something physical to give Nelsen? Since her apartment was tossed, maybe she left whatever it was with her mother?"

*

Sgt. Jim Nelsen felt he should be the one to tell Mrs. Chambers of her daughter's death. Of course, feeling a bit guilty that he had to inquire about any knowledge she may have about who would have wanted Alison dead and why.

Nelsen parked his squad, and slowly sauntered to the entrance of Green Gables with a heavy heart. Telling someone their loved one was deceased was a heart wrenching task, in which no matter how many times you do it, it never gets any easier. Especially, when telling a parent, it was *their* child. Jim placed his hand on the brass handle, but before he pulled open the door something made him turn back and look out over the parking lot. It took him a minute to realize what he was seeing. A red 2006 Volkswagen Bug parked right up front. "I'll be damned!"

Sgt. Nelsen radioed dispatch letting them know he found Alison's vehicle and to have it impounded. Jim had a nurse accompany him while he spoke with Mrs. Chambers. The nurse confirmed that 'yes', Alison was there visiting her mother the night she was killed. And that there were numerous witnesses to verify she left around 7 o'clock.

Although Mrs. Chambers' physical condition was such that she was unable to care of herself, her mind was good. Jim did his best, taking great care to inform Mrs. Chambers of Alison's demise. She was grief stricken, but was still able to answer some of Jim's questions regarding Alice.

"Could you tell me if Alice's behavior was unusual?"

Mrs. Chambers' mouth was uncooperative and forced her answers. "No, she seemed fine, but preoccupied."

"Did she give you anything?"

The woman sadly shook her head no.

"Then, did she say where she was going?"

Having difficulty, "No, just that she had to leave." She forced herself to answer.

Jim thought to himself, *"Yeah to meet me, but was she meeting anyone prior?"*

He gave her hand a warm squeeze, "Thank you for your time. And, Rebecca, I am truly sorry for your loss."

Sgt. Nelsen left Rebecca Chamber's room unaware the key to the entire investigation was shelved in a bookcase along with *Sense and Sensibility* and *Wuthering Heights*.

*

Chapman and O'Brien went to Puss 'n Boots to question management and its employees.

Randy was focused, "This doesn't feel like Richie did this. But I can't believe anyone would have been stupid enough to kill Richie's girl without his consent!" He was just talking out loud, more to himself than to Cal.

Stating the obvious Cal commented. "Two of their dancers met with violent deaths, someone here knows something!"

Randy started to question the employees of the club while Cal spoke with the club's manager, for the second time. Manny's lack of cooperation struck a nerve with Cal. He was obviously not being forthright, and his attitude about Alice's death was remiss.

Randy suspected one of the strippers, a petite brunette known as "Bo" might know *something*, but she was definitely afraid. Randy turned-on his charm to make her feel more at ease; it was futile; however, he handed her his business card anyway. "Feel free to call me if you can think of anything that could help us."

She took his card, although there was no way she would ever chance talking to the police.

It was no surprise that Manny proved to be uncooperative. Everything about Manny's demeanor told Cal, he knew *exactly* who was responsible for these girls' deaths.

Cal was determined to find the killer, every fiber of his being told him it was Charlie Nix, and in his experience when a man takes something that does not belong to him, from *animals* such as the 7 Sons of Sin...he ends up dead. Chapman needed to find Charlie before the bikers did.

8

Taking leave from the strip club, Chapman and O'Brien headed over to the industrial park to meet Officer Gentry. Gentry had been waiting at the site where he believed Alison was killed.

O'Brien was unusually silent. Chapman understood the need for quiet reflection and did not question.

The sound of the squad car's doors closing brought Officer Gentry outside.

"What do you have?" Chapman asked Gentry.

Officer Gentry explained while Chapman and O'Brien followed along. "The foreman came in this morning to find a pile of burnt lumber. At first, he thought it was a bunch of kids having a party, but after he started to clean it up, he found what appeared to be a blood-stain and called us. It looks like she was killed here, and then the perp tried to cover it up with a fire. We've bagged a roll of duct tape and that roll of plastic looks to be the same grade as what the body was wrapped in. I bet they'll find prints to match the ones on the duct tape found on our vic."

Now that Sgt. Nelsen found Alison's car, O'Brien was eager to get to get to it.

*

Tanya was not sure what the nature of Billie and Jack's relationship was, but regardless of their lack of affection at work, she knew there was more to it. She was so jealous; she could not stand it.

Since the very first day Jack brought TJ on board as a bouncer for the Brick Yard, Tanya had been toying with him to get back at Jack. She craved the attention and would do anything she could to get any reaction from Jack. To her dismay Jack could care less about what Tanya was doing or to whom she was doing it with. The fact was, since their break up Jack said very little to her. Determined, jealousy was the best way to get him back; Tanya openly threw herself at TJ.

TJ was well aware of the brief affair Jack had with Tanya. However, he also knew the entire premise for their break-up, which was why he allowed Tanya to flirt and toy with him in the first place. It made it easier to keep an eye on her. He suspected she was the one behind the bindle Billie found in her apron, and the intermittent flow of narcotics that passed through the doors of the Brick Yard.

Seductively, Tanya slunk across the front of the upstairs bar, with the roll of her hips showing off her long silky legs. Her black spandex boy shorts left little to the imagination, along with her tight-fitting half-shirt in-which she cut a 'V' in the neck to show off the overflow from her deep cleavage. The smoldering expression in Tanya's eyes told TJ the vixen was on the prowl.

She made him feel like he was her prey as she wrapped herself around his well-defined muscular body. She nipped at his ear lobe and in a heavy hot breath whispered, "*I – want – you!*"

TJ beamed, knowing full well the slut only wanted to push Jack's buttons and use him to do it. He tipped his head down to her, just enough to make her think he might kiss her, but then stopped short. "That sounds wonderful, Sweetheart…but now is not a good time for me. Maybe later!" TJ said with an impish gleam in his eye.

Not sure if she should be offended or if possibly, he was only toying with her. She shrugged it off as she uncoiled herself from him, like the snake she was. Her pouty lips twisted up in a faint smile, "I'm ready whenever you are, big guy."

To keep her on the hook, TJ gave Tanya a smack on the ass, just for good measure. "Sugar, you'll be the first to know!" he flirted.

Jack who had been deep in conversation with Erik witnessed the cheap show.

Erik knew TJ and Jack were old friends from back in the Marine Corps, but was unaware, like everyone else of their outside work relationship. "Doesn't that bother you, Jack?"

"What?"

"Your buddy, messing with your EX!"

Jack turned back to Erik with a smile. "Not in the least."

TJ strolled over to Jack wearing a shit-eating grin, "Ready to open the downstairs?"

Jack just gave Erik a cool smile, "Later!" he called over his shoulder as he headed down with TJ.

Jokingly Jack ribbed TJ, "Do you have to enjoy it so much?"

"Hey, I might have to take one for the team!"

"I can almost guarantee it! She's gonna make you pay dearly, my friend!"

TJ belted out a hardy laugh, and slapped Jack on the back. "I'm sure I won't enjoy it."

Jack just rolled his eyes at TJ's sarcasm.

The sight of Billie always put an extra bounce in Jack's step. Tonight, the girls wore denim skirts with matching plaid shirts. The lace-trimmed camisoles they wore underneath drew attention to their bare necklines.

Except for Billie, who wore a simple silver chain with a Celtic cross around her neck.

TJ kept a close eye on the girls. He noticed Jack was too, one in particular.

Although Katie was physically at the Brick Yard, her mind was wandering somewhere back at the white brick building, thinking about why someone would hide the entrance to a basement. It took her a moment; however, with the sight of Charlie coming down the stairs snapped her back to the present. Thinking to herself... *"Just what I need!"*

The very sight of Charlie Nix made Katie's skin crawl.

TJ and Jack had equally become aware of Charlie's presence downstairs.

When Katie came up to the bar to order a round of drinks, Jack reminded her, "Don't let that asshole bother you! If he lays a hand on you, TJ will be more than happy to bounce him."

Katie smiled, "I know – TJ is just waiting for an excuse to hurt him."

Jack gave her one of his cautionary looks.

"Okay - okay, I hear ya Jack – no worries!" She said, as she walked away with her tray of drinks.

Getting around to serving Charlie, she noticed how scabbed over his knuckles were. One hand looked worse than the other, like he had gotten into a fistfight with a cheese grater. Knowing what she did about him, it was obvious to her that he had to have beaten somebody badly to get those injuries. She smiled graciously and took the tip he gave her, before quickly moving on to the next table.

Concerned, she made her way back to the bar. "Jack, call Cal, I think he might want to talk to Charlie. His hands look like he beat someone up pretty bad!"

Jack nonchalantly approached Jessica at the till, and privately spoke to her, sending Jessica up stairs to have Erik discretely call Cal. He did not want Charlie to know Katie had anything to do with the police coming for him.

Charlie had been ogling some of the women standing near his table, when he caught TJ eye-balling him. That is when Charlie knew it was time to leave, something was up, and he was not about to stick around to find out what that was.

TJ followed Charlie up the stairs; debating whether he should detain him. He chose to engage in a conversation with Erik and stopped at the door, allowing Charlie to leave.

By the time Cal arrived at the Brick Yard, Charlie was already gone.

"Sorry, man." TJ offered.

"What's the deal?"

"We called you because Katie noticed Charlie's hands were pretty messed up. She brought it to Jack's attention, and then you were called."

"Do you think he suspected anything?"

"He did leave rather quickly. I'm sure he probably suspected I was watching him."

Disgusted that he missed Charlie at the bar, Cal got on the radio, to put out an APB on him. Hoping now that Charlie was not going to run, he sent Gentry to Charlie's address.

9

Charlie made his way down the apartment steps with a quickly packed duffle bag. Even though it was a cold night, the sweat poured off of him. Huffing and puffing he pushed his way through the back door only to find Richie Collins and his enforcers patiently waiting for him, as they casually leaned up against his Buick. He stopped dead in his tracks, as his heart tightened in his chest.

"Going somewhere?" Richie called to him.

"Ah - yeah, just leaving for a few of days until things cool down."

"Is that so?" Richie gave pause, "Know what I think? I think you and me are gonna have a little chat."

"'Bout what?"

Richie looked down at the injuries on Charlie's hands, and then said, "I think we both know."

Charlie knew he could not run even if the thought did cross his mind, Brock made that decision for him. Brock had a way of looking right through you with an evident look of hate in his eyes that left you cold and empty. He could have been the Grim Reaper...maybe he was for some.

Adam grabbed the duffle from Charlie's hands, while Luke stuck a .45 in his side; taking Charlie's own .9mm from inside his jacket.

Luke ushered Charlie forward, "Get in!"

Brock slipped in behind the wheel of Charlie's Buick. Adam tossed the duffle bag into the trunk and rode shotgun.

Luke was all smiles, "Move in Tubby and slide over."

Then Luke climbed in the back seat beside Charlie. He enjoyed the look of fear Charlie was trying to conceal.

The old Buick reluctantly started with one of its pistons loudly rattling under the hood. The exhaust strained to expel from the single tail pipe. Using Brock's red Caddy, Richie led the men in the Buick out on to some back - country roads leaving town.

Charlie knew his fate, but was still hoping this was only a scare tactic. When you work closely with a group such as the 7 Sons of Sin, you are living life on the edge as it is. At any time, your number could be up, and he had been running on fumes since the break-in back in December.

Charlie kept checking the rearview mirror trying to read Brock, except Brock never bothered to look back at Charlie. Definitely *not* a good sign!

They slowed, driving over the single lane stone bridge that crossed a stream. Charlie did not recognize the area. There was nothing but rough snow-covered fields that backed up to dense woods of leafless trees.

Richie pulled off and parked. Brock pulled up beside him and parked.

Richie got out and then motioned to Luke.

Luke got out of the Buick, pointing the .45 in Charlie's face. "Get out!"

Charlie did what he was ordered to do. He glanced over to Richie, recognizing the fixed glare of revenge in his eyes.

Charlie had no choice; he would hope for the best but knew the best just might be a bullet to the back of the head.

Brock stood by the open trunk of the red Caddy ready to do whatever was asked of him while the others walked Charlie out a short distance to a snow-covered field.

The men stopped by a frozen marsh. Thick cattails poked through the snow and ice, straining to break free from their frozen restraints. Luke and Adam both had their guns trained on Charlie, while Richie took his time sizing him up, flipping his Zippo open and snapping it shut, repeatedly.

Invading Charlie's personal space, Richie asked in a soft yet gruff tone, "Now - Charlie, what did I ask you to do?" He then leaned in real close, putting his hand to his own ear, "I can't hear you!"

"I don't have the book yet, but I'm working on it!" Charlie's fear showed by his snap response and the waver in his voice.

Richie gave a quick snuff through his nose. His eyes narrowed, "Didn't I tell you to bring Alison back? Now, tell me how she ended up *dead*!"

In a panic Charlie blurted out, "It was an accident! I swear to you, I never meant to kill her...she was playing games!" He knew there was no use denying he did it. "I can still get the book back for you."

"You stupid – fucking – bastard!" Richie hit Charlie in the face with the cold steel of his pistol so hard it split his cheek open, and the force behind it spun Charlie around.

Richie reached out for Charlie's coat with his left hand and clubbed him again with his .45, bringing Charlie to his knees.

Charlie spat blood onto the snowy ground.

Richie still held the front of his coat and maneuvered him to address him on his knees. Getting right in Charlie's face, "When I give you a job to do, you follow my direct orders to the *letter*! If I wanted to kill her...I would have done it myself! You took something from me, Charlie.

"What did I tell you? What did I say was going to happen if you fucked this up?"

"Richie, listen to me...it was an accident! I never meant to..."

"No, Charlie, it wasn't an accident. Courtney wasn't an accident either. You should be happy I'm dealing with you and not Manny! Those Latino boys can be sick fucks!"

"It was an accident! I can fix this!"

Richie burst with a loud disturbing laugh. "It's just a matter of time before the cops link you to their murders, and *then* to *us*! *You're* the accident. But I'm going to correct that." Richie snapped his fingers.

Obediently, Brock brought over a red plastic gas can from the trunk of the Caddy.

"You know what, Charlie? I'm doin' you a favor. Manny, wanted to gut ya while you were still alive, and then strangle you with your own intestines! But I thought that was a bit too extreme."

Charlie's eyes grew large with terror. While Brock walked the distance to where they were he pleaded, "No, don't do this, Richie! If you're trying to scare me it worked, I get your point. It'll never happen again, I promise!"

"You're right, Charlie...I know you'll never do it again...you took something from *me*! *No one* takes from me! And you're gonna *pay* for Alison." Richie's tone was cold and hard.

Richie stepped back; taking the gas can from Brock.

Adam and Luke made sure Charlie didn't stand up.

This had gone too far. Charlie knew he was doomed. He begged, "Please just shoot me. Just fucking shoot me!" Spittle flew from his lips as he cried out in terror.

As Richie poured gasoline on Charlie, he continued begging to be shot.

Richie got a perverse pleasure in the ultimate fear this pathetic loser had in him. He finished by dumping the remaining gas over Charlie's head.

The fumes alone were too much as Charlie gasped and gagged for air. The gas burned his eyes, blurring his vision and caused intense pain from the fuel getting into his cut-open flesh.

Handing Brock, the empty can, with a dark cruel pleasure Richie reached in his pocket for his Zippo lighter, flipped the top up producing a flame, but then paused. The sick sadistic bastard gave Charlie a split second to grasp for some hope that he really was not going to light him on fire. Then an evil twisted grin tugged at the corners of Richie's mouth as he tossed the lighter to the sniveling waste of life in front of him, sealing Charlie's fate.

WHOOSH!

Instantly set ablaze, the flames consumed Charlie. The angry flames licked and swirled about in a foreboding dance, as his screams quickly died out.

Richie's men did not respect him as much as they feared him. But they stayed loyal to him out of that fear and that was good enough for Richie.

"Brock, when the flames burn out dump the body, and dispose of his car. You know what to do. Oh, and retrieve my lighter." Richie hopped in the Caddy and casually drove away.

Adam and Luke stayed to help Brock dispose of Charlie and his car.

Once the flames died out, Charlie was frozen in a silent scream with a blackened grotesque crust covering what was once his skin.

Moving him was not going to be easy.

In Adam's over zealous act to be done with the disgusting task at hand, he grabbed Charlie by one of his legs to pull him along. To his surprise he was left holding a handful of cooked flesh that easily slipped off like the covering on a toasted marshmallow.

Luke laughed at his friend's expense. Adam's gagging and round of vomiting only increased Luke's amusement at the situation.

Brock was annoyed with having to deal with these two dumb asses. He was sickened by the entire ordeal, not that Charlie didn't get what he deserved, but he had a job to do...what he always did...clean up after everyone else's mess.

*

It was late when Cal came in, but Katie was just glad he was home.

Hondo happily greeted Cal, eager for a good scratch. After vigorously playing with his dog for a few minutes, Cal looked up to find Kate standing on the stairs. They exchanged loving smiles.

"How was your day?" Katie asked.

"Let's just say I'm in dire need of one of your hugs right now."

Reaching out to him, Katie met Cal halfway. They held each other tight.

She could feel the tension he held through his embrace, and gave pause as she affectionately asked, "Is everything okay?"

She stepped back to look him in the eyes.

Cal did not want Kate working at the bar anymore, however, this was not the time to have that conversation. She needed to be made aware of what was happening. He could not keep her in the dark even if he thought he was protecting her.

10

Jack Carter laid awake most of the night thinking about all the bodies that were starting to pile up. There was no doubt in his mind that the 7 Sons of Sin were behind these murders in one way or another.

TJ had already gotten a couple of good drug buys working the Tanya angle, but it was not enough. The murders and the guns were top priority. It bothered him that they did not have the evidence they needed to stop this.

How in the hell are they able to conceal their drug lab? Their intricate network seemed to be flawless, but Jack was determined to take these bastards down.

When Courtney had confided in him, he was hopeful for his first real break, but then she was murdered before he could get anything tangible on them. Now, with Alison's murder his anxiety was at an all time high. The sheer brutality of it worked a knot in the pit of his stomach.

The things he did, and saw while he served his country left him with scars, both mentally and physically. That was war, but this is not. This was just some sick scum-bag who thinks they are above the law, doing whatever the hell they wanted.

Jack also thought about Billie, and her safety. He knew how dangerous this biker gang was. His mind kept flashing back to the night Adam Knox tried to assault Billie at the bar. How easy it would have been for him to beat the life out of Knox. That was the night he realized how much he truly cared for Billie, and could not bear to have anyone hurt her. It was getting harder to keep his secret from her.

Keeping his cover as a bartender, Billie only knew what he wanted her to know. His father was the medical examiner, and that Jack had been in the Marine Corps, which he did not talk about. He was not one to talk about much.

She really had no clue *who* he was. Jack kept things to himself and was even taking their relationship at a snail's pace. Committing to Billie was not something he would do easily; however, if he *was* going to take their relationship to the next level, he would have to tell her the truth. Honesty was the most important thing to him, and it needed to start with him.

His cell rang, interrupting his thoughts. He cleared his throat before answering, "Hello?"

"Good morning, Jack!"

The sound of Billie's joyful, bubbly voice on the other end brought a boyish grin to his tired unshaven face. "Good morning, Blondie! To what do I owe the pleasure of this wake-up call?"

"I was hoping you'd join me for breakfast?"

"I suppose that can be arranged."

Jack could hear the happy tone reflected in Billie's voice, "Sonny's around 9?"

He looked over to the digital clock on the nightstand that read 7:45 a.m. "Sure – I'll meet you there."

He hung up the phone, exhaling heavily, before rolling out of bed.

*

When Jack entered the little café, he was first greeted by an overly tanned older waitress reeking of cigarettes, then spotted Billie sitting alone in a booth directly behind her. He gave a nod to the booth, "I'm meeting someone, thanks." He smiled as he walked purposely towards Billie. His heart began to race at the sight of her beautiful smile and those clear blue eyes welcoming him to her table.

He slid in behind the booth's fixed little table across from Billie. He returned an easy smile, "Thanks for the call this morning. You must have been reading my mind."

She giggled, but quickly turned it into a soft little laugh. "Oh?" The butterflies in her stomach fluttered and made her feel a little queasy. Having Jack so close to her made her titillatingly nervous.

He liked the way she tried so hard to keep some self-control.

The waitress waddled over to pour them a cup of coffee. Billie quickly protested, putting her hand over her Caribbean blue mug, "I'll take some hot tea please."

"I'll take the coffee, thanks!" Jack waited for the waitress to leave them before he reached his hand across the table for Billie's. Her warm, soft, delicate hand was a contradiction to his rough strong hands. Hands that had been through much; hands that have killed. He started to doubt what he was about to do.

His silence puzzled Billie.

Jack locked himself into Billie's deep ocean-blue eyes, knowing how he felt about her and sighed. Truth, was she made him feel like a kid again, yet confused and nervous all at the same time. He could not deny the attraction. He wanted more. It was the feeling of not being in control that frustrated him. His reservations were justified, but he wanted to take his chances.

"*Billie?*" Jack started to tell her what was on his mind, when his 'Spidy senses' told him they were being watched. He paused to glance over to the opposite side of the room. They *were* being watched.

Richie Collins sat facing Jack, with Manny and Brock holding court.

Seeing them unnerved Jack. He wanted to keep Billie out of their reach.

Jack forced himself to return his attentions back to Billie's angelic bright face. He attempted to focus on her, ignoring the animals across the room, yet he was fully aware of them at the same time. This was not going to be easy. Suddenly, what he wanted did not matter anymore. His conscience told him he could not risk telling Billie he was an ATF agent working undercover, at least not yet.

"Jack?" Her voice snapped his attention back to her and the lovely hand he held. "Is everything alright?"

He gave her hand a little squeeze before letting it go, "yeah, fine." He sipped his coffee, and quickly burned his lip, and winced, "Ah, hot!"

Their waitress returned with hot tea for Billie, and took their orders.

Jack kept their conversation light and easy. "So, what kind of trouble do you plan on getting into today?"

She coyly batted her eyelashes at him. "Trouble? Me?"

He gave Billie one of his looks. "Sure...I may be slow, but I'm not *that* slow!" Then he flashed her one of his sexy smiles.

She could not resist that smile of his; it turned her into a silly fool every time. "To be honest I'm not quite sure what we're doing today."

"We?"

"Katie and I...who else would I be with?"

"Wasn't sure...just checking." He joked.

She cocked her head giving him a quizzical look. He surprised her sometimes, but she was learning he was not as hard-assed as he led on to be. A big smile spread across Billie's face as she picked up her tea to sip it and her playful eyes flashed at Jack.

"How is she by the way?" Jack quickly skirted the playful direction they were headed.

"She's going to be okay. Katie's a fighter. I am amazed at her strength. I do not know what I would do if I had been through what she had. She's not talking about it, but who could blame her? I think that's why she's been so preoccupied with researching that white brick building on Milwaukee Ave. Before Eddie took her, we found a secret door to the cellar. Now I am helping her document everything we find. There are these strange archways in the walls that are all blocked-up. It's been driving her crazy trying to figure out what it was used for and why someone would have hidden the door down there."

"What door?" Jack was trying to wrap his mind around what Billie was saying. This was the first he'd heard about it.

Billie quickly put her hand up motioning for Jack to quiet down. "Shh! Not so loud. Katie does not want anyone to know about it yet." Making air quotes, "She says she wants to get all her 'ducks in a row' before she says anything."

"I don't think you two should be messing with a mysterious basement without someone else being there with you. What if that hidden door closes while you two are down there? People do not just hide doorways for no reason. Maybe, you guys should rethink your plans?"

"Jack – it's just an old dusty basement. There were some old wine racks down there with a few old bottles of wine. I didn't see anything dangerous. I am sure we'll be fine."

"Yeah, well...still...I think she should at least tell that Paul guy she works for about it. Does Cal even know what you two are up to?"

"He knows about the basement. Just promise me you won't say anything? I told Katie I wouldn't, but I just don't like keeping things from you."

Those words struck a nerve with Jack.

Billie continued, "I really don't know what the big deal is, but for some reason it's important to Katie."

Jack studied Billie for a moment, contemplating her request. "I don't like it...trouble...isn't that what I said?" A little smile pulled at the corners of his mouth.

Billie flashed Jack a warm but impish smile, "Okay, so I *am* trouble. Whatch-ya gonna do?"

Jack leaned in close, drawing Billie near and whispered, "I'm not sure yet, but I *know* you're going to be a challenge." He still wrestled with the idea to move forward with their relationship, considering their 10-year age difference, his real job and the threat of Billie getting hurt by that job.

Jack had become accustomed to being alone. He did not have to lie or hide who he was. Of course, ever since Billie walked into the Brick Yard, he had been denying the attraction he had to her. Who was he fooling? The bubbly fun-loving blonde stirred things in him he was not ready to feel. He was surprised she still showed any interest in him at all. Most women would have moved on by now, not only tired from his lack of commitment but also his disinterest in the casual affair.

Billie had fallen hard for Jack, harder than she had for anyone before him. He was different. Not only had he not pursued having sex with Billie, he turned her down on numerous occasions. This frustrated her and had her questioning her womanly charms. Jack had the ability to bring out the best in her and balance her idiosyncrasies.

She could stare at his handsome face forever. The juxtaposition of his messy hairstyle and neatly trimmed unshaven face held the sexiest smile a man could have. Eyes being the window to one's soul, she found his to be mysterious. At times they could be warm yet then again appear to be dangerous. She fondly remembered how he intimidated her once upon a time, and that too was part of the attraction. Over these past several months she was getting a sense for who he truly was, even if she didn't know everything about him, she knew he was a good man, and a dependable man, but one who was also well guarded.

Once Richie Collins and his hierarchy left the restaurant, Jack was finally able to allow himself to relax and really enjoy Billie Jo's company.

"You never told me what you have up today?" Billie questioned.

Jack, who was slightly distracted, brought his full attention back to the cute pert blonde sitting across from him. His face softened with that sexy smile of his, "I hadn't thought past having breakfast with *you*. Although, I did tell Bob I would help him inventory the stock room today."

11

Jim could not help but feel somewhat responsible for Alison's death. "We need to find Charlie, but that son-of-a-bitch hasn't shown up for work in three days or gone back to his apartment!"

"We've got an APB out on Nix; it's just a matter of time before we find him." Cal answered.

The phone rang interrupting their conversation.

In a distressed tone Jim said, "You better answer it, it's probably the Chief wanting an up-date on our investigation."

Cal shot Jim a disapproving glance before picking up. "Chapman!"

Of course, the look on Cal's face proved Jim right. Nelsen formed a gun with his fingers, put it to his temple and made like he just shot himself.

Cal hung up the phone, sat back in his chair and tipped his head back blowing a long breath from his lungs.

"Let me guess, the Chief wants us in his office ASAP!" Jim's comment was full of contempt.

Cal acknowledged it was.

In frustration, Jim shook his head, "This week I don't know who is worse...the damn Chief or my wife!"

Cal was stunned, "Your wife - everything okay with you and Kristine?"

"Yeah – I guess! She's just being difficult about all the time I've been spending working these cases. She thinks I am obsessing and gripes about how I'm never home any more. Kristine expects me to be home for dinner every night and have time to go to her mother's on the weekends! Of course, when I am home, I can't even let off any steam. Sometimes I just need to vent! She thinks I'm yelling at her! It's probably just *that* time of the month; she knows this isn't a 9-5 job! I could be retiring right now – but *no,* she's the one who wanted me to stick it out the full 25-years! If Chief Murphy was still here it'd be a cake walk! But with Perry - I'm working in *Hell*!"

Cal empathized. He could tell by the look on Jim's face, his home life, the one thing he could always depend on and seek refuge, was now wearing on him. Work was stressful enough, but your home life should not be.

*

Chief Perry arrogantly sat behind his desk; his wire rimmed glasses perched on the end of his nose critically reading through the case file Sgt. Nelsen obediently handed over.

Detective Chapman dutifully and silently sat beside Nelsen anticipating the wrath the Chief was about to unleash.

Sgt. Nelsen did his best not to show the contempt he had for their Chief.

After a redundant amount of time, Chief Perry removed his glasses, crossing the bows and finally tapped the file lying on his desk. "What exactly is this?"

Jim restrained his initial response and spoke slowly for the Chief. "*That* is the information you requested, *Chief. That*, is an accumulation of all the written files we have thus far on the two murders."

"Is that so, Detective Chapman?" Perry's tone was condescending and untrusting.

Cal was formal and direct. "Yes – Sir, you have everything."

"Then why do I think you're hiding something? What have you left out?"

"What do you think we're hiding, Sir?"

Perry despised a subordinate answering a question with a question. "That is what I'm asking *you!*" He then turned his attention back to Nelsen. "Sergeant? What else do you have?"

"Chief, you asked us to bring you everything. *That's* what we did. If you feel there is something missing that's because you're tying our hands on this! By not allowing us to seek help, you've impeded our investigations!"

Cal was almost as surprised as the Chief with Jim's directness.

The Chief shot out in anger, "What are you inferring, Sergeant?"

Jim smirked with the satisfaction that he just pushed one of the Chief's buttons. "*Not a thing,* Chief. I'm simply stating a fact; we haven't gotten too far. We have a suspect and his DNA is linked to both murders. Of course, we have not been able to locate him. Now, if you would allow us to ask for assistance from outside agencies?"

"No! We don't need any external help on this. We can handle it ourselves."

Cal piped in, "Chief, we're working two murders here and the County has offered their assistance..."

"I told you, *no!* Now - that's – that! Keep up the good work. You're dismissed."

Jim and Cal exchanged perplexed glances, got up and left the Chief's office.

Dotty watched from behind the glass in dispatch as Chapman and Nelsen made their way through the station.

Cal made a point to stop and say *hello.* "Anything new, Beautiful?" Cal always said the right thing to brighten her day.

Dotty just smiled, but her troubled eyes told Cal she sensed there was something more going on.

This was neither the time nor the place to talk about it. Chief Perry had eyes and ears everywhere. She politely answered, "Not really, but let Katie know I found that recipe she asked about. I'll swing by with it later."

Cal's steely grey eyes creased in a friendly smile, "I sure will."

Jim waited until they were in the parking lot before his aversion for Chief Perry came out, "What the hell was that?"

"He's fishing for how much we know." Cal knew Jim was not asking about Dot.

Jim's tone was flat and angry, "I don't trust the chief! That rat-bastard has an ulterior motive here."

Cal could not deny it; the problem was proving it.

12

Once again Billie met Katie back out at the 480 building on Milwaukee Ave. They had opened seven of the eight rooms on the second floor. The rooms all seemed to mimic the same vacant space, apart from the different wall-papers or degree of damage.

When they opened the 8th and final room, Billie got chills followed by the heebie-jeebies. She knew Katie would tell her she is just imagining things, so she kept it to herself.

Little did Billie know, Katie thought this was the same room she had been dreaming about, and deliberately saved this room for last.

They continued with the picture taking, and Katie noted everything or lack of, in her notebook.

Billie felt an invisible cold brisk hand upon her back. Startled, she quickly turned her head to face an unseen foe. An ominous abandoned framed picture hung on a blank wall by the door, drew Billie's attention. Its dirty glass dimmed the image behind it. The woman in the painting had her bare back to the viewer, looking forlorn at her own reflection in the mirror. Its colors were muted and calm; however, Billie could not pull herself away.

Katie took notice. "What is it?"

"I don't know. This is the first room we have found with anything in it. Don't you think there is something daunting about this picture?"

Katie stepped beside Billie to take a closer look. After a few seconds, she reached out to take it off the wall. "There's nothing behind it?" Billie sounded a bit disappointed.

"Well, let's go back up to the third floor - BJ could you grab the hammer I left by the window?"

"Yeah, sure." Billie sulked across the room. She grabbed the hammer, and as she turned back Billie stepped on a weak spot in the floor. Not thinking much of it, she absently looked down to where she had just placed her foot. It was not a weak spot; the floorboard was actually loose. "Hold up – Katie!"

Billie knelt down and played with the loose floorboard. It easily pried up. "Katie, there's something in here!" Billie reached her delicate hand into the space below. Her fingers felt for the object and pulled out, what appeared to be a book wrapped in a tattered piece of cloth.

The fabric almost disintegrated as she carefully unwrapped the book. The book's leather covers were cracked and worn with age. The pages were crisp and yellowed. On a few pages watermarks left the stain from what looked like tears that ran the ink and blurred the written words. "It's an old diary!" Billie's thoughts ran wild, her pulse quickened. "How cool is this?" She excitedly flipped open to a page.

Katie glanced over Billie's shoulder as she read aloud. *"May 7th 1928. I've been watching the hotel fill up with distinguished looking men. They all seem to be waiting for something."* Billie got Goosebumps.

"Oh my God, Billie! This diary could have the information I'm looking for!"

Enthusiastically Billie flipped to an entry in the back. *"December 12th 1928. I'm meeting Cliff in the east tunnel. He told me not to wait for him if he wasn't on time. I don't know if I could ever leave without him. I know he's scared. He's put on a brave front, but he's in too deep."*

"East tunnel?" Just saying it aloud gave Katie goose bumps.

"I'm gonna take this home and read it. If there is any other mention of the tunnels or this building, I'll flag it with one of those sticky note thingies."

"Okay, you take the diary and see what you can find. I'm going home to let Hondo out and then go back over those pictures we took when we first found the basement."

*

Katie had been worn out from her and Billie's endeavors. Lying on the couch she had fallen asleep, no nightmares, no restlessness, just sound sleep. It wasn't until much later when Hondo rested his head on the sofa cushion; letting out a subtle whine, that woke her up. "Thanks, boy." She said as she reached out to stroke his face. She had just enough time to change and fix her make-up before heading off to the Brick Yard.

Next to the crock-pot, she left a note for Cal just in case he came home before she did. He was supposed to be on light duty but still managed to put in 12-hour days. Luckily his shoulder was healing just fine. It was only a flesh wound he told her, but a 30-06 to the shoulder was a little more than a flesh wound and caused him pain, even if he wasn't willing to admit it. The doc put him on antibiotics and said to give it 2-months. However, Katie worried how he'd handle it *if* he didn't regain full use of his arm.

*

"Hey - Red!" Erik greeted Kate with a warm friendly smile.

"Hey – Erik, staying out of trouble?" Katie flashed one of her playful looks.

He teasingly reached out to swat her in the arm with his rolled-up flyers.

Katie laughed with a carefree air about her. It felt good to laugh. It had been a while. "What's with the flyers?"

"We've got a new band booked for the weekend so I'm passing them out."

"That's great news!" Katie yelled over her shoulder as she bounded down the stairs. "The weekend should be pretty busy!"

Downstairs, Jack was already tending bar. Katie grabbed her apron and tied the strings behind her back. "Hey, Jack, where's BJ?"

"Don't know." Jack's answer was short, and he seemed to be in a foul mood.

Katie raised a brow to him, turned on her heels and strolled right past the bar to the storage room. She found TJ easily stacking half barrels against the back wall.

TJ's bulging muscles and ripped body stopped Katie in her tracks. He was a very fine specimen. Even his easy smile could melt the coldest of hearts. She had almost forgotten what she was even doing in the storage room.

"Did ya need somethin', Red?"

Kate shook the almost indecent thoughts from her head and came back to her original train of thought. "Ah, yeah...is there something wrong with Jack? He seems crabbier than usual."

TJ shrugged his shoulders. "It's Jack", he said with an amused expression.

"Have you seen BJ? She should have been here by now."

"Nope - can't help ya there, either."

Katie stepped out of the storeroom to see Billie bounce in for work.

Jack looked up from behind the bar to flash Billie a curt and frosty glare.

"I'm late – I know...*sorry!*" Even Billie noticed Jack's surly mood.

Katie impatiently waited for Billie to clock in. When she could not contain her eagerness any longer, she pressed, "So, what did you find out?"

Billie had a twinkle in her eye as she told Katie what she read thus far. "I'm pretty sure the woman who wrote it was a prostitute!"

"Seriously?"

"Yep, and she fell in love with one of her Johns. Cliff somebody? I don't know his last name, but I think he was in the mob! It is pretty interesting though, and I've just begun! I must have fallen asleep, because I think I was dreaming about it."

"Anything on the tunnels?"

"No – not yet. So far, it's about this young woman who found herself in a situation she couldn't get out of. She started out at a 'turn-key' establishment called the Plush Horse. But some important John liked her and moved her to Deuces. That must be the white brick building that is left from the fire that took the Jones House Hotel."

"Anything else?"

"Well, actually she said something about the front being a Western Union and a barber shop."

"Sounds like I need to spend a day at the Historical Society! I don't suppose you know what's up with Jack?"

Billie just shrugged her shoulders. "Wish I knew."

The bar was not too terribly busy, mostly filled with the regulars like Brandon Holtz, and Reggie. Katie and Billie had plenty of time to discuss what they were going to do next. They were eager to get back to the 480 building and were surprised at how fast closing time came. The night seemed to fly by.

Billie was sucked into this love story belonging to a woman of ill-repute, and wanted to know how it all ended. She was fascinated with the diary and excited to get back to it. She could not wait to get back to her apartment. "I can meet you tomorrow morning at your place about 10?"

Billie looked back to Jack washing glasses as she left, trying not to be concerned with Jack's foul mood. Something obviously troubled him, but she knew it was not her. "G'night Jack! See you Friday!"

He gave her a head-nod, "Have a good night, Billie." His tone was more distant than usual, and she sensed whatever it was, really bothered him.

TJ escorted the girls out. Katie wasted no time as she jumped into her Jeep, revved it up and took off for home. Billie on the other hand, fumbled with her keys, debating whether or not she should ask TJ about Jack. Her curiosity finally won out. "TJ, is everything okay with Jack? He seems ornerier tonight than usual."

TJ gave her a reassured smile, "Don't worry pretty lady, Jack gets that way sometimes."

The look on Billie's face told TJ she was not completely convinced.

"Blondie, Jack likes you. Just be patient, he's workin' things out." He added.

Divulging more than she wanted to, "You know how I feel about Jack. I have done everything I can. I've given him space, I don't ask questions about what he's doing, and I haven't even been to his apartment. Come to think of it, he hasn't been to mine either! I guess what I want to know is, if I'm just wasting my time, hoping for something that's never gonna happen?"

Billie's troubled blue eyes wore at the soft spot TJ had for her. "Billie, do you remember how upset Jack got when you pulled a bindle from your apron?"

"How could I forget!"

"I'm going out on a limb here to give you a little insight in to Jack, only because I know how he feels about you, too."

Billie's bright eyes grew wide, anxious for new Intel on Jack. She leaned up against her car's door, eager to hear what TJ had to say.

"Jack and I met in the Corps, and became fast friends. He used to talk non-stop about his girl back home, and how he was going to marry her when he returned." TJ gave pause to look around in case someone; mainly to see if Jack happened to be within earshot of what he was telling her. "Well, while we were over in Iraq, his high school sweetheart, died from a drug overdose. When he got the news, it changed him. He had no reason to come back home, so he re-upped. Look, all I'm sayin' is to be patient with him. If you care for him like I think you do - give him some time. He's a good guy, really. He just needs to work some stuff out."

Billie frowned, "He told me he was seeing Tanya, and he caught her strung out with a prospect for the SSS."

"That's true, he did. After Jack came home, he tried to date again only to find the second woman he tried a relationship with was also into drugs."

"That explains why he flipped out, but why didn't he just tell me the whole story?" She gave pause, and then sighed, "Well, thanks for telling me, TJ!" Billie gave TJ a big hug, "I really wish he could talk to me."

"You have to understand - Jack is a very *private* person."

Billie's big blue eyes got their spark back, "I can wait...I'm not going anywhere."

"Well, I see he's finally found himself a good woman!" TJ's words brought a smile to Billie's sweet face.

"Have a good night, TJ - I'll see you Friday!" Billie's mood was joyful as she buzzed off in her little Escort.

TJ made his way back into the bar to find Jack in the office. He sat himself down in a chair in front of the desk.

Jack did not bother to look up, "Did the girls take off alright?"

TJ just sat with an all-knowing look stamped on his face.

His silence finally motivated Jack to look up from what he was doing. "What are *you* lookin' at?"

"How in the hell can a hard-ass bastard such as yourself string along a fine little lady such as BJ?"

"You got something to say?"

"Your damn right I do."

"So - let's hear it!"

"What is your issue?"

"No issue, I've got a job to do. I don't have time for..."

"For what, Billie? Are you frickin' kidding me?"

"What do you want me to say?"

"Jack, I love ya man, but you're a dumb ass!"

Jack just glared back at his Marine brother.

"That girl is *in love* with you, and the way you've treated her..."

"The way I've treated her?" Jack snapped back. "I've been a complete gentleman with her, I've never taken advantage even when I knew she was more than willing – I wouldn't! I like her, but I am keeping my distance so she doesn't get hurt."

"Yeah, you keep tellin' yourself that."

"Look, she'll just get in the way! Besides, love just doesn't work for me. You know what happened to Karen, and then Tanya."

TJ gave a hardy laugh, "Are you kidding me? You're seriously going to compare Billie to either one of them?"

"Like I told you, she'll be a distraction. She'll only get in the way and could get hurt."

"Okay, you keep thinking like that and you *will* lose her. She's a sweet gal and for some reason she actually likes you, in *all* your glory!" His tone was deep with sarcasm.

"She doesn't even know me. She doesn't know who I am or what I've done."

"Jack, you keep lying to yourself, and only telling her half truths, and you'll lose the best thing that has ever happened to you, buddy."

"Why the sudden interest in my love life?"

"I could care less about your love life, but I do find myself interested in Blondie's."

13

Keeping to the shadows and alleyways, Midas made his rounds like a stray dog that nearly all the neighbors took pity on. He was invisible to most, neglected and even ignored by others. However, Brandon Holtz was one of the few who took the time to befriend the homeless man. He brought him food, blankets and occasionally hired him to do odd jobs. Midas was great with his hands. He could get damn near anything broken to work again, from transistor radios to computers. The man was a genius with electronics, but socially inept. His social anxiety was not the only thing that kept him from the normal life he had prior to the war.

Before the war with Iraq, everyone knew him as Kelly Green, the handsome extraordinary high school all-star. Now, this war hero was living in the long-forgotten tunnels under Burlington with deep physical and emotional scars.

His family home had been destroyed by fire, and the property is where Green Gables currently stands. Shortly after the fire, he lost both parents. He had lived in Burlington all his life, where was he to go?

When Midas was thirteen, he found an entrance into a tunnel while making a fort out of an underground shelter. This discovery led him to a larger network of tunnels. He would spend endless hours, day after day exploring these tunnels. He found some of these tunnels just ended, blocked off from the basements to the buildings downtown.

One went out to the Fox River by the Jefferson St. Bridge. Another tunnel led out to Hillcrest Bed and Breakfast. He thought he had hit the jackpot when he discovered an underground bowling alley left over from the 30's or 40's.

These tunnels were now his home. Over the years a few of the tunnels had collapsed, and one he avoided at all cost. It was a bad place with hidden secrets kept from those above.

*

Once again, Cal left early for work. His shoulder wasn't going to slow him down; he now had two homicides to solve.

Keeping the chief at bay and out of his investigations was almost as difficult as the investigations themselves.

Through the front window, Katie watched as Cal pulled away. She sighed deeply out of concern for him and all the time he was spending at work. Leaving early and not returning home until real late. Running on little or no sleep, she knew was going to take a toll on Cal.

She poured herself another cup of coffee, padded into the living room and curled up in Cal's over-sized leather chair. As she sipped her coffee, she scrutinized over each one of the photos she had developed before Eddie had taken her. They were not great photographs, just snap shots in a dimly lit basement. The auto flash highlighted the arches, but did not really show much detail. In her disappointment she tossed them aside.

Hondo must have sensed her mood, for he rested his head on her lap, and then looked up at her switching his eyebrows back and forth. Instantly her mood lightened. She gave him a loving smile as she stroked his soft fur and toyed with his big ears. "You're good boy, aren't you? Do you want to come with us today?"

He lifted his head and wagged his thick tail in complete understanding; her tone meant he would be going for a ride.

A knock on the door sent Hondo running to investigate who had come. Katie followed behind, "It's just Billie, relax!"

"I'm here...sorry if I'm late!"

Hondo excitedly pawed at Billie to get her attention. She bent down to scratch him behind the ears. "Hey, buddy boy!"

"You're not late at all. I was just going over the snap shots of the basement. How much time do you have today?"

"Until whenever you want to quit!" Billie answered while petting Hondo, who had dropped to the floor enjoying all the attention she was giving him.

Billie followed Katie into the living room to take a look at the pictures of the basement. Billie spotted one still in the envelope. "Do you have this one separate for a reason?"

"Huh - No," Katie took it from Billie. "None of the pictures show anything interesting and..." Katie paused taking a closer look at the photo. There was something odd about it.

"And?"

"And what?" She absently answered, still studying the photograph.

"That's just it...you didn't finish your thought."

Katie handed over the picture, "Billie, what does this look like to you?"

Billie studied it. It was not a good picture of anything. It was dark and grainy. She could barely make out the outline of the wine racks. She shrugged, "Katie, really, I don't know what you're asking me? The picture is too dark to see anything. The wine rack was the only object in the photo I can make out. It looks dusty and grey. What am I supposed to be looking at?"

"Here...take a look at these photos." Katie laid a few out in front of Billie. "Notice the position of the wine racks?" Katie pointed out the direction of each one. Then the rack in the photo Billie held, the wine rack stood out vertically from the wall. "Something just isn't right about this wine rack."

"Oh - I see...it's an illusion."

"Illusion? No, Billie...don't you see there is something special about the way this one is different from the rest?"

"Yes, Katie – an illusion! See how much darker it is behind the end of the rack? Looks like there could be a void back there, otherwise the wall would have been present."

Katie took another look. They were both looking at the same photo, but they each saw something different. "Let's head over there. I want to take a closer look."

*

Katie and Billie locked the door behind them, with the still quietness amplifying their movements. Their heightened anticipation transitioned over to Hondo. Katie still carried the Smith and Wesson Cal gave her, just in case there were any unwelcome surprises.

Billie had her camera charged and ready to go. Both armed with flashlights and extra batteries, this time. They cautiously opened the hidden door to the basement.

Hondo's ears stood alert. A faint whine escaped from him as he looked up to give Katie a cautionary glance.

"It's okay, boy." Katie reassured him by rubbing his face and neck.

Once again, they headed down into the forgotten basement. "You know what really puzzles me, Billie?"

"No – do tell, as we head into a dark creepy basement that someone hid years ago!"

"Sarcasm, nice! Duly noted."

They paused when they reached the bottom of the stairs to shine their lights around the quiet space.

"Billie, what I was going to say was, why hasn't this building been used since the 1940's? Nothing has been done to it, other than up keep on the exterior. Why would someone pay taxes on an abandoned building all these years? Weird - right?"

With hair raised along the ridge of his back, Hondo gave a subtle growl. He made a bee-line for the old wine rack in question. Katie held his leash as he led her.

Billie with camera in hand started snapping pictures. The flashes lit up the dark space a split-second at a time.

That is when Katie saw Billie was right. There was a void behind this wine rack. Hondo sensed it too. His muscles tensed and twitched under his bristled coat. His shiny black nose flared, and his ears kept moving forward and then back.

They concentrated their light to the space beyond the rack. Katie was determined to see what was back there.

Billie did not have to ask, she only studied Katie to know they were about to do something not *too* bright.

Then, Katie confirmed it. "Help me move this rack away from the wall."

In the back of Billie's mind, she knew after reading about the tunnel in the diary, Katie would eventually find a way into the tunnel, maybe this was it. She just did not think it would be today.

The heavy wooden rack creaked and moaned when they forced it to move. They moved it enough to squeeze between it and the wall and then pushed with their legs. With some effort they made ample room for them to pass from the basement to enter into the void behind.

Katie was amazed when the light from their flashlights illuminated a brick and mortar arched ceiling and walls. "Do you see this? You need to take pictures of this!"

"I'm on it!"

With each flash, the strobe of light bounced off the walls leading them down long forgotten paths under the town. Hondo quietly padded along between the girls, keeping

7 Sons of Sin

attentive. Although he was only 6-months-old, with his innate protective instincts, he would alert them to possible trouble.

They came to a junction where the tunnel branched off into three. Here the ceiling had beautiful brick vaulted arched ceilings. The mason work alone was worth seeing.

Katie was thrilled at finding this and tingled with excitement.

Billie snapped pictures of this junction from all angles.

Katie gave Billie a hesitant look. "Now what?"

Billie shrugged her shoulders and looked down at Hondo. "He's not growling...maybe we should start with the left one, first?"

Katie agreed with a nod, and held Hondo's leash tight. If she felt him protest in anyway, they would turn back.

To keep from freaking themselves out, they discussed what this could mean. Billie's nervousness had her talking a mile a minute. Today, she incessantly yammered on about what she read in the diary. Telling Katie, she felt a connection with the woman who wrote it.

Katie sensed Billie was now fixated with this diary.

Soon their voices seemed to be bouncing back to them. "There's got to be something up ahead. We haven't gone too far, so I think we're only under the building next door?"

Billie became quiet. She took up her camera again ready to snap a few pictures. Suddenly, Kate's light revealed what they were walking into.

To their disappointment, this first tunnel seemed to have been caved in. Trying to peer through the collapsed tunnel walls with their lights, it didn't look too promising.

Katie blew out a disappointed breath, "Well, let's turn back and try the second one."

They knew they were across the street, somewhere under the St. Vincent DePaul building. Once again, their voices seemed to bounce back more quickly. They stopped; their flashlights revealed dulled images painted on a block wall of bowling pins being struck down by a black ball in motion.

"Do you see this?" Katie could not contain her excitement.

"Yeah, I see it, Kate!" Billie snapped a few pictures.

They continued to investigate. There was a window with old advertisements. The door seemed to be locked; and it was too dark to peer through the window; however, Katie was determined to find a way to get in.

They walked totally around the side of the underground building; then they found a side entrance.

Before trying the knob, Katie pointed to it for Billie to take a picture. "There's no dust on this knob. Someone has to have been here recently."

"If you're trying to encourage me to go with you...you're not helping your cause!"

Even though both were very apprehensive, the two sleuths slipped in through the open door. It was as if time stood still. They stepped back in time to an era where women were called dolls or dames, and men wore suits with fedoras. The bowling alley was quiet now, abandoned through the years. The shellacked wooden lanes beckoned to be used. It appeared one night they closed up, and no one bothered to return to reopen.

Hondo was busy nosing a wrapper. Billie picked it up, confused, "Ah, Kate?"

"Huh?"

"Did they have plastic wrapped snacks back in the 40's?"

"I doubt it – why?"

"Then where do you suppose *this* comes from?" Billie held out the discarded wrapper.

Katie walked over to a trashcan and peered down inside with her flashlight. The modern-day trash turning up in a place from the past was all she needed to see. "Billie, I don't think we're the only ones who have recently been down here."

"I'll take a few pictures, and then I think we should go." On the way-out Billie found switches on the wall. She just happened to try them. With a flip of a few switches, a buzz and hum echoed from the back of the alley, all the way up to the exit where they stood.

Katie gave Billie a surprised look, "Really? You just walked over, flip the switch and the lights turn on!" Katie frowned. "How can that be?"

Billie only shrugged.

"I think I know who I should ask about these tunnels."

"Who's that?"

"Stella, from the city clerk's office. If anyone knows about these tunnels - she would, and I think she might talk to me."

"Well, we know they exist, now! We'll have pictures to prove it." She said as she held up her camera. "I think we need a map of town. Then we can highlight each tunnel and where they lead."

"That's a great idea."

"I can't wait to tell Jack what we found!"

"You can't! At least, not just yet."

Billie did not see what the big secret was. After all they could trust Jack and Cal. Billie just would feel better if one of them knew they were going exploring in tunnels under Burlington that supposedly do not exist.

"We *will* tell them, but I want to know more before we share. Besides, Cal knows we're doing research. If we let him know what we've found now, he'd tell us to stay out, and then the police would investigate!   I'd like us to be the ones to investigate these tunnels!"

14

Katie and Billie had discovered something quite incredible. However, she would have to wait until Sunday to go to the Historical Society, since that was the only day, they were open. Instead, she made a call to Dotty's friend Stella, and then drove over to the town hall to search their records for any mention of tunnels or connecting basements between buildings. There were a few things she knew for sure; someone hid the entrance to the basement, and basement walls do not have arches, egresses do. Now that she found an entrance to the tunnels, she was determined to find out what else was down there, why they were built, who built them, and why no-one seemed to know anything about them.

She was not ready to let Paul know about it just yet. It was important to Katie to get as much information as she could before sharing their discovery.

Stella was the City Clerk from Mayor Dunn's office but also the records clerk at the town hall. She wore a few different hats and somehow managed to keep it all straight. Although she was pretty old, she was still working and sharp as a tack.

When Katie arrived, Stella was standing on the sidewalk smoking a cigarette and drinking a cup of Annie's coffee. She took a deep drag to finish it off and dropped the lipstick-stained remnants of her cigarette onto the wet sidewalk. Her thin-lipped smile greeted Katie warmly.

"Hi, Stella! I appreciate you letting me search through the records," Katie said returning the friendly smile she had received.

Stella answered in her husky voice, "It's not a problem, Hun. Dotty says you're working on a project with that architect fella."

"I am."

Stella held open the heavy door for Katie. "Is there anything specific I can help you with?"

Katie knew if anyone could help her find what she was looking for, it would be Stella. She was born and raised in Burlington. Katie's eyes twinkled with the prospect of what she could learn from the woman. "As a matter of fact…"

Stella had listened to Katie's thoughts about the bricked-up archways in the basement of the building, leaving out the fact that she just left one of those tunnels.

"There is no record of any underground tunnel system. There was an underground bowling alley many years ago, but it is long gone. It would have been under where St. Vincent DePaul stands now. To be honest, Katie, I can't say for sure why there are bricked up archways down there; other than the egresses between the buildings that were used to transport coal. However, I do know something about a tunnel from when I was a little girl."

Katie, of course, was very intrigued to hear it.

"I'll never forget what I'm about to tell you. At the time it scared me, and to think about it now, it is still a bit disturbing." Stella cleared her throat as she glanced around making sure they were alone, so that no one might overhear her. "I was a young girl, probably 8 or 9 years old, we lived just a few blocks from here. My grandfather came to stay with us for a while.

I was an inquisitive child, and one night after being put to bed, I snuck back downstairs. I heard my father talking to another man at the kitchen table. I'm not quite sure *how* I *knew*, but there was something about this man that told me to stay hidden and not let him know I was listening in on their conversation."

"Anyhow," Stella took a breath, "This man had told Dad he needed to handle this matter with Grandpa. They needed something; I never heard what that was. Their voices were hushed and very secretive, until that man got angry and raised his voice to Dad. That was the wrong thing to do. I'd never seen my father get so upset. He told that man, he'd kill him if he so much as came anywhere near his family."

"Oh my gosh! That had to be quite a surprise to hear for a 9-year-old?"

"Let me tell you, I high tailed it back up stairs. The next morning, I got up and headed outside. When I saw Dad and Gramps discussing something in the garage, I crept along the side of the garage to the little window, so I could hear what they were being so secretive about. That's when I heard Gramps telling Dad to 'stay out of it'. Dad was mad, and blamed Gramps for getting his family involved in this thing that he did. They argued and the last thing Gramps told Dad was not to worry, everything would be taken care of. I could have sworn he said something about it being hidden down below."

Katie got excited about what she was hearing.

Stella continued, "Then one day I was riding my bike downtown here and saw my gramps coming out of a tavern with a package under his arm. I, of course, followed him for a few blocks, but then he disappeared."

"How can he just disappear?"

"Here's the thing. That's the part of my memory that gets a little hazy. I thought I saw him enter a building, but he never came out. It got dark and I had to go home for supper. And *there* was Gramps, sitting at the kitchen table. I never saw him leave the building! I did a very foolish thing...I started to spy on Gramps. I wanted to know where he went and what he was doing. After a few days I followed him into that same building. I was very good at being sneaky. I followed his shadow down a corridor, but there were cement steps. I remember taking the steps, careful not to let him hear me. Then, I lost him. I found myself in a maze of brick passages with arched ceilings."

Hearing Stella's words gave Katie the chills.

"There was very little light, and I remember being afraid of getting lost down there. That's when I heard my grandpa's voice. He was arguing with another man. I followed their voices to a grate in a wall. I climbed up on something to peer in. There was a whole other room behind the room I was in. There were men in suits, and they all had guns. Grandpa's voice was stern and had upset one of the other men. I tried to hear what was going on, but I only heard bits and pieces."

Katie was caught up in Stella's tale, "What did you hear?"

"I really don't remember...all I know is Gramps had something they wanted, and he didn't trust them with it. I've never told a soul about what I heard. Now, you're telling me there was a hidden passage to the basement of this building and blocked-up archways. I may not have a record of what you're telling me; but, it sure sounds like perhaps there was a passage leading to something...maybe I found myself in one of these tunnel years ago?"

"Stella, if there are tunnels under Burlington, wouldn't the historical society have it in their archives? I mean - that would be such a draw to this town. People eat that stuff up. Why wouldn't they advertise it?"

"Katie, I'm not saying there are tunnels under Burlington, but if there were..." Stella trailed off with her thought. "If there were tunnels, someone would have made it public awhile ago. It would be hard to keep something like that a secret."

"I have to ask...was your grandfather involved with the mob?"

"Well, after that day, I always had my suspicions. I remember him and my father being very guarded, and at times we'd be places when my mother and I would leave them alone for a while. Mom would always say we were going off to have "girl time" but I knew it was so Dad and Grandpa could have some space to do whatever it was they were doing. Now mind you, prohibition ended in 1933. Burlington was no different than any other town of that time. From the '20's until '33, we had Speakeasies and women of ill-repute, along with visiting gangsters."

Katie was in awe of Stella's vivid tale. "Did you ever go back to that building you followed your grandfather into?"

"Oh – no, I couldn't even tell you which building it was, or if it is even still standing. I stayed clear of that building, and I never followed Grandpa again! I don't even remember if I heard them right. I was 9!" She tapped a finger to her head, "The mind remembers things differently through the years."

"You could have fooled me, you tell that story like it was yesterday!"

"I wish I had some sound information for you."

"Well, the main questions I have are really about the white brick building. Do you know anything more about that particular building? All I have is what the Historical Society gave me from back in 1845 when it was part of the Jones House Hotel."

"Of course! That entire block was known as the Jones House Block. Later it was the Badger Hotel and after that, the Coach Lamp, but in 1968 a fire destroyed the upper two stories. They didn't rebuild or use it as a hotel anymore. Only the one level remained, and that is now the sports bar and grill attached to your white brick building. One thing you might want to check into is the underground bowling alley."

"Seriously?"

"Well, there really was an underground bowling alley. It was part of an old speakeasy from back during the Capone days. It's long gone now, but it was somehow accessed by way of the sports bar attached to your white brick building."

"Thanks, Stella! It looks like I have a lot more research to do. By the way, did you ever find out what *it* was, that was hidden down below?"

Stella sadly shook her head, "No, Dear, I never did. Strange thing, not long after that Gramps left, and I never saw him again! He just disappeared. I always thought one day he'd come back, but he never did." Stella left Katie to her devises.

Katie had spent most of the day going through boxes of files searching for anything that would suggest there were tunnels under Burlington. Stella's words played over and over in Katie's head; tunnels left behind from Al Capone's prohibition days, and a hazy memory from her childhood, which of course only motivated her to search even harder.

She came across the tax file for the 480 building. Her heart beat a little faster, maybe she would find out who owned it and why they anonymously hired Paul to research it. Unfortunately, all she found was a name for a corporation. This same corporation has held this property since 1935. Just one more puzzle for Katie to solve.

Until her stomach growled, she completely forgot about meeting Cal for dinner. Checking the time, Katie realized she was already 15 minutes late. Quickly packing up and rushing out, Katie would not have time to clean up. Luckily, they were only going to Doug's.

Excited to tell Cal about the conversation she had with Stella, Katie spotted him sitting at their usual booth in the back, but she soon realized he was already deep in conversation with Jim Nelsen, drinking a beer.

Katie smiled, "I see you've had one of *those days*...do I even want to know?"

Cal's steely grey eyes softened as he smiled back at the beautiful woman standing before them. He quipped back in an amused tone, "I see you've had one of *those days,* too!"

Jim looked up to see what changed his partner's expression and had to grin at Katie's disheveled appearance as well. "What in the *hell* have you been into today?"

Katie held up a finger to excuse herself, "I'll be right back." She turned on her heels and headed for the lady's room.

"Cal, I thought she was doing some research for that architect?"

"She is, on that old white brick building on Milwaukee Ave. by the sports bar."

"I didn't realize research was such a dirty job?" Jim chuckled.

"I didn't either!"

Katie looked at her messy and dusty appearance in the mirror. Even she had to laugh at herself. She quickly washed up and finger-combed through her hair only to pull it back into a neater version of a ponytail before rejoining Jim and Cal at the table.

Upon her return, O'Brien had been added to their group. Even Randy looked a little haggard around the edges. These murder investigations were obviously wearing on all of them.

Kate sat down next to Cal. Doug brought a round of beers for the three off-duty officers. "What can I get for ya, Katie?"

"Actually, I'll take one of those." She exhaled deeply blowing up at tendrils of red hair that hung in her eyes.

"You too, Hun?" Cal asked as he wrapped his "good" arm around her.

Katie had not realized how exhausted she really was, until she sat down, resting her tired head on Cal's shoulder.

15

Lately, Cal's disquiet thoughts had him anywhere but home. Katie was feeling distracted herself this morning - mentally preparing for another visit to see Doctor Sylvia Reynolds.

Cal took his coffee to go, as he rushed off to work, but suddenly stopped at the front door. He almost forgot something. Cal turned back to Katie who was absently staring out the window.

It just dawned on him that today was another counselor day, and he would be missing it. Cal set his keys and coffee down as he came up behind Katie. "Kate?" He placed his hands on her hips, and spoke softly in her ear, "Is everything alright?"

Katie nodded, and then leaned back into him. "I'll be fine."

"I'll go in late today...I want to take you."

Katie sighed, she knew he wanted to go with her, but she also knew Cal was troubled with work. She turned to give Cal a reassured smile, "You go - I'll be fine. I can do this today."

Cal felt torn, but Kate was always honest with him. If she said she would be fine, there wasn't some hidden underlying code that he had to guess. Cal kissed her with warm, tender lips, which let her know he fully supported her and loved her.

As soon as Cal climbed into his squad and backed down the driveway, he punched up Jack's number.

Feeling the pressure from Special Agent in Charge Wesley Cooper, Jack had not gotten much sleep. He just lay in bed staring at the white ceiling, thinking back over some info he might have over looked, or angle he could work to move this investigation along; when his cell phone rang.

He answered, "Jack!"

"It's Cal, are you up?"

"Yeah - I'm up."

"I need your help."

Jack cleared his throat, "Yeah?"

"Can we meet – just the two of us?"

There was a long pause on the line. Cal could almost hear the heavy sigh escape from Jack, "Sonny's in an hour." Then he hung up.

Before he could make it across the room to the shower, his phone rang again. "Aw - hell!" He grabbed it and answered with irritation, "Now what?"

TJ sounded amused. "Good morning to you, too, Jack!"

"Sorry – man, how did it go?"

"I'm getting closer. She is such a slut for attention. Our fishing expedition has started to pay off. I've gotten two good buys and the 'ice' I got last night directly leads to the SSS."

"Is that so?"

"Let's just say I got a little more than a lap dance at Puss 'n Boots last night."

"I really don't need to know. What about the other thing?"

A hardy laugh came through the phone. "Yeah, about that...the other night I thought I would watch Brandon Holtz from Fox's Liquor. He's been behaving suspiciously, and knowing how he feels about Charlie... I followed him."

"Okay, so?"

"So, I followed him to the river's edge and then lost him. He's up to something."

Once again, he snapped his phone shut.

Although, TJ's tid-bit of good news brought a smile to Jack's scowling face; Jack was frustrated with his own investigation. He did not like having to keep Chapman out of the loop, and that was no easy task. Other than his military brothers, Chapman was the one-man Jack trusted.

*

Stella came in early to finish some filing at City Hall. Somehow a file was misplaced and she was diligently searching for it. Thinking back on Katie's inquiry as to the possibility of tunnels under Burlington, Stella's *quiet* was suddenly disrupted.

She did not think anyone else would be down there this morning. She stopped what she was doing to take a look around, when she spotted Mayor Dunn as he disappeared behind a false wall. The hair on Stella's arms stood on end.

"What the hell is he up to?"

It was just last week over lunch when she and Dotty, had compared notes about their bosses. Dotty even had a long list of grievances with the Chief. They had joked that both the mayor and chief of police were probably corrupt.

In the last few months Stella had also found the mayor to be acting peculiar, even more secretive than usual. Now, she was sure he was hiding something.

She might have been an old woman, but there was a storm brewing, she felt it. She decided it would be best *not* to be in the records room when the mayor returned.

Seeing the Mayor leave through a secret passage down in the records room was unsettling, especially considering the conversation she just had with Katie about the possibility of tunnels under Burlington. She did not believe in coincidences. She needed some advice. Back at her desk, Stella picked up the receiver and dialed Dotty at the Police Station.

"Dot – it's Stella. Let's have lunch today. You are not going to *believe* what I have to tell you!"

Dotty heard something in her friend's voice. "Of course – can we do it early, say 11:30?"

*

Cal was already seated at a back booth when Jack strolled into Sonny's.

Jack winked at the shriveled up older waitress, and asked, "Can I get a cup of coffee, Beautiful?" His devilish grin and easy, confident swagger told Cal that Jack was unhindered.

She flashed Jack a smile the size of Texas, as he slid into the seat across from Cal.

The waitress poured a cup for Jack and topped off Cal's. Then they placed their orders with her.

Cal took a sip of his coffee as he waited for the waitress to take leave.

"Thanks, Hun!" Jack responded with one of his sexy smiles.

Cal just rolled his eyes.

Jack looked down into the hot dark brew, "Let me guess, you think I know where Charlie is?"

"You don't?"

"Nope! I don't doubt he pissed off some very dangerous guys, but what happened to him...that I don't know."

"Look, Jack...I've now got two missing persons on top of two homicides, and my only lead is one of the missing persons!"

"Who is your second missing person?"

"Cory Walker."

Jack took a slow sip of coffee.

Cal knew Jack well enough to know he was struggling with something. "Jack, I could really use your help here. Our first murder vic, Courtney Roberts was a dancer at Puss 'n Boots, the girlfriend of Nick Bolen, and you dropped a huge hint that we should look further into the break-in at Pioneer's Inn. Charlie Nix was the chef there. We know he had sex with Roberts the night she died, and there was a trace of meth found on her."

Jack sat quietly listening to Cal, and sipped his coffee.

"Cory Walker was one of the boys we questioned about the break-in, also about Courtney's death and her connection to the drugs. Now, he's been reported missing. Our latest victim, Alison Chambers also danced at Puss 'n Boots. She had information she was going to give Nelsen but was killed before she could. Charlie Nix's DNA was all over Alison's body. He's our main suspect here, and we can't locate the son of a bitch. The viciousness of these murders and in so short a time requires a damn task force of cops from all over the county working on these murders, and now two missing persons!"

Cal sat back, after he revealed everything about his case so far. "Perry has tied our hands. He wants this kept quiet for God's sakes!" Cal looked directly at Jack. "I can link Nix to both bodies, one more circumstantial than the other. What I need to know is why? Jack, can you give me *anything*? I'm drowning here. Is Cory missing because there were drugs stolen from the Pioneer's Inn? My guess is that there were drugs stolen by Bolen and his friends, and then Nick used his girlfriend to sell them, which - therefore got Courtney killed! Am I warm? I know you know the connections here. I've seen your files on the SSS. This all leads back to the damn strip club, doesn't it?"

Cal studied Jack for any offered assistance, but was perplexed with how reticent Jack was.

Jack sees Cal is tired of treading water. He felt bad; after all, they were on the same side. Jack's expression altered, although he did not look up from his cup. "Chapman, I trust you implicitly which is why I agreed to meet with you. Do you realize I can't even ask for an exception for you? There are things I can't tell you..." Finally making eye contact with Cal, his tone was low and strong, "You have to promise me, whatever you do – don't compromise me on this. Don't quote me! It's vital that you give an independent source how you learned this information."

Jack studied Cal, taking his time he coolly took a long drink of his coffee, and then continued. "We only have one judge and one felony States Attorney in on this, and the players meet regularly."

Cal instinctively knew he was only scratching at the surface of something bigger.

"I don't doubt Charlie is responsible for the girls' deaths. And I can damn near bet that kid isn't coming back. The drugs Charlie was dealing out of the restaurant were part of the items not reported stolen. Those same drugs belong to the SSS. If he was fingered for being there, they've already killed him. The same goes for Charlie Nix. He's fucked-up too many times for the bikers to give him a pass. They would dispose of him just to keep you guys out of their business."

Cal was silent.

Their waitress brought their food.

Jack set his coffee to the side for a refill.

Cal once again waited for their waitress to leave them. "Are you any closer to finding their cookers?"

Jack busily salted and peppered his potatoes as he pushed things around on his plate. Without giving Cal his full attention, he answered in a hushed tone, "This Meth lab is supplying a huge area. They can take it anywhere, but they're here for a reason. This segment of organized crime has roots here."

It was what Jack was not saying - that told Cal he was right, there *was* more to it. He also understood the position Jack just put himself in by telling him as much as he did.

"We already know Charlie killed Alison because of the DNA we got, but can't find the bastard. Now, it sounds like Charlie is the common link in all of this!"

"Courtney was my informant. She had linked the drugs stolen from Pioneer's Inn to the SSS. Yes, her boyfriend, Nick Bolen, gave her some 'ice' to sell to her clients. She had something to tell me, but you know *that* never happened. Cory was just in the wrong place at the wrong time."

"Jack, do you remember back to freshman year in high school?" Cal realized Jack knew exactly what he was talking about by the smirk that spread across his face. "I still owe you!"

"So, you remember it correctly." Jack mused.

"If you need me...you know I'll do what I can. You know we can trust each other. I'm asking if we can share info on this; just between you and me." Cal studied Jack for a moment, "Now, what aren't you telling me...I know there's something else going on here, Jack?"

"I told you - I'm limited, Cal. I could lose my job, just with the information I gave you."

Cal was right; there was something more going on. As much as Jack trusted and respected Cal, there was only so much he could tell him. Jack had suspected there was someone inside the department helping these bikers to keep their secrets hidden. There had been too many things sugar coated or swept under the rug in Burlington to bring anyone else in on what he was really doing. Finding the arms stolen from the weapons depot was his main focus. There was too much at stake to risk a leak.

*

Katie did not want to think that seeing her shrink was a waste of time – even though she felt fine, she knew it was a very important process that she had to work through.

"Good morning, Katie!" Dr. Sylvia Reynolds said, with a little too much cheer for Katie's liking, this particular morning.

"Morning!" Katie replied, as she sat down in one of the patterned fabric chairs in front of the large window.

Sylvia had a peachy complexion, and short spiky Chestnut colored hair that gave her the look of a younger woman. Her friendly hazel-brown eyes were framed with severely waxed, dark, penciled-in eyebrows, which gave her a permanent "eye-opening" expression. Katie focused on the bright coral lip-stain that brought way too much attention to a large gap in Sylvia's front teeth. It made it difficult for Katie not to stare.

Doctor Reynolds was a nice lady, but she had not seemed to offer Katie anything relevant. She would just ask the same questions and listen; however, this morning she surprised Katie by changing things up. "How are you and Cal doing?"

Katie's puzzled look prompted Sylvia to revise her words and ask a more direct question. "How is your intimate relationship with Cal, have you made love since your return?"

Reacting to the question - instead of answering the question gave Dr. Reynolds more insight than Katie knew. "Why is *that* the subject of this session?"

"Katie, you and Cal are newly engaged, and the stress of your kidnapping along with his job can interfere with your relationship. I just want to know if you have resumed your intimate relationship, or if there is something that is hindering that. Having a healthy relationship is also part of the recovery process and is essential to moving forward."

Katie's troubled stare partnered with silence was an automatic give away that she and Cal had not been sexually intimate since her return.

"Katie, I know talking about your sex life to a therapist isn't the easiest, but know I'm not judging here. I'm only trying to help you work through whatever could be obstructing that part of your relationship."

Being reluctant to openly discuss her sex life or lack there of, Katie responded with, "We've been pretty busy with work, and the puppy, but we do unwind with each other at the end of the day and talk."

"Okay, so you're back at work. How's that going?"

A spark in Katie's green eyes ignited with the excited promise of exploring the tunnels, which she could not conceal. "Work is good. I love what I'm doing."

Sylvia read there was something more to it. "How is your working relationship with your boss, Paul?"

"I haven't really seen Paul much. He told me to take as much time as I needed, but what I really need is to keep myself busy. That's why I went back to work. I'm back at the Brick Yard, too."

"How is that going for you?"

"What, the bar?"

"Yes, the bar. How did you feel your first night back?"

"How did I feel?"

"Katie, why are you answering my questions with questions?"

"Sylvia, I really don't understand why you're asking me these types of questions. Cal and I are good. No, we haven't been sexually intimate, but there is so much going on right now. We have an open line of communication; we snuggle and have our intimate moments. Work is good. I don't have issues at either job. My customers at the Brick Yard are great. Why don't you ask me about how I'm sleeping? Or about the nightmares I'm having?" Katie's tongue was sharp.

Katie was a strong-willed determined woman, and Doctor Reynolds was beginning to learn just how strong she was. Katie had bared her soul in the first few sessions, but now kept certain things private, which didn't help her counselor. "All right, tell me about these nightmares you've been having."

"They've gotten more intense, but I don't have them all the time. The last one turned into a night terror. I relived everything I experienced while Eddie had me. I physically felt grief from losing Cal."

"You didn't lose Cal."

"I know that, but that doesn't prevent me from having these very vivid dreams about it. I know they scare Cal. I see the worry in his eyes."

Doctor Reynolds wanted Katie to meet with her twice a month to help Katie regain control of her life. Subconsciously, Katie felt out of control, which is what Eddie had done to her by taking her from the safety of her home. The idea of losing the one man she so deeply loved and needed was triggered by the traumatic experience of him being shot while saving her. Although Katie already knew the triggers, she needed to focus on how to control these feelings and underlying thoughts in order to relieve her from the nightmares.

*

Sgt. Nelsen and O'Brien were walking out of the Substation when Chapman pulled in.

He lowered his driver's side window, "What's up?"

Nelsen barked with an agitated abrupt tone, "Don't bother parking. Just head to the main station! We have been summoned to the Chief's office!"

"Summoned?" Cal repeated.

Randy just shrugged his shoulders.

This is just how Cal wanted to start his day; missing Kate's appointment, verification about what he already suspected but could not prove, and now having to deal with the chief's negative agenda.

Dotty's friendly face smiled at the officers when they came in. She was getting ready to leave for lunch with Stella but made sure to exchange pleasantries with her officers. "I'll let the chief know you're here."

Deputy Chief Dan Dogget was making his way down the hall when he saw Chapman, Nelsen, and O'Brien. "Don't bother Dot – I'll take the *Three Musketeers* back." He turned on his heels fully expecting the officers to just blindly follow him.

Dotty knew the Chief was screwing with her men, and she did not like it. Not one bit! She exchanged a look with Cal. She held up crossed fingers and mouthed, "Good luck."

Sgt. Nelsen was already agitated, and the Deputy Chief's insolence toward them now had him fired up.

*

Dotty and Stella preferred Polly's Deli. Not only was it with-in close walking distance from both the police station and City Hall, but there was plenty of privacy to talk. The crabby woman who worked the lunch counter kept most people from dining in.

They sat at their usual table quickly getting into their lunchtime groove.

Stella got right to it, commenting on the unsettling chance of Katie inquiring about the tunnels under Burlington and then witnessing her boss disappear behind a false wall in the basement of City Hall.

Dotty was utterly speechless.

"Dot what the hell is going on here in Burlington? I heard your guys are now working two homicides?"

"They are...but what about tunnels under Burlington? I thought they were only rumors?"

"Time will tell!"

Dotty took a sip of her iced tea, "Now Mary's boy is missing. If the tunnels really exist, that would be a great place to start looking!"

"How is Mary taking it?"

"Not well. She knows he's gone. She blames the Reid boys."

"What's the chief doing about it?"

Dotty laughed, "That damn fool doesn't do anything unless *your* boss tells him to."

Stella nodded in affirmation, "I've been thinking about that." She ran down her list of insight to the Dunn's miraculous success in real estate, owning the three grocery stores and of course his political career. "It never smelled right to me, but what do I know? I only work for the man...although lately he has been extra cranky and likes his privacy."

"I never liked his wife either."

"Oh yeah, she's a real piece of work; that up-tight boney assed witch!" Stella laughed at her own reference to the mayor's wife.

"The one I feel sorry for is Mrs. Perry and those kids. I don't think they know the real Dennis Perry. I have got a stack of reports Perry made the officers change that were suppose to be shredded. To top that off – he's purchased all kinds of new equipment for the department. The latest things I've had to sign for were new cameras! And guess what...only one of the two made it into our inventory! I know that weasel ordered one for himself courtesy of the department. The way he treated Cal when Eddie had taken Katie, I'll never forgive him. I'd love to see that man gone! What he is doing to my guys makes me so angry!"

"Dot, we know our bosses are no good, but unless we have something to take higher...you know the village idiots won't do a damn thing. They *love* the mayor. He has got his hands in everything! Including the local press! The editor in chief is his best friend, hell - his only friend! His wife is successful in real estate, his brother-in-law owns B & B Construction, and whom do you think approves all these contracts to them? The wife holds the properties, and the brother-in-law builds on them. That, and he monopolizes the grocery markets...he doesn't just run Burlington he owns it!"

"Stella, you said the mayor left the records room - through a false wall? Where do you suppose he went?"

"Hell, if I know!"

"Do you *really* think there are tunnels under Burlington?"

"I'm sure he's been keeping all kinds of secrets."

"Stella, we need to find out for sure."

"If Katie keeps pushing, she'll be the one to find them. You know that girl is determined!"

"Do you think you can figure out how Dunn opened that false wall? You have to see what's there; it may be nothing, just a hidden room in the basement. But - if it is an entrance to a tunnel, I don't want Katie snooping around. She could get hurt."

*

Detective Chapman was beginning to despise the chief like Sgt. Nelsen already had.

The chief made it clear to Sgt. Nelsen, Detective Chapman, and Officer O'Brien that he wanted these two murders minimized, basically covered up. After all, they were only a couple of strippers associated with a biker gang. They were not getting anywhere, and he wasn't going to waste any more of his resources on this, when their time could be better served writing tickets to make the village money.

Sgt. Nelsen was seeing red, "They were young women who did not deserve the brutality and deaths they received! It doesn't matter what their profession was. And neither one of them had a record, not even a speeding ticket!"

"That's enough, Sergeant!" Chief Perry was agitated but dismissive.

"The County offered their help on this, and we should take it. Otherwise, you're just setting us up to fail!"

"Regardless of how *you* think we should handle this...ultimately it is my decision! When you get to be chief Serge, you can make the call!" The chief was clenching his jaw in agitation with Nelsen. He then turned his attentions to Cal, "Detective, when you have something, I want it. I will look it over, and decide how we're going to proceed. Until then anything said here, will stay here with us. You aren't to discuss these cases with anyone except yourselves and me. If anyone speaks to the press, you're done. I will be the only one talking to the press. Do I make myself clear?"

Chief Perry did not like anyone questioning his authority. "When I give an order, I expect it to be followed!"

O'Brien obediently sat quietly, while Sgt. Nelsen glared at the Chief with hatred in his eyes.

"And another thing, Jim, I've noticed the ugly hand-made signage in town is still posted. I told you to remove those. The Village has ordinances against using handmade signage. If they want to post any signage, they must use the Village's sign company to do so."

In disbelief, Jim fired back, "Are you frickin' kidding me? We are in the middle of two homicides and you're worried about signs?"

Chief Perry added insult to injury with a crooked smile, "Sergeant, if you can't handle your duties, I do have someone else in mind that can. You're dismissed!"

Whatever conflicts Cal had had with Chief Perry in the past, Cal did his job first and foremost. This was not personal; this was different and highly suspicious. Now the chief seemed to be playing some kind of game to prevent them from doing their jobs.

The three officers had quietly left Perry's office. They left the station separately, only to meet up at Doug's for a late lunch.

Randy had remained silent since the meeting in Perry's office. Now, that he was not under any scrutiny he vocally questioned their chief's motives, "Why is he sabotaging these cases?"

Cal was disturbed by Perry's indifferent attitude towards the investigation. How could the chief just want to bury these girls' murders? The only press it had gotten was a small paragraph on page 7. The paper made it sound like the police already had it taken care of, an "isolated incident". That was a joke, one – maybe, but two?

Nelsen had all he could take, "Someone else can do my job? What the hell was that – a threat? That rat-bastard! And, how dare he hinder our investigation! He's obstructing justice! What's this bullshit with the signs? He's fucking with me again; threatening my job! I'd like to see that piece of shit hang!"

As amusing as Sgt. Nelsen's ranting could be, Cal did not want any attention brought to them. In a calm voice Cal redirected Nelsen, "Look, Jim, I agree with you, but you need

7 Sons of Sin

to take it down a notch. We can't have anyone hear what's going on. I'm tired of Perry's lackadaisical managerial oversight, too."

Nelsen knew Cal was right. The chief knew how to push his buttons and turn him into an angry manic. He took a breath, "Sorry, you're right; he just gets under my skin!"

"His micro-managing is tying our hands on purpose! I know what the chief said; however, we do need help and we're going to seek it without his permission."

Jim gave Cal a squinty-eyed glance. "What are you up to, Chapman?"

Randy and Jim both sat up straight, and leaned in close across the table.

Cal mirrored them, "I'm not up to anything, yet! But Randy is right, the chief's motives are wrong. If he *is* up to something, we need to figure out what that is. This is more than just stacking the books."

16

Randy O'Brien's suspicions about the Chief of Police were eating away at him. There was something going on and he was resolute to find out whatever that might be.

Tonight, was not the first time Randy had followed his chief. As Randy sat in the parking lot across from the Cotton Picker Restaurant, he watched Dennis Perry enjoy an expensive dinner with his wife.

There were things that Chief Perry had done, that at first did not seem too terrible. After all, he only wanted Burlington to look like a town where everyone wanted to live, or visit. But then, he used his power of authority to manipulate the good men in his department; which meant certain ranking officers were severely discredited, dismissed or forced to resign, even demoted in place by job description, or forced into early retirement, until the chief had the solid chain of command he wanted.

The first real sign something was amiss was the number of police reports he ordered changed, making them misdemeanors or some village ordinance violation. Randy regretted following Perry's orders, and was glad he kept copies of those reports he was ordered to change. When Perry asked O'Brien to spy on the Substation and report back to him, Randy knew the chief was a no-good son-of-a-bitch.

When equipment, previously requested and then denied had suddenly shown up, another red flag went up. Randy was personally told these things were *not* in the budget, then two cameras arrived for the evidence truck and one quickly disappeared into the chief's possession. Perry not only had the audacity to take the camera on a family vacation, but then showed his minions back at the station the pictures he took with it.

Now, with the way the chief was handling the murder investigations of these two young women Randy was appalled. There was more to the chief's micro-managing the officers' investigations than they knew. Randy was determined to find out what their chief was hiding, through any means necessary; all on his own time, of course.

*

Katie could not wait to tell Cal about the tunnels and the underground bowling alley. Stella's story was still playing over in her head. The endless possibilities of a mob connection thrilled her. Tonight, when Katie pulled in, she saw Cal had visitors.

Cal was discussing work with Sgt. Jim Nelsen and Randy O'Brien, when she came in. Sharing her discovery would have to wait until later.

"Hi, guys!" Katie greeted everyone with a pleasant smile.

"Hey, Katie!" came in unison from the men sitting in the living room.

Katie tapped her thigh, calling Hondo to go out one last time before going to bed. He readily trotted to the back door.

Cal excused himself to give Katie a proper 'hello'. From behind, he put his arms around her, letting her ease back into him as he kissed the side of her face. "How was work?"

"Probably better than yours...is everything alright?"

"We've just got some things to discuss. It might be a while."

Katie turned to face Cal and smiled, "Take your time, there is always tomorrow." She let Hondo back in, and gave Cal a proper kiss good night before heading upstairs.

He thought she was awesome, so understanding. He watched her walk away, taking Hondo with her. Cal felt guilty for not being with Kate at her appointment, and now when he knew he should really take the time to be with Kate, he was dealing with work. He better not screw this up with her.

Cal took three beers out of the fridge and returned to the living room.

Randy shared his thoughts, "Think about it; the chief moves into a very nice house in an uppity neighborhood, buys two new vehicles; a Cadillac SUV of all things and a loaded Dodge truck. The kids now have new quads, a dirt bike, and then the wife, who doesn't work by the way, buys one of those expensive foo-foo dogs! You tell me how a cop, even the chief of police can afford all that? He's nothing more than a legal criminal!"

Jim had despised the man. It was more than just a personality conflict between them. The chief screwed with his men, who were good cops and his friends. "Well, that rat-bastard is getting his money somehow, and we *know* it ain't his salary - paying for all his toys!"

Cal did not like what he was thinking; but, the truth of the matter is, it fit.

17

With Easter coming soon, the mayor wanted to insure everyone's attentions were focused on the Easter Day activities and not the homicides the police were working.

He would make sure most were gearing up for it, participating in it, and then talking about how great it was afterward. They would start the Easter celebration off with a special service at his church. He and his wife would even help make pancakes for the Easter brunch, and then the mayor's crème de le crème; the Easter Egg Hunt which he hosted every year in Echo Park.

Mayor Dunn knew it all had to do with perception. He was the ideal politician. He could charm a rattlesnake, just so he could make chili out of it later.

The 7 Sons of Sin were just like that rattlesnake. They served a purpose until they no longer made it worth-while for the mayor to conceal their activities. He was very displeased with all the attention the deaths of the two strippers brought.

The problem with Mayor Dunn was his self-proclaimed control he had over Richie Collins. Richie allowed Mayor Dunn to push his weight around only out of necessity. Mrs. Dunn's access to properties for show, made it easier than ever to conduct private business at a number of locations under the radar of the LEOs (law enforcement officers). A couple would pose as prospective buyers during the dinnertime showings. Then leave after brokering a deal. They easily moved large quantities of drugs this way, and thought the unsuspecting cops were a joke.

When the Mayor scolded Richie like a child for letting things get out of control, Richie reminded him of their long business history.

Mayor Dunn never took kindly to being told anything, and being reminded of their first business endeavor struck a raw nerve with the mayor. There were skeletons stacked a few deep in the mayor's closet, and he would be damned if a low life such as Richie Collins was going to reveal what he had stored in there.

There really was not much difference between Richie Collins and Mayor Patrick Dunn. One wore a suit and the other one wore colors. They were both twisted businessmen who did not trust the other, but only one would personally dispose of the other.

*

Billie and Katie had decided to leave Hondo at home today. Katie carried the .357 in an inside jacket pocket just in case they would need it. Billie had brought the map and an extra roll of film. Their excitement about the discovery of these tunnels, over ruled the natural fear they had for exploring the unknown.

Billie happened to look at the time on her cell when she realized she did not have any bars. "Do you have a signal, Katie?"

Katie opened her cell to check, "No", she answered flatly.

"Isn't that just great! What if something happens? No one is even gonna know we're down here!"

"Do you want to turn around and head back?"

"I'm not sayin' that...besides, I told you I'd help you document whatever you find. I'm just along for the ride!"

Katie sighed, "The first tunnel was collapsed, the second tunnel led us to the bowling alley, and the third one is also collapsed. That's the one - which ended under the sidewalk by the bank. It must have collapsed while they were building that ATM."

"Yeah, I marked it here on the map. We'll check it when we get top-side."

They chose to explore a narrow tunnel - which branched off from where the third one had collapsed. They followed this one for a few minutes when it turned from brick and mortar to earth and timber. This tunnel was cold, almost damp.

Billie was feeling a bit claustrophobic. "It feels like a crypt down here!"

"BJ! Really?"

"Well, it does!"

Katie was thinking the same thing, only Billie said it aloud. "Do you mind if we just finish this one tunnel until it ends? Then we will head back."

"Well, okay but it's already going on 2 o'clock, and we both have to work the Brick Yard tonight. And after this – I need a shower. I think I have cobwebs in my hair!"

Katie and Billie continued to cautiously follow the tunnel that went in a north-eastern direction. They didn't seem to get too far when they discovered another brick-and-mortar section of the tunnel that widened. Not only did it widen, but there was another branch that seemed to veer off to the south.

Billie took several pictures. "I know it's not logical, but instead of following this one to the north, I'd like to check this one out when we come back tomorrow to finish."

"I guess, but you're the one who only wanted to go another 30 minutes!"

"I really need that shower, I feel icky!" Billie giggled. In truth, she was anxious to read more of the diary before having to go to work.

"There's a new band playing this weekend. We should be busy at least!"

"Oh yeah, Erik was passing out flyers for that. A band would be great! Bob has not booked a band in a while."

"Maybe because he knows how crazy busy, we get, and I wasn't around to help you."

"That could be..." Billie trailed off into silence.

Katie was suddenly feeling guilty for not being there to help her out, "I know working a busy floor by yourself isn't easy."

Then Billie's voice became low and even, almost a whisper. *"Come take a look at this!"*

Katie could not believe she missed it. She was too busy watching the ground and looking up ahead to notice the walls. A black metal grate was bricked in place. Billie had a concerned look on her face. "There must be something on the other side of this wall. It's like a little window. There's a faint draft, too."

"I wonder? Can you see anything in there?" Katie was too short to peak in, and BJ could barely look in standing on her tiptoes.

"We'll need something to stand on to get a better look. Just mark it on the map where you think we are," Katie told her.

They traveled only a short distance before Katie sensed eyes upon her. Even in the dark, Katie could feel someone watching her. She switched hands putting her flashlight in her left hand and kept her right hand on the gun she carried. Katie's breathing slowed to where she was almost holding her breath, and allowing her other senses to kick in. Every whisper, every echo, every step seemed to radiate caution.

"Okay, I don't think we have much further to go, we're getting a bounced echo. The end should be near." Although Billie's voice was soft, it made Katie edgy.

Sure enough, the tunnel came to an end. They found another bricked up passage topped with an arch in the wall. Billie snapped a few more pictures as the flash bounced light down the tunnel.

That is when Katie saw another black metal grate. She tapped Billie on the shoulder. "BJ, get a picture of this, too", she said as she focused her light on it.

"Katie, there must be other rooms down here, and I'd love to find a way into them." Billie's focus had changed direction; now she wanted to find the East tunnel and what had happened to Cliff from the diary.

That unsettling feeling that they were being watched kept Katie on edge. "Let's head back. I'm sure there is a way to get in, but we'll have to bring some tools down, and something to stand on."

*

Chief Dennis Perry had been stewing in his office. His approach to control his men, was not working. Dennis was feeling a bit transparent, and he did not like his subordinates challenging his authority. Both Sgt. Nelsen and Detective Chapman were good cops, and the chief had a feeling that neither one would back down. The more he thought about it the more irritated he had become.

Picking up the receiver of his desk phone - with quick, angry fingers he jabbed numbers that would connect him to Mayor Dunn.

Stella answered in her deep raspy voice, "Mayor Dunn's Office!"

"This is Chief Perry," he barked. "Put me through to the mayor!" His tone was sharp.

Stella was immune to the chief's venom and remained undaunted, and professional. "Good afternoon, Chief Perry!

The mayor isn't in right now. Would you like to leave a message on his voice mail?"

"Where the hell is he?"

Quickly changing her demeanor to one who was dealing with a spoiled child ready to have a temper tantrum, "I'm sorry, Dennis, *that* I cannot say; but if you'd like to leave him a message..."

Dennis had not let her finish, "No, I'll call back!" he snapped.

Pleased with herself for agitating the chief of police, she simply hung up the phone and went about her business.

18

After having witnessed the mayor sneaking out of the records room through a false wall, Stella started to pay closer attention to the mayor's comings and goings. She even kept a notepad writing everything in shorthand. Stella and Dotty had decided to keep a log of everything their bosses did, from phone calls to meetings, both in and out of the office. With all her snooping around Stella felt like that little girl who spied on her grandfather so long ago. There were advantages to being old and being a kid; people seem to underestimate you.

Stella thought about Dot's warning regarding Katie getting in over her head. She felt the need to seek out Detective Chapman. After all, she liked the girl and respected Cal.

Today she ran into him, accidentally on purpose, at Polly's Deli. She remembered Thursdays were his usual soup and sandwich pick-up.

"Hello, Detective Chapman! How are you?"

Cal gave her a friendly smile, "Good, Stella - and you?"

Her deep raspy voice ground out. "Any day I wake up breathing, is a good day in my book!"

Cal had to chuckle at her cynicism.

"Say, I've been meaning to ask, how's Katie's research on the tunnels going?"

Puzzled, Cal furrowed his brow, "Tunnels? What tunnels?"

"Oh, I thought you knew Katie was doing research on that old white building that used to be part of the Jones House block years ago?"

"She is, but this is the first I've heard about tunnels."

"Oh - well I was just thinking she should know that there could be some hidden sub-basements and such in some of these older buildings in town. Why, just the other day I saw the mayor disappear from our records room!"

Cal was stunned. He quickly put a quieting hand up and then politely escorted Stella off to a quiet table. He offered her a seat as he sat down across from her. "Okay, Stella, what's this all about?"

"You see, Dotty and I were having lunch here a few days ago, having our usual bitch session about the bosses. We both feel something is hinky with them two. We may be old, but we are not blind or deaf! We hear and see things others wouldn't, and because we're old – people don't pay much mind to us."

Cal intently listened to what Stella was saying.

"Katie came to see me wanting to search the records, and asked me questions about 480 Milwaukee Ave. You know, I've lived in Burlington all my life, and I've only heard rumors of tunnels being under town.   But then the other morning when I was in that same records room at City Hall - I heard a noise. When I looked up, I saw the mayor. I was surprised to see him there so early. I was about to ask him if he needed some help finding something when he stepped behind a false wall! I was not about to let him know I saw him. I felt it was a little too coincidental to have happened the day after Katie asked me about it. Don't you think?"

Cal never thought about there being tunnels under Burlington. If there were tunnels under town, somehow that rumor would have gotten out. Being a cop, made him privy to certain things the general public would not always know, but this was a new one. "So, Katie asked *you* about the tunnels?"

"Well, she said there were bricked archways in the walls of the basement in that building, and thought they were doorways out. She asked me if I knew to what?"

"Tell me again about the mayor?"

"Like I said, Cal, I didn't stick around! He's a snake, and I trust him as far as I can throw him!"

They sat in silence for a few seconds, while Cal absorbed everything Stella had told him.

Stella sat forward, "Oh - and another thing, the second Thursday of every month, he has an open appointment marked on the calendar. I happened to mention this to Dot and it turns out your Chief does, too! I just thought I'd bring *that* to your attention. If you ask me, them two are up to somethin'!"

"Stella, why are you telling me all this?"

"Well, Dot and I think all the hullabaloo that's been happening this past year has Dunn's name all over it! And, that Chief of yours is Dunn's puppet. I'm just sayin'...these old bones feel there's something funny going on! If we're right, that means Katie is going to dig up something in her research she shouldn't!"

*

Katie and Billie spent the morning going over what they had found and highlighted where they had gone on their map. Billie had only developed one roll of film and needed more time to develop the other two. However, at the moment Katie was insistent on going back into the tunnel that led northeast.

"I have some tools in the back of the Jeep, and I brought a collapsible step stool. I want to see what's behind that grate!"

"Shouldn't we bring Hondo with us?" Billie was just as curious, nevertheless she would feel a whole lot safer if they had a dog to warn them if someone else was down there.

"Next time we'll bring him."

Billie was not feeling very brave today. The more she read the diary, the more she became emotionally invested. There was not much written about the tunnels, but what there was left Billie feeling cautious.

Billie would follow Katie anywhere. Apparently even into the depths of Hell, which was Billie's new nickname for the tunnels.

Sure enough they found their way back to the first metal grate in the wall of the tunnel. Katie set-up the step-ladder, so they could easily peer though the grate; however, it was still too dark to see anything. As slight as it was, there was a definite draft coming from behind the wall.

"What do you see?" Billie asked.

"I think it's a *room*? I'm not sure; it's really small whatever it is. But there is something definitely behind this wall! Somehow, we need to find a way around this to get inside."

"Why not just remove the grate and get in that way?"

Katie was not thinking of the obvious. "Billie – you're a genius!"

"I can't tell, was that sarcasm?"

"Not at all...well maybe just a little bit. I don't know if we can squeeze through there, though?"

"I'm game - let's find out!" Billie said as she started to tap on the mortar joints around the grate.

Katie took out a screwdriver and a hammer to chisel away at the joints while Billie started to carve around the crumbling joint that held the grate in place with her pocketknife. It was not long before the old mortar crumbled away.

They pushed and pulled working the grate loose. They worked until the grate popped out.

With thrilling anticipation, Katie tingled with goose bumps. "Billie...what do you think, should we?"

Billie's curiosity got the better of her, "I think - hell yeah! This is so cool! Where do you suppose it goes?"

Katie's desire to find answers squashed any doubt she would have normally had. In her obsession, she lost all sense of reason.

Billie laced her hands to give Katie a leg up so she could squeeze through the small opening they made in the wall.

Neither one wanted to admit they were both a little afraid.

"It's your turn, Billie. I'll try to help you through."

Billie first passed through her camera bag and then with some effort, Billie squeezed and wiggled through the opening. Both of them were scratched up, but they didn't care.

"Billie, these are pretty old tunnels. Look at the brick work." The walls were brick and mortar, with a beautifully bricked archway over the door.

"I wonder who built them and when?"

"That is what I want to know." Katie followed her light along the floor and the wall. The room appeared to be empty. However, it was clear to her that others had been through here. There was a path from dusty foot traffic down the center of the floor from the door.

Billie panned her light across the floor. Off to the back of the room was a trap door in the floor. "Here, take a look at this!"

Katie was excited to discover something new. She pulled the latch over and lifted the old heavy wooden door. She illuminated the space below with her light.

"What do you see?"

"Not much, I need to get down there."

"Are you sure you want to? How are you going to get back up here?"

Katie shined her light on the floor below, "It doesn't look very deep."

Katie lowered herself down through the hole. "Well, it's not a sub-basement, more like a deep crawl space."

Billie handed her the flashlight. Then she laid on the floor of the little room and cautiously stuck her head in the hole so she could see what was down there. She was grateful there were no spider webs in her face.

Katie panned her light across a stack of boxes along the wall and froze her beam on them. She read the yellow spray-painted stenciled letters on the boxes, which looked military. "Billie?"

Billie was reading the same thing that she was. "I see it, Katie! Are those military boxes?"

"Looks like it."

"Why would there be military boxes down here?" Billie asked as she snapped a couple of photos. "Now - what?"

"Well, now we're going to have to tell Cal, but first we need to get out of here! Should we find out what's behind that door or climb back out the way we came in?"

Billie looked up to the void where they came in and then over her shoulder to the door. "I vote we use the door." She offered Katie a hand and helped her out of the hole. They replaced the trap door the way they found it.

A nagging feeling of dread stopped Katie at the door.

"What are you waiting for?" Billie whispered.

Katie turned back to the trap door, then to the exit. Carefully, she checked for anything that might be a booby-trap. It was not that she was paranoid; instinct told her she just could not trust the obvious right now.

In a hushed yet nervous tone, "Are you frickin' kidding me? You think the door might be trip wired?"

Quietly Katie snapped back, "Billie, with what we just found - I just don't want to take any chances!" Katie shared a look with Billie before turning the knob, "Ready?"

"Not really – but I'd really like to get the heck out of here."

The old heavy wooden door seemed to have swelled shut. It was very tight and took some effort to open. Full of apprehension, the hair on the back of their necks stood on end. Fearful that the noise they were making might alert someone that they were there.

They pulled the door open with a loud thud. The girls sucked in a deep breath with the anticipation of being discovered. When nothing happened, Katie peered out into the hall.

This part of the tunnel was very dark; to the left, darkness; to the right, more darkness. They chose left. The girls quietly exited the room, closing the door behind them.

Katie knew they were now in over their heads. This was huge. It was not just the history behind an abandoned building any more. There were unanswered questions and too many possibilities to what they just found.

They walked cautiously and silently through some narrow passageways, and occasionally found another hallway that branched off into another direction. For fear of getting themselves lost down there, they kept to their left. The tunnel was dank, and barely lit by a few bulbs strung along the top. Katie was concerned with why abandoned tunnels would have electricity, just like the forgotten bowling alley.

Billie started to regret urging Katie to take the door instead of climbing back through the grate.

They vigilantly walked along the wall; pausing every few steps to listen. Katie knew they should not be down there, but her curiosity had won out.

They came upon an intersecting tunnel which offered only two options. Having to choose right or left, they had not gotten far when they caught wind of an odor. This odor grew stronger the further in they went.

Billie hissed, "Eeew! What's that smell? It's like cat pee on steroids!"

"I don't know!"

"Maybe we *should* go back the other way?"

"Why? We're here now?"

"But - that smell?"

"Come on...just a little further. Then if you want to turn around, we will."

Soon they could see a faint light.

"I don't know about this?" Billie cautioned.

The smell in the tunnel was getting so bad, that Billie held her sleeve to her face as not to breathe in too deeply.

Katie had also covered her nose. Her heart was beating hard in her constricted chest. She was not feeling very brave at the moment. The further down the tunnel they got, the more tense she became. Something was not right, maybe this *was* a bad idea, and they should turn back.

"Kate, I think we need to go back." Billie said, sounding more nervous than she wanted to.

Then in the distance a shadow appeared and started to grow across the ceiling, the girls froze. They quickly turned off their flashlights.

Voices traveled, bouncing up and down the tunnel. Not sure if the voices were coming from up ahead or from behind, they needed to make a decision – fast.

Katie looked to the floor of the tunnel they were in and found it had a recess. She tugged on Billie's sleeve for her to follow her. Carefully, the girls stepped as close to the wall as they could without making a sound, slipping into the recess.

Katie took a breath, centering herself. She turned to whisper in Billie's ear, *"I'm going to take a look up ahead."*

Billie grabbed Katie's arm and shook her head 'No'.

Instinct told Katie this was not a good idea, but curiosity was the over-powering force right now. After all, they did not really know who could be down there. She hugged her body close to the wall and crept cautiously, as she kept to the shadows. At the end of the intersecting tunnel was a much wider tunnel blocked off with heavy clear plastic flaps like she had seen in a slaughterhouse. The pungent aroma was so sickening; it gave her an instant headache, even her eyes watered.

The sound of someone wheeling a large cart with loud squeaky wheels came from the right of the tunnel. Katie held her body tight to the wall.

After several minutes a man returned pushing the cart heavy with packages. That is when she realized they were in real danger. These were the 7 Sons of Sin, and this is where they had their Meth lab. The police could not find it because the bikers used the tunnels to hide what they were doing.

She was rightfully scared. These bikers could not know the girls had been there. She never should have seen what she did. Now, as swiftly and quietly as she could, she backtracked to where Billie was eagerly waiting for her.

"What did you see?" Billie asked in a whisper.

"We need to find a way out of here, now!"

"But what did you see?"

Katie put a finger to her lips, shushing Billie.

Even in the dim light, Billie could read Katie's grave expression, and the unease she was feeling just escalated.

Feeling along the tunnel walls, they didn't turn their flashlights back on until they stepped into the smaller tunnel. There had been little or no light after they left the northern tunnel. They cautiously panned their lights along the floor and occasionally up ahead.

Back to where they started, they could finally breathe fresher air. Frantically, they tried to open the heavy door, but it was no use. Katie knew the danger they were in and moved Billie forward. Keeping tight to the wall, they took their time cautiously feeling their way out of this maze.

Now the tunnel branched off to the east or was it the west? Katie tried to figure their whereabouts by what direction they had traveled and how far down they had gone. She was completely turned around. "Do you feel that?"

Billie paused, "Yeah, there's a slight draft. That means there's an exit right?"

As gingerly as they could they followed this new tunnel. It was concrete and definitely smaller than the others, more like a wide hallway.

Midas was working on one of his listening devices when suddenly, he sensed another presence. He hastily shut off his task light and stealthily made his way into the cover of the shadows.

Katie froze when she realized there was another opening.

Billie just about ran Katie over before she came to a halt. *"What is it?"* she asked in a hushed whisper.

Katie put her index finger up for her to be quiet and once again turned off her light.

Billie did the same.

Fighting the fear she felt, Katie began to break out into a cold sweat. Her heart pounded hard in her chest. She had a bad feeling about this. There was something very wrong with what was going on down in these tunnels.

They remained silent. Neither one moved a muscle; they just listened to the dark.

Although Midas did not like intruders, he especially did not want the girls to get caught by the bikers. He reached out, taking a heavy metal nut off his workbench, and tossed it out towards the exit that led to the river's edge.

Billie and Katie both turned to each other in the dark.

Katie spoke softly into Billie's ear, "Did you hear that?"

Billie nodded 'yes'.

Alarmed, Katie tugged on Billie's sleeve to get her to turn back the way they came.

Midas could not let them turn back; it was much too dangerous. He tossed out another one. This time it bounced and rolled down the corridor he was trying to keep them out of.

It worked. The two sleuths quickly changed their course and slipped silently through his chamber, as they stayed close together exiting the same tunnel in which his friend, Brandon Holtz would enter.

Finding themselves at the mouth of a newer concrete formed entrance, they were relieved to be out of the underground tunnels. Both took a deep breath of fresh air.

They climbed out and up the river's edge to the newly built condos on Jefferson Street. Katie looked around the area. She smiled when she spotted the Malt House Theater directly across the way.

Billie noticed how shaken Katie was. "Hey – what did you see?"

"Something I shouldn't have!" Katie pulled out her cell to call Cal. "No answer, it went straight to voice mail."

Billie pointed to Fox's Liquor across the river. "Maybe Brandon or Fox could give us a ride back?"

The little brass bell on the door announced their presence. Brandon was stocking the cooler when they came in.

"Hey, ladies, it's been a while!" Fox's smile was genuine and friendly.

"It has been a while!" Katie changed her mind about asking for that ride. Whatever was going on down in the tunnels, the last thing she wanted to do was get either one of these guys involved.

Brandon looked back to the girls and smiled wide when Billie called out, 'Hi, Brandon!'

Katie just grabbed a couple of waters from the cooler and handed one to Billie.

"What have you ladies been up to?" Fox asked as he rung them up.

"Trying to stay out of trouble!" Billie answered.

Katie laughed it off. "It's such a nice day we thought we'd just take a walk."

Fox could not agree more. "Well, don't be strangers!"

The little bell rang again as they took their leave. Brandon watched them walk past the front window before he went back to what he was doing.

Billie turned to Katie, "So now we're walking to the substation? What *did* you see?"

"Billie, let's wait until we're alone. Cal is going to have a fit!"

19

TJ had been watching Brandon's comings and goings for days, and now brought Jack on board to help tail him. Brandon's car turned off to the left, pulling into the lot for the new condos along the river. Jack continued over the bridge to follow the curve in the road. They pulled into the car lot on the corner and parked. Then slipped out of Jack's truck, quietly closing the doors. Checking their weapons, they both wore .45's at their hips and compact .9mm's on their ankle.

Jack followed TJ and jogged to the backside of the little building. He spotted Brandon's vehicle parked at the far end of the lot for the new complex.

"I thought *I* lived a dull life!" Jack griped.

TJ chuckled at Jack's grumpy mood. "Explain to me again, Blondie's interest in you?"

Jack reached out and smacked TJ's arm.

Razzing Jack was easy for TJ. It was the little things he found highly amusing. But for now, he needed to focus on what they were doing. He scanned the area for Brandon and then spotted him. "Psst! Over there!" He pointed across the river.

"Yep, let's go."

Brandon was suspiciously carrying a backpack along the river just south of the Jefferson Street Bridge. This time of night, the town was pretty well closed down. No one would have even noticed him if they were not already watching him.

TJ and Jack kept to the shadows, parallel to Brandon on the opposite side of the Fox River. Once they made it to the back of the Malt House Theater, they lost him.

"Son of a bitch!" Jack expressed his dismay under his breath, "Do you see him?"

TJ once again spotted movement, "Down there." He directed Jack to look at the base of the river's edge. They observed as Brandon moved a large metal grate aside and crawled inside.

Jack shared a look with TJ. "Let's get over there." Jack was determined to get in there, and hurriedly made his way across the next bridge and down the embankment.

TJ did his best to keep up with him.

When they reached the large grate Brandon had entered, they paused.

"What's the plan, Jack?"

Only the look Jack gave TJ told him there was no plan.

"Oh – I see – we're just gonna wing it?"

Tactically they maneuvered inside, guns drawn, stepping silently into the dark. Alert to the faint light up ahead. They approached with caution, listening to muffled voices, which echoed down the cement tunnel as shadows moved in and out of sight.

It was apparent, Brandon was meeting someone down here. Jack was going to find out who and why, as they cautiously listened in on Brandon's conversation. None of it seemed threatening in any way, until Jack heard the unidentified man say, *"Those girls are getting too close. They can't come down here anymore."*

In that instant, Jack reacted.

Jack swiftly holstered his weapon as not to reveal it to Brandon. TJ could not stop Jack as he entered the room.

From behind, TJ could see Jack's fully lit silhouette. He hated it when Jack pulled these stupid stunts.

The conversation died the moment Jack stepped into the light.

Brandon was completely dumbfounded to see the Brick Yard's bartender down there. "What the fuck, man?" What the hell are you doing down here?"

Jack was utterly silent; his eyes fixed on Kelly Green; the man Brandon had been conversing with. He thought he was seeing a ghost. It could not possibly be; the man that stood before him had been dead for six years.

After a few moments of uneasy silence, TJ cautiously came up behind Jack. That is when he too, recognized the man Jack was staring at.

"Midas?" TJ questioned in a shocked yet puzzled tone.

Brandon looked to Kelly, and then to the guys from the bar. Confused, he asked, "Midas, you know these guys?"

It was TJ who had given Kelly Green the nickname, *Midas*. They had met in the Corps, and quickly made friends. Kelly had a talent for fixing damn near anything. When their unit came under fire, losing contact when their equipment got shot-up; he worked his magic. His ability for getting the damaged equipment to work well enough to call in support - saved all their asses that day.

Midas hadn't moved a muscle. He appeared to have lost himself in a memory.

Brandon was quite perplexed; he exchanged his glances between the three men in silence.

Jack spoke low and slow, "How is it even possible, you're dead?"

Recognizing his comrades, Midas glanced from Jack to the large muscled man behind him, in an almost joking manner he said, "TJ – Jack, what's the matter? Haven't you ever seen something so hideously ugly before?"

TJ with his happy, yet loud booming voice answered, "Are you kidding, Buddy, you're beautiful! Absolutely gorgeous!"

Midas was so elated to see his Marine brothers he dropped his guard to openly greet them.

The men happily hugged each other, joyful for their reunion. Midas, full of emotion had tears in his eyes.

TJ was speechless. That aching knot that had been in his gut was now lodged in his throat. He felt responsible for Midas's death and there he was, in flesh and blood standing before him.

"But how? We saw *you*..." Jack trailed off.

"No – you didn't." Midas answered soberly.

TJ's tone was almost angry, "We looked for you! We found a boot with your tag."

"You didn't happen to find my ear did ya?" Midas laughed.

TJ lovingly punched his friend in the shoulder, "Asshole...seriously, where the hell have you been?"

Midas pictured himself in uniform, fighting side by side with these men back in Afghanistan. When he was with Jack and TJ, he was strong, invincible. He could handle anything when they were by his side. He repressed all the pain and torment he endured so he could function with his brothers. Remembering himself as he was before he suffered brain trauma; before he was disfigured, before he was, broken.

"We just want to know what happened to you, man." TJ was adamant.

After an uncomfortable amount of time, Midas who wasn't fully ready to befriend his estranged brothers did gradually opened up to them.

Midas stood there with an empty defeated silence. He was not comfortable talking about it, so he shook his head in a dismissive manor. Seeing them triggered something in him. Slowly it was all coming back like blood rushing through his veins. With tears in his eyes he finally spoke, "I don't know...last thing I can remember is the flash, and then pain. The doctors said I was in a coma for about a month. I didn't know who I was or where I was." He looked to TJ, and in a surprisingly witty tone said, "The force of the explosion must have blown me clear out of my boots! I was told the clean-up crew found me."

Then Midas got really serious, "My back, face, neck and arms were badly burned. I've had over 30-different surgeries and numerous skin graphs, spending nearly 3-years in recovery. When they sent me home, I was still pretty messed up. I was supposed to follow-up and take my meds." He gave a long pause, swallowing hard. "But, when I got home, there was no home to go to. The farm had burned down when we were over seas, Dad was ill, so Ma just let the property go, and Dad passed while I was recovering! I stayed with her at her little apartment until she died last year. That's when I met Brandon."

Jack turned to Brandon, "What are you doing down here?"

Not quite sure as to why Jack was asking him that, he answered any way. "Midas is my friend. When he came home, he found his family farm was gone. Green Gables was already being built on his land, and he had no where else to go. He moved down here after his mother passed away. I bring him what he needs." Brandon wanted answers of his own and asked, "What are *you* doing down here?"

Choosing his words carefully, Jack told him, "We saw you enter down here by the river and just thought we'd check it out."

The look on Brandon's face told Jack he wasn't convinced, but he didn't press.

TJ was still in shock. Midas had been his best friend, and TJ owed him his life on numerous occasions. Although he had many questions about what had happened and how he came to be *here* of all places, he saw the signs and knew his friend suffered. Whether he was diagnosed with Post-traumatic stress disorder or not, his friend needed support.

TJ wanted to keep his newly reacquainted friend talking. "Man, I can't believe you're here! Alive! Damn – I've missed you, Buddy!"

The four men copped a squat on the floor of the tunnel and leaned against its walls, rehashing old memories.

"How are you doing?" TJ wanted to know.

"Just taking one day at a time."

TJ prompted Midas with excerpts from their last mission. "There isn't a day that goes by I don't think about that day. We were ordered to clear out. After I sent you on ahead, Jack and I were the last ones, humpin' it back to the L.Z. (landing zone). Most of our platoon was already loaded on the Chinook. We had no visual, but we heard it...it came right over our heads. In an instant we lost 2/3 of our brothers."

There were no words to describe the look in Midas's eyes. He had never heard a first-hand account of what happened.

Jack shifted the conversation. "How long have you lived down here, Midas?"

Midas looked to Brandon for confirmation, "Maybe a year."

Brandon nodded in affirmation.

Jack asked, "Didn't you check-in with the V.A.?"

TJ shot Jack an agitated look for asking the question.

"Yeah, I did, and I was going while Ma was alive. They had me on all kinds of shit...Lithium, Depakote, even Venlafaxine. I didn't like taking them. I don't like the way they make me feel. They made me fat, and if I had hair, I'm sure it would have fallen out! They caused some pretty bad hallucinations in my sleep – when I could sleep."

143

Hearing Midas admit that he has not gotten the help or meds he needed in nearly a year, up-set TJ. He wanted to help his friend. He did not want to hurt Midas's feelings, he just wanted to clean him up and take him out of here. "If the drugs you were taking were that bad, maybe a doctor will find others with fewer side effects, but you should trust the VA hospital. There has to be alternate drugs, and you need to talk to a counselor sometime, at least for a while. Give it a chance man, don't be ashamed. You've got three friends here that love you, man."

Jack was desperate to learn more about this tunnel system, and if the girls he had mentioned being down here *were* Billie and Katie. "What is this place? How'd you even find it?"

Midas gave Jack a puzzled glance. Memory flashes of the past started to poke holes through his mind. "I've known about them since before high school. After Ma passed I had no where else to go."

"You're really living down here?" TJ could not hide the surprised tone from his question.

"I like it down here."

TJ pushed. "We're gonna help you, if you'll let us?"

Midas was hesitant, even somewhat ambivalent.

Brandon remained quiet, but observed how Jack controlled the conversation. There was something more going on here, and it was not sitting right with him.

TJ placed a friendly hand on Midas's arm. "Don't worry man; we just want you to know we've got your back. We'll help you out anyway you'll let us."

Jack continued, "You shouldn't live down here any more."

"No...they leave me alone."

Jack quickly shared a look with TJ and then asked, "They who?"

"The bikers, they leave me alone."

"You mean the 7 Sons of Sin? Are they down here, too?" Jack shared a look with Brandon.

Brandon had been suspicious that they knew about the Meth lab the bikers had down there, but now was not so sure.

TJ's gut was in a knot. "Man, you really can't be down here. It's too dangerous."

"Look, Midas...they're bad men and could get tired of you. Brandon here would be the only one who would notice if you disappeared." Jack's tone was even and sincere.

Midas felt the concern his old friends had for him. He knew they meant well.

"Midas, I have to tell ya, we *are* in this tunnel for a reason!" Jack said as he shot a look back to Brandon. "Who else besides the bikers have you seen come down here?"

"I don't want to see anybody, that's why I'm here!"

"Midas, do you trust us?" TJ asked, offering his large strong hand.

Midas clasped their hands in a brother/soldier honor of trust and camaraderie. With tears in his eyes, he answered, "With my life."

Jack pushed a little harder, in an almost pleading sort of way. "Can you give us any information?"

Feeling their strong plea for his help, "I'll tell you anything I know."

TJ gave Midas an accepting nod, happy that the circle of trust was still there.

Brandon Holtz must be trust worthy, or he would not be Midas's friend. That still did not make Jack completely comfortable to have to ask these questions in front of him.

"Tell me about these people who come down here."

"I stay out of their way. They don't see me. They're too busy cooking drugs. They don't wander too far in the dark. But, I'm not afraid of the dark – I like the dark – I see in the dark just fine."

"Can you tell me anything else about these guys? Like how many are there?"

"It changes...but usually 8-10 men come and go. There's a guy in a suit that talks to the leader. But he comes in from a different way."

"There's other ways to get down here? Can you tell me about them, do you know where they are?"

"Sure, I know these tunnels – it's my home."

"Yes, Midas – it's your home, but these are bad men. How are *these* guys getting into your home?"

Midas placed his head in his hands. After a moment, he looked to TJ and then to Jack, stroking his scruffy face. "There is an entrance under the old grainery. That's where the bikers come in. There's this one, which only Brandon and now you came in. Crest Hill Bed and Breakfast has one, Kane Street, oh and the girls come in through the one on Milwaukee Ave."

Before Midas could continue listing other entrances Jack stopped him. Now was Jack's chance to ask, "Okay – back up there! *What* girls?"

Midas looked over to Brandon for some support.

Brandon answered for him, "I think its Katie and Billie. They somehow found the entrance through the basement of that old building she's been researching."

Burlington was a relatively small town, and everyone pretty much knew what everyone else was doing. Brandon had known Katie since she moved to town. He was the one who initially warned her to stay away from Charlie Nix. He also did not want to see BJ or Katie get hurt by coming down into these tunnels.

Jack clenched his jaw. "How far have they gotten?"

Midas wanted to help TJ and Jack, but he was reluctant to say something that might put them all in danger. "They almost found the biker's lab today. There are parallel tunnels, and they were in the one where the man in the suit comes down. I've been watching them. They don't see me, but I think the redhead senses they're being watched. The blonde one takes lots of photos and almost caught me today. But she didn't!" He said in a pleased manor.

"Brandon – you knew about this and didn't say anything?" Jack was furious.

"Hey, man – I only found out a couple of days ago!"

"But you knew about the Meth lab!"

Brandon narrowed his eyes, "I knew! But me and cops just don't get along. Besides I wasn't about to have the cops raid these tunnels! What about Midas? They would have locked him up!"

"No - they wouldn't have! They would have gotten him the help he needed."

Midas didn't like them arguing. He didn't like a lot of talk or noise and their voices were in danger of setting him off. "Hey – I'm right here! Do you mind not talking about me like I'm not?"

Jack instantly apologized to Midas, "I'm sorry man. I didn't mean any disrespect." His focus returned to Brandon. "Do you know who the man in the suit is?"

"I have never seen him. Midas has only told me he comes down here – but rarely. Something must be going down with the bikers 'cuz he's been down here twice this month."

"Let me get this straight...the bikers use the grainery to gain access, some guy in a suit visits the biker's Meth lab, and Billie and Katie found a way in and are getting close to discovering this lab? I understand you want to protect Midas, we do too; but we can't have the girls wandering around down in these tunnels. The SSS wouldn't think twice about killing them to keep their secret! Is there anything else happening in these tunnels under Burlington I don't know about?"

Brandon said nothing. He never got too far in the tunnels. Midas would not let him. He only knew what he did, because of Midas.

"Damn it!" Jack stood up. He did not like the unknown.

Everyone watched Jack pace like a caged animal.

Midas had a strict set of morals and a fierce loyalty to those that earn it. These men, his Marine brothers he'd do anything for. Midas then stood and reached out to Jack, placing a hand on his shoulder. "What can I do? I want to help you, I will tell you anything I know, but I won't talk to any cop. I won't go to court. You can't get me into court!"

Midas was feeling a bit overwhelmed, although he was happy to be reunited with his Marine brothers. They gave him a purpose, a reason to live.

"Can you take us to their drug lab?"

"Sure, I'll take you to it."

Brandon did not like what he was hearing. "Jack, are you fuckin' crazy? Now why in the Sam Hell do you want to mess with Richie Collins and his business? The 7 Sons of Sin will kill you!"

Midas found some humor in what Brandon said. "Of course, Jack is crazy – that's what made him so damn good!" Midas was proud to have served with both Jack and TJ. Right now, he felt like he did back in the Corps, he had a purpose. He turned his attention back to his fellow soldiers, "You guys come back here tomorrow afternoon. I will take you. There is less going on during the day."

Brandon just glared at Jack. It was not just that Jack ignored what he asked; he did not like that Jack was involving Midas with whatever he was doing.

There was so much more Jack wanted to ask Midas, but he knew he would have to do it in small doses.

20

Billie had enough excitement for one day. She had been busily working on developing her own film. It was a way for Billie to disconnect and relax. Her little make-shift darkroom was efficient, and her cat, Torre, knew when the heavy black fabric curtain closed, she had to keep out.

She was so engrossed on her task at hand that she did not bother to answer her ringing cell phone. When she finally had a moment, she saw she had three missed calls, all from Jack.

Billie was thrilled that Jack had called her, but she fought the urge to call him back. Katie did tell her not to be so eager. Looking down at Torre washing behind her ears, "You know what; I think I'm going to jump into the shower, and then I'll call Jack back!"

After the dirty dusty excursion, she and Katie had today, the shower felt good. She even conditioned her hair a second time and made sure to rinse her long hair thoroughly. Taking her time, she combed through her tangled wet hair before drying it; all the while day dreaming about Jack. She did not want to get too excited about Jack's calls, after all he probably only wanted to talk to her about work.

She bent over and started drying her hair first upside down to get the underside dry and then straightened back up so she could finger fluff her waves dry. The entire process for drying her hair took about 20 minutes. In that time, she missed Jack's fourth and final call.

It was not until there was a knock at her door, did she realize she was about to get company. She quickly wrapped up in her oversized towel and hustled her bare feet across the carpeted living room floor to the door.

Peeking out, she saw it was Jack. She tested her breath...it was good. Taking a breath and blowing it out, "*Okay.*" She opened the door.

To Jack's surprise, he was greeted by a practically naked Billie. "Do you always open the door to strangers just wearing a towel?"

"Well, technically you're not a stranger."

Jack held up a big brown paper bag, "Can I come in? I hope it's not too late?"

Billie sheepishly smiled, "Sure." She stepped back to let him enter and then closed the door. She looked down at her towel, "Maybe I should get dressed." She wrinkled up her nose pointing to her bedroom and excused herself, "I'll be right back - make yourself at home!"

While Billie got dressed, Jack glanced around her little Bohemian apartment, looking for a place to set down their dinner. "I brought Chinese. I wasn't sure what to get so I have quite a variety, I hope you're hungry?" He hollered from the other room.

Billie pulled on a pair of comfy jeans and a long sleeve tee accented with shiny *bling* in the design. "I'm famished!"

She entered the living room fluffing her beautiful long wavy hair. Jack was still standing holding the bag of Chinese food. She blushed with a slightly embarrassed smile. "Sorry, I wasn't expecting company." She said as she tucked a tendril of hair behind her left ear, and then took the bag from him, before taking it into the kitchen. It was one of the few areas that did not have something cluttering it.

Billie returned to grab a pile of clean clothes she had been folding a day earlier, "Here, let me move this out of the way."

A sexy lacey bra fell to the floor, at Jack's feet. Amused, he bent down to pick it up and handed it to her with a grin accompanying a raised brow.

Once the couch was cleared, he sat down. Glancing around her apartment he noticed her camera equipment. There were photography magazines laying on a table and stacked up in a corner next to the couch. The coffee table was covered with photos and a map with a couple of lines highlighted.

Billie quickly gathered up the papers and magazines together and cleared off the table. She came back adorning a wine cooler and a beer in one hand and the take out in the other.

"I didn't mean to crash in on you tonight. I tried to call you, but you didn't answer. When I went to pick up dinner, I saw your lights were still on so I took the chance..."

She unpacked the contents of the bag and handed Jack a plate. "This is nice...I love Chinese!"

Jack loved Billie's easy yet beautiful smile and could lose himself in those eyes of hers. There was so much more to Billie than he ever realized. She was sweet, young, cute, and smarter than he gave her credit for. She kept him interested after all these months of putting her off. Amazed he had no idea what her interests were. He had to ask, "Are you into photography?"

"What was your first clue?" She laughed as she looked around her humble abode.

"Sorry I didn't answer the phone...I was in my dark room developing some photos I took today. I didn't take my phone in with me and I can't break the dark seal once I'm working."

"So, you develop your own film?"

"I sure do. It's getting harder to do that these days with the chemicals I use. Homeland Security is probably watching me as we speak." She joked.

Jack was impressed. He took notice of the framed photos on her walls. "Did you do these?"

"Every one of them!" She said proudly.

There was an awkward silence.

Jack sipped his beer to wash down his pork-fried rice.

Billie sensed there was something on his mind, so she broke the silence. "The other day when we went for breakfast, and I kept thinking you wanted to tell me something. Is that why you're here? You've never come over before."

Jack was a no-nonsense guy, and when it came to women, he was never any good with relationships. However, Billie stirred something in him. He didn't have any control over it, and he didn't like *not* having control.

Knowing her strong attraction to him, he had to ask in the most sincere, heartfelt way he could, "What do you want from me, Billie?"

She had been chasing him for eight months, and now that he was in her apartment, which felt like a date, she was not sure how to respond to that.

She thought about it for a moment, smiled and said, "Hold that thought, I have something for you." Billie hopped off the couch and jogged into her bedroom. When she returned, she held a large matted and framed photo approximately 24" X 36".

"Now, ask me again."

Curious, he played along. He asked again, of course with that sexy grin of his, "Billie, what do you want from me?"

She held out the framed and matted black and white photo to Jack. The look of recognition in his eyes with what the subject of the photo was, took him completely off guard. He was utterly speechless.

"It's your spot! The one you go to when you need to sort things out." As if she had to explain what it was.

"You took this?"

Her big ocean-blue eyes sparkled as she answered him with a happy smile, "That was the moment I knew."

"The moment you knew what?"

"That whatever happens or doesn't happen, I'm better for sharing that moment in time with you."

"But nothing happened...Billie, we just talked."

"Exactly."

Jack was moved by the gift, but confused as hell when it came to women. He felt deeply for this goofy blonde, and his conflicted feelings for her were going to drive him mad.

"How long have we been doing this?"

Billie took a sip of her wine cooler. "I don't even know what *this* is?"

"Well, now that I've finally been invited over to your apartment, I see we really don't know much about each other."

Billie giggled, "Actually you invited yourself – but I'm not complaining. If you want to know me, all you have to do is ask!"

They shared a flirtatious look, and smiled at each other.

While they ate, Jack asked Billie about her photography and her other interests. He already knew by looking around her apartment she was quite the opposite of his utilitarian way of living. There were colored glass vases in her windows, and candles everywhere. On the side table she had incense burning, it was not too strong, but he was super sensitive to scents. Her furniture was soft and easy. From what he could see through the door, she had a decent electronic set-up in the other room. Her taste in music was quite diverse. He already knew she listened to AC/DC and danced to country, but she had been listening to Loreena McKennitt when she answered the door.

Once again, he found himself engaged in an easy conversation with this lively, enchanting woman. "Is there anything you want to ask me?"

Of course, she did. Billie was dying to know more about Jack, like where he went and what he did when he was not working. But she did not ask. "I know all I need to know about you, Jack."

"Is that so?" He raised a puzzled brow.

Now was her chance to take the bull by the horns. She reached down and found the courage to finally tell him, "I like you, Jack; I have for some time now. And, I think you like me, too. I enjoy your company and I'd like to take a chance with you; see where it goes."

"How can you want to be with a man you hardly know?"

"Jack, everyone has a past. It's not about knowing everything up front; it's the journey of getting to know each other along the way."

Billie continually amazed and baffled Jack. He was not sure if her carefree spirit and surprisingly insightful yet naive ways were not part of his attraction to her. She was so far removed than anyone else he had ever been interested in before. Maybe he *could* chance a relationship with this bewildering woman.

21

Cal had been working non-stop on the Courtney Roberts and Alison Chambers's murder cases. Now that Cory Walker's disappearance had been added to his already overly cumbersome work load, he barely came home.

Katie was eager to tell him what they had found, but once again she found herself sleeping alone. The night dragged on with so many thoughts running through her mind, if it were not for exhaustion, she would not have slept at all.

Waking up early with the hope to find Cal - quickly turned to disappointment when Katie discovered his side of the bed was empty and cold. She felt anxious. Katie knew she needed to let Cal know what they had found hidden in the tunnels. She tried Cal's cell, but it went right to voice mail. Then Katie called the station.

Dotty's friendly voice answered.

"Good morning, Dot! It's Katie."

"Good morning, Katie dear! What can I do for you?"

"I don't suppose you've seen Cal this morning?"

"He didn't come home again last night, did he?"

Katie sighed, "No...and he's not answering his cell either."

"If it's important, I'll see if I can track him down?"

Katie knew Cal was already treading on thin ice with Chief Perry, but this *was* important, "Can you just give him a message for me?"

"Of course, Sweetie! What's the message?"

"Could you just tell him he needs to get a hold of me as soon as he can?"

Frustrated, she tried to keep herself occupied until she could talk to Cal. Katie busied herself putting together everything she and Billie had on the 480 Milwaukee building. Organizing all their notes and even the photos Billie had taken.

The one photo, in particular, that started this whole inquiry into the tunnels, Katie placed in a plastic sleeve and then wrote notations on it in red.

This basement was deliberately hidden. Whether it was to conceal its contents or to hide the entrance to the tunnels, Katie felt there had to be a much more interesting story behind them, than access to the Meth lab. Her thoughts drifted back to what she had seen. The whole thing was troubling to her, especially the round-about way in which they stumbled upon the Meth lab. There had to be an easier way to get to it.

Realizing what a cluttered mess she was making all over the dining room, Katie reeled in her scattered thoughts. She needed to focus on her research, and decided to find a space where she could spread it all out and leave it out. That way she could surround herself with all the images. Sometimes taking a step back to look at them from different angles, gave one an added perspective on what they were seeing.

She thought about the attic, but Cal stored a lot of boxes up there, mainly old case files. The basement was the only other logical choice. She had never been down there, but as far as she knew Cal only stored carpentry tools and boxes of decorations down there.

Katie unlocked the door to the basement, and switched on the lights. The old wooden steps were solid but slightly worn in the middle of each tread. She stood at the bottom of the stairs observing what she had to deal with. Behind the staircase to the back there was an area she could use. Of course, Cal had everything in order. Everything seemed to have its place. There was a large workbench along one wall with a stool that looked promising. It was cleared off but she wiped it off before bringing down her muddled mess of papers.

Katie took inventory of some things she needed to buy, and then called Billie to see if she wanted to tag along.

Billie had spent the morning developing the pictures she had taken of their latest excursion. When she got to the pictures of the military boxes, she blew them up so the lettering could be easily read. She knew this would be important for Cal to trace these boxes. She was hanging the last of her photos when her cell rang, "Hey, Kate!"

"Are you busy?"

"Not any more, why?"

"I need to pick up a few things, I'll pick you up on the way, and then we can do lunch."

"Sure!" Billie giggled. "I can always eat!"

With-in minutes Katie pulled up to Billie's apartment. Billie was already waiting and climbed into the Jeep. "So, where are we going?"

"I need some office supplies – then we'll stop for whatever you're in the mood for!"

"There's a cute little café right in town that now has Chicago style hotdogs, let's have lunch there on our way back!"

Her intent was not just to create a work space in the basement, but to make it more of an office. Katie hated to shop so she was quick with her purchases. Luckily everything fit in her Jeep. "Now, where are we going for these hotdogs?"

Billie sheepishly answered, "The Sci-Fi Café!" She knew Katie was not going to be thrilled to go at first, but that was part of the fun, having BJ for a friend.

"The what?"

"I know what you're thinking, but I want you to keep an open mind. I found this place when I was looking for my teas and incense. One side of it is a cute little shop and the other side is the café. Besides they're good people and have good food too!"

Luckily there was parking right across the street from the Sci-Fi. Katie was surprised she never really noticed this place before. Out front they had a couple of little bistro tables with chairs, and an American flag hung outside their entrance. Katie was now a little less skeptical as she followed Billie inside.

The interior was decorated exactly as the café's name had implied. There were little green spacemen and science fiction memorabilia, from Star Trek to Star Wars and even Doctor Who. However, there was much more to this café. The owner, Mary, was heavily involved in the research of strange and unexplained mysteries, and set up a research center where a few people were working while enjoying their coffees.

"Hey, Billie!"

Billie returned the friendly hello, "Hey, Mary!"

"Are you having lunch today?"

"You bet – I even brought my friend, Katie, with me today!"

"Well, have a seat – I'll be right with ya!"

Mary brought over a couple of menus.

"You know what, Mary? I think we're just gonna have two of your Chicago style hotdog specials with root beers."

"Sure, Hun – you got it!"

Katie turned to Billie, "I take it you've been here once-or-twice?"

Billie giggled, "Yeah, have you seen my fridge? I don't cook – I usually get take out or come here!"

Mary brought over their drinks, and then went back to the counter to give her husband, Brad, the order.

Katie observed the people in the café while they waited for their food. Noting some books with the name of their author matching the owner of the Sci-Fi, she had to ask, "Is Mary an author?"

"Yeah, she just published her 5th book. She's researched all kinds of interesting things, like lost worlds and ancient man. I just love to talk to her. Mary is one of the coolest people I've met in this town!"

The friendly, charismatic woman returned with their hotdogs and took a seat next to Billie. "So, what are you girls up to?"

Billie didn't think twice, and with an impish grin she said, "Trying to find the truth behind the rumors of tunnels under Burlington."

Katie instantly kicked Billie under the table, a little harder than she had planned to.

"Ouch!" Billie shot Katie an angry look.

Mary laughed. "Oh sure – I know about the tunnels! When you're finished with lunch, I'll take you girls downstairs and show you the blocked-up archways in my basement!"

Katie was surprised at how candid Mary was, "So, you know about there being tunnels under Burlington?"

"Honey, I've been researching the strange things that happen in or around Burlington for over 15-years! There are people who know about the tunnels, but most of them won't talk about them."

"Really?"

"Sure, I've even got pictures of the underground bowling alley! They say it's not there any more, but I know better! I'll show them to you if you want?"

Katie and Billie just shared an all-knowing look and smiled.

*

Being short staffed, the chief had loaded Cal down with following up on loss prevention cases. Driving all over, visiting the local business that had property stolen, kept him from working the murder cases. Cal's days had all been merged together; he couldn't be sure what day of the week it was. His head throbbed and his shoulder ached, letting him know he was pushing himself too hard. He poured his mentally and physically drained body into his desk chair. Opening his top drawer to retrieve some Advil, he noticed there was a message waiting on his phone. He popped the pills before listening.

When he heard the scolding tone in Dotty's voice, he knew he messed up. Exhaling a defeated breath, he quickly called Kate, ready to take his lumps.

Katie's cell rang, and she answered with a smile, "Hello, stranger!"

"Is everything okay, Sweetheart?"

"Maybe I should be asking *you* that question? You didn't come home last night."

"I should have called...I've been tied up and was supposed to be in court this morning, but now that got cancelled. I'm sorry, Honey, is this something that we can discuss later tonight?"

"It can wait until tonight."

"Thank you...I love you!"

She smiled, "I know!"

*

Midas had anticipated Jack and TJ's arrival.

Jack was grateful for Midas's assistance, "Midas, we couldn't do this without you!"

TJ put a strong reassuring hand on Midas's shoulder. "It's great to have you with us again."

Pride filled Midas's chest. He felt useful once more, as he led them through his chamber. He was used to the dim light, but his friends were not, so Midas turned on a second light so they could see on what he'd been working.

TJ and Jack shared an astonished look.

In amazement, TJ asked, "Where did you get all this stuff?"

"I've picked up a few things along the way and what I don't have, Brandon will find for me."

Jack saw an old transistor, "May I?"

Midas gave him an approving nod.

"This is damn near an antique! Does it still work?"

"It all does!" Midas boasted.

Then Jack noticed the boxes of old Cunningham radio tubes on a shelf.

TJ picked up an unusual piece of equipment, "What the heck is this?"

"This is so cool – it's one of the first wireless electronic stethoscopes!"

"Where in the Sam Hell would you find something like this?"

Midas' excitement quickly changed, ignoring the question all together. "If you want me to show you where the Meth lab is, we need to go."

Jack sensed there was more to Midas's abrupt misdirection but let it go for now.

As Midas led the way, Jack and TJ tried to take in all that they were seeing.

They knew they were getting close by the toxic odor that hit them. Midas took them down a narrow corridor to bypass the tunnel the bikers used for a lab. They came up behind a brick wall with an iron grate for a window.

Peering in, Jack and TJ were surprised at the magnitude of their operation. At the moment, Jack only counted six-men, but then two more came in with a hand-truck to pick up another load.

"I'll be a son-of-a-bitch!" Jack said under his breath. In the back of Jack's mind, he kept thinking how the girls could have been caught by these assholes.

They stepped back.

Jack turned to Midas, "Can you show us how they're getting down here?"

*

Late in the afternoon, Chapman got called out to Holtz's farm to respond to a complaint. Just before reaching the Holtz's driveway, he saw the reason for the call. Coming into town where there used to be a population sign standing, was now a pair of broken off stumps with drag marks gouged into the blacktop leading right into the gravel driveway of Holtz's farm.

Following the trail that led into Holtz's, Cal sighed heavily shaking his head with the obvious foolishness of their local menace, Davey.

Old man Holtz was raising hell with Davey, his youngest son. The kid's pudgy cheeks were flushed from being scolded. His impish blue eyes peered out from an unmanageable mane of brown hair. Seeing that Chapman was not in uniform – kind of surprised him.

Tom Holtz was so angry with his son; Cal thought he'd better step-in before he witnessed the whipping Davey was about to receive. "Good evening, Tom! What's happening here?"

Davey was a 14-year-old boy who was notorious for finding mischief in one form or another. Although unintentional, he was forever giving his parents a hard time. This evening Davey wanted the road sign and decided to use the big John Deere tractor. He had wrapped chains around the posts and took off thinking it would pull right out of the ground. He did not figure they would snap off and almost hit an on coming car. If it were not for that car, he swore he'd been in the clear.

Cal fought back a chuckle as he took Davey to the side to talk to him about what he had done. "You were very lucky no one got hurt! Other than the sign, no damage was done. Now, Davey, you know you're going to have to pay for that sign. What do you think we should do about that?"

Cal did not want to give Tom Holtz any more grief. His son was not a bad kid; he just had to learn every lesson the hard way. Cal worked out a deal that Davey would work every weekend washing and waxing squad cars, fire trucks, and ambulances until the sign was paid for. Tom was grateful Cal was so lenient with his son.

Feeling guilty for not coming home last night, he was looking forward to seeing Kate before she left for work. Naturally, he now had to respond to a call that would keep him at work a little longer.

*

Margarita Night at the Brick Yard always brought on a special kind of entertainment, usually closer to closing time.

Jessica had said all the craziness was the Tequila talking, 'it did more than just make their clothes fall off'.

The energy was building at the bar, gearing up for the band that was to go on at 10 o'clock. Floog was a local band gaining much popularity all over southeastern Wisconsin. Their original music had been described as a blend of Island/Reggae/Rock. They also played song requests from bands like Sublime, Smashing Pumpkins, Nirvana, and others.

Billie grooved to their music while working through her tables and back up to the bar to retrieve more drinks.

Jack enjoyed watching Billie, with her carefree spirit; she cared less what anyone else thought. She was having a great time, and the way her body moved, Jack could see she took pleasure in the music. When Billie pulled her long hair off to the side exposing her bare neck, Jack felt a twinge. The mere thought of her drove him crazy. He could not get her out of his mind.

When she came back around, the lead guitarist, Jim, came out into the crowd and stopped Billie in her tracks. He recognized her from high school, but it took her a moment to register the familiar face in front of her. Her joyous squeals could almost be heard above the music.

Jim smiled, as he strummed away on his guitar and then gave her a wink as he made his way back on stage.

Billie flitted over to Katie with such enthusiasm, "Oh my God - Katie! Do you know who that was?"

"Who?"

"The guitarist! That's Jim – from high school!"

Glancing over Billie's shoulder to the 4-men on stage, taking a good look at the guy Billie pointed out. "It sure is! I'll be damned. That's great that he still plays!"

Billie was her usual bubbly-self and could not wait to get reacquainted with an old friend.

The dynamic vibe in the bar was electric. The crowd was a lot of fun, and kept Katie's mind from the conversation she was going to have with Cal when she got home. It was nights like these that reminded her why she liked working here. It was not just the money; it was the friendly and lively people.

Katie delivered 3-pitchers of Margaritas to a large table in the back as Brandon flagged her over for another tapper. Katie liked the regulars. As a rule, routine becomes mundane, but in a bar, your regulars get you through the evening with a smile or some quick wit.

Katie returned with Brandon's mug of beer.

He reached out for her arm, "Hey, I want Cal to know my family appreciates that he let Davey off easy today."

Katie smiled, but did not have a clue as to what he was talking about. "You know Cal!" was all she could say. She realized that although they were now living together, she and Cal still really didn't spend a whole lot of time together. She was going to have to change that. Homicide investigations or not, they needed some normalcy. Well as relatively close to normal as the two workaholics could.

Katie joyfully watched Billie dance around to the beat of the music, as she made her way to the bar.

Catching up to BJ at the bar, Katie checked the time; it was already after 1a.m. She flashed Jack an all-knowing grin.

"And what is *that* grin for?" Jack asked.

Katie tapped her wrist where a watch would be and held up an empty pitcher of Margaritas.

Jack caught on, and shook his head. "Oh...don't you dare jinx it!"

Katie shrugged her shoulders, flashed Jack one of her mischievous smirks as she walked away.

Sure enough, not 10 minutes later TJ escorted a loud-obnoxious, half-naked, inebriated college kid up the stairs.

Followed by a co-ed carrying some of the clothes her friend had discarded along the way.

On cue, Floog started singing, *"Tequila makes her clothes fall off..."*

Katie pointed to Jack back at the bar and mouthed, *"I told you so!"*

Jack shook his head trying to contain that smile pulling the corners of his mouth. Surprisingly, he was in a great mood tonight and was hoping nothing would spoil it.

Billie had a couple of girls 'gone wild' she was trying to deal with until she finally gave up, and then fetched TJ to take care of them.

Erik came down to assist TJ, who had gotten mobbed by the horny intoxicated bimbos.

When one started to inappropriately paw at Erik, Jessica shot daggers in their direction that could kill.

Katie just laughed, enjoying the show like everyone else.

It was just about 2 a.m., before the tequila gave voice and courage to a few more souls. Some learned what their friends really thought of them, and a few seemed to enjoy the uninhibited exhibition of others. This was the entertainment factor of Margarita Night. It was also always one of the busiest nights.

One scantily clad young woman who had lost most of her clothes on the dance floor, or in the bathroom had to be escorted up the stairs by her entourage before she was physically removed from a table top by TJ. Her hair was matted down with sweat from dancing, and her mascara smudged giving her drunken raccoon eyes, but she looked like she was having a great time.

Billie and Katie had a blast tonight, but were grateful for last call. They hustled to clean up empties and wipe down tables. The dance floor was a sticky mess and was left for morning cleaning.

Floog was packing up when Jim snuck up behind Billie and grabbed her, making her squeal. "Wow, BJ! I think I'm deaf in that ear now!" Jim's ease with Billie got Jack's attention.

Billie greeted Jim with a big hug, "Hey – you, can ya stick around for a little while? Katie and I would love to have a drink with you and catch up!"

Katie brought up the last tray of empties from the bathrooms. "You guys were great! This was such a nice surprise to have your band play here. Can you hangout with us for a little while?"

Jim laughed, "Alright, ladies, I'd love to have a drink with you, but first let me help these guys haul everything out!"

"They're invited, too!" Billie happily announced.

Jack glared as Jim returned to pack-up the band equipment. "How do you girls know him?" He ground out.

Billie's face lit up, "We went to school with him. He played back then, too! We all thought he was really good. I'm glad he continued playing."

"Don't worry, Jack – they didn't date!" Katie's snarky tone told him he was showing some jealousy.

"Well, I've got frozen strawberry margarita left in the machine, are you ladies interested?" Jack asked.

"Oh hell - yeah!" Jessica piped up. "After all that – I sure could use a drink!"

"Sounds good! Are you in, Billie?" Katie asked.

"Oh-what the heck! One won't hurt!"

Jack finished washing up the glasses as Jessica dried and put up. It was not long before the after-bar party grew, when Jim and the rest of Floog came back down, filling in the seats at the bar.

Billie was already sipping a frozen margarita through a straw. "Ooh, brain-freeze!"

Katie just shook her head, "Come on, BJ, keep up!"

Knowing BJ did not really drink much; Erik had some fun teasing her, and drank a beer while he waited for Jessica. The other band members were entertaining and had some interesting stories of their own to tell.

Katie enjoyed the visit with their old classmate, but was anxious to see Cal. "It was great seeing you again," she said as she hugged Jim good-bye. "Maybe you'll come back to play for us?"

*

Cal had been waiting up for Kate to come home. His open arms and sexy smile met her at the door. "How was work?"

Seeing him gave her a renewed vigor. She smiled wide, "It was good!"

Katie loved Cal's easy smile and sexy grey eyes. It was those wonderful playful eyes that had attracted her to him that first night they met at Doug's.

He bent down to kiss her full soft lips. In that simple, tender moment Kate's blood heated, her pulse quickened. The wanting she had been suppressing was rushing to the surface. Cal took her breath away.

Then, he had to ruin the mood, "I'm worried about you going back to work so quickly." Like nails on a chalkboard, the moment fleeted.

"Working two jobs; I feel it might be a bit much for you right now. Promise me you'll take it easy, even slow down," Cal said, as he led Katie into the kitchen.

Kate held her tongue. She knew he cared; he meant well, but only *she* knew what she really needed.

She had something very important to tell him. Kate tried to be patient, not wanting to blurt out what she had been anxious to tell him. She decided to lead up to it slowly. "I know - but I can work at my own pace for Paul. He's been really good about letting me do things on my own. I only have to meet with him once a week." Katie could not help but smile. Cal was worried about her, and he was the one who was supposed to take it easy. "Now, what about you?"

"What about me?"

Katie wrapped her arms around Cal's neck, looked up into his steely grey eyes, "You know *exactly* what I mean."

Cal's apologetic eyes locked with Kate's look of concern. "I really am sorry about the last couple of nights. A night without a phone call won't happen again." He promised her as he leaned in, resting his forehead to hers. Then he gave her a little kiss on the nose, and winked. Cal took down two wine glasses and offered one to Kate. "Red or white?"

She really did not want any wine after having a Margarita, but they still needed to talk. Unwinding at the end of the day with a glass of wine was their thing. It was their way of connecting with one another through all the chaos. "White, thanks!"

He poured her a glass and handed it to her. He was hoping he was not in too much trouble with her. He also hoped she would finally tell him about what she had been doing. "How's the research going?"

"Slow. I haven't gotten too far. I found some of the folks in town don't want to divulge any information. It's like everyone is keeping the same secret, and I'm irritating them." She needed to tell Cal what they found, but she wanted to test the waters first. She did not know what he had been dealing with at work or how this new information could affect things.

"You, too?" Cal replied.

"What's the Chief done now?" She asked, before taking a sip of wine.

"We're getting no where with our investigation. Our only suspect is missing, and Perry won't authorize any outside help. He's also burdened us with other work to keep us from working these murders, on top of it!"

Cal never discussed the details of police business, especially on-going investigations. She sensed how deeply troubled he was. She took Cal by the hand and led him to the living room. Her intention to snuggle on the couch was clear. Hondo trotted in behind not wanting to be excluded.

Katie tucked her legs under her as she nestled into Cal, and he put his arm around her. She was trying to be attentive to what Cal was saying; however, Cal sensed she was distracted. After the conversation he had with Stella at the deli, he had a feeling he already knew what she wanted to tell him. "Darling, why don't you tell me what's on your mind?"

"I don't know where to begin, and you're not going to like it!"

"This can't be good? Now, what did you do?" He joked trying to lighten the mood.

Katie could not even crack a smile; she had been holding it in for too long. She turned to face Cal sideways on the couch. "You know the building I'm supposed to be researching?"

Cal raised a questioning eyebrow, "Yes?"

"Well, Billie and I found an old diary that mentioned a tunnel. When we found the building had a hidden entrance to the basement, we found an access to a tunnel. But, it's not just one tunnel; there is a network of tunnels under Burlington! We have even found an underground bowling alley!"

"I knew about the bowling alley, but that's been gone for years!"

Katie shook her head, "No – its still there! Billie took pictures of it! We were in it - but that's not all..."

Cal could tell it was important. He could see the seriousness on her face.

Katie took a moment to formulate the words to tell him. "Cal, I think we also found boxes of military weapons."

Cal swallowed hard, "You – what?" He sat up straight, setting his wine glass on the table in front of them.

"Billie and I were documenting everything we learned about this building. And then when we found the tunnels, we mapped out where we went and what we found. We found a large metal grate in one of the tunnel's walls, and found it was to a room. These military boxes are under the floor in this room."

Cal did his best to hold back the over whelming apprehension he felt hearing about all this. Then in a calm cool tone he asked, "Okay, so tell me about this room?"

"Well, it was all brick, just like the tunnels. They are well constructed, and I wanted to find out who built them and why. After BJ and I climbed in through the grate we saw there was a trap door in the floor that led to a deep crawl space. That's where we found the boxes stacked up against a wall down there, with stenciled lettering spray-painted in yellow. We didn't open the boxes. So - I can't tell you what was in them, but Billie did take pictures of the boxes."

"Kate?"

"Hold on – there's more!"

Cal was shocked at what she was telling him. What more could there possibly be?

"When we left that room, we first went to our left and somehow we ended up behind a wall that concealed the Meth lab you've been looking for."

Her words knocked the wind out of him, "Damn it, Kate ..what were you two thinking?"

"Cal - I was doing the research and following it where it took me!"

Cal took Katie's hand in his. She felt how shaky he was. With gentle eyes he said, "Kate, I'm worried about you. You're taking unnecessary risks and taking these risks with Billie. Why didn't you tell me you found these tunnels before you went off exploring?"

Katie raised her brow and gave Cal an exasperated look that told him she tried, but he had been too wrapped up in his own work.

Katie knew all along she should have tried harder to tell him. "I attempted to tell you - a few times...besides I *knew* you would tell me to stay out of them and *I* wanted to explore these tunnels!"

Cal did his best not to raise his voice. Keeping a stern yet even tone he said, "Kate, of course I'm going to tell you to stay out of those tunnels! I just got you back! I'm working two murder investigations, and I have two missing persons! And now you just stumbled across cases of guns and the Meth lab that we've been looking for! There could be more to these tunnels than you think. Do you realize how dangerous they are? And if the 7 Sons of Sin are using these tunnels, there could be booby-traps down there! If you two found a way in, then others have too!" Cal sighed deeply to calm himself, and then wrapped his arms around her. "Kate, I just couldn't bare it if anything happened to you again."

22

Billie was just about finished with her second margarita when Jim and the members from Floog said their good byes, and TJ walked them all out.

Earlier, Billie had kicked off her shoes and sat with her long legs stretched out across to the next bar stool. She uncrossed her ankles and wiggled her freshly polished toes. "It feels so good to be off my feet!"

Jack came around to Billie, and studied her adorable face, which had a permanent happy smile plastered on it. She took a finger and wiped some sugar off the rim of her glass. Flirtatiously gazed into Jack's eyes, and then slipped her finger into her mouth as she sucked off the sticky sweet sugar.

"Seriously?" He said to Billie as a playful grin spread across his face.

TJ was observing from the bottom of the stairs as he loudly cleared his throat, "Am I interrupting something?"

Billie let out a giggle, and then quickly covered her mouth.

She placed her empty glass on the bar and reached out putting her hands on to Jack's shoulders. "Jack?" She concentrated hard to articulate each word. "I - think - I - need - a - ride - home..."

TJ was now standing next to his partner with his large imposing muscular arms folded across his chest. With a smile he said, "Jack, I think you better drive the lady home."

Jack sighed, as he helped Billie down off the bar stool.

Billie looked down at her pretty polished toes. "Where – are – my – sha – shoes?" She asked, as she looked around her.

TJ bent down to fish them out from under another chair. "Here ya go, Sweetheart." He said as he handed them to her.

She got the biggest grin, "Thanks, TJ!"

Billie started for the stairs, stepping cautiously across the sticky floor.

Jack caught up to her; "I'll take ya home, Bright Eyes!" He said cheerily as he tossed her over his shoulder. Her shoes loosely dangled from her fingertips, and she hung on to her purse with the other hand as he carried her up the stairs.

TJ hit the lights and locked the door on their way out. He helped Jack get Billie into his truck.

Jack hopped in behind the wheel and saw that TJ was itching to say something, "Don't!"

"Don't what?"

"Just – don't!"

TJ let out a hardy laugh, "Whatever you say!"

*

Billie did not drink much. She was not drunk, but tequila made her very loopy. She knew she was not sober enough to drive herself home, and the idea of having Jack take her home was an added bonus.

Jack helped her up the stairs to her apartment. After standing on the landing for a couple of minutes watching her unsuccessfully find the right key, he held his hand out.

Billie giggled as she gladly gave him her keys so he could unlock the door for her.

"Are you going to be alright?"

"Of - course!" She leaned against the open door. "Aren't you going to come in?"

He raised his brow to her. Jack wasn't the kind of guy to take advantage. He had real feelings for this goofy blonde. Realizing he was taking a little longer to answer than he should, he said, "On one condition."

Billie coyly pouted her kissable lips. "And what would *that* be?"

"You have to promise me you'll behave yourself and not take advantage of me." He flashed her one of his sexy grins.

She knew he was only toying with her; she wasn't *that* drunk. Billie put the hand holding her shoes behind her back and crossed her fingers. "Okay - I promise."

Jack laughed, "Yeah, right! Come on, let's get you inside."

As Jack shut the door behind them, he found Billie's cat glaring up at him. Torre meowed in a sassy tone, as if to scold him for bringing her home late. "What are *you* looking at?" It was not that Jack didn't like cats; he just wasn't use to them.

Torre got up in a huff and meowed one last good complaint, before strutting away with her tail held high in the air like she told him a thing or two. Jack chuckled to himself, "I guess it's not just dogs that are like their owners."

Jack sat down on the sofa, while Billie changed out of her bar clothes in the other room. On the coffee table he noticed an old diary with a worn leather cover. Sticking out were a few colored post-it notes marking some of its yellowed pages. Beside it was a map of Burlington oddly folded, and a few lines were marked, highlighted in neon pink. Under the map were some photos protruding from a folder.

Billie entered the room wearing a baseball jersey with yoga-pants, and had her hair put up in a messy twist on top of her head held with a clip.

Jack thought she looked sexy just the way she was. He held out his hand to her. "Come; sit with me for a while. I can't stay long."

Billie happily sat on the sofa next to him. She knew he had his secrets, well maybe not secrets, but she did not know where he lived or what he did after hours. She just wanted to enjoy whatever time or consideration he had for her.

Jack was curious about the diary lying on the table. "That looks pretty old. Where did you get that?"

Billie had been obsessing over this book and could not conceal her excitement when he inquired about it. "I found it in one of the rooms in that white building Katie's been researching." She blurted out, eager to share.

"Really?"

"Yeah, didn't you grow up in Burlington?"

Jack, who had always kept a low profile and did not talk about his past, was now being asked what would be considered an easy question. He decided to open up a little and answered her, "Well, Junior High and High School anyway."

"Did you ever hear about there being tunnels under Burlington?"

He was not completely truthful, "Rumors maybe...why?"

Billie slipped off the couch and sat on the floor settling between Jack's legs. She grabbed the diary, "Here, let me read part of this to you...do you mind?"

Jack looked down at the perplexing blonde, he flashed her one of his tired yet sexy smiles and shook his head, "Not at all, sounds like you're captivated."

"Oh, my goodness, Jack! This is the coolest story! I found out the woman who wrote it was a prostitute, and she lived in one of the rooms in that building! Her name was Sadie, and it's not just about her being a prostitute, it's her love story from 1928. I know it takes place during Prohibition, but some of the things she mentions, gives me the chills."

Jack could see how intrigued she was with this diary. "Where did you say you found it?"

"Oh, under some floorboards in one of the rooms on the 2nd floor, that must have been her room."

The mystery behind it now spurs Jack's interest as well, "What were you going to read to me?"

"I'm looking for it...here we go.

> December 12th 1928. Tonight, I'm meeting Cliff in the east tunnel. He told me not to wait for him if he wasn't on time. I don't know if I could ever leave without him. I know he's scared. He's put on a brave front, but I know he's in too deep."

Jack listened to her words. Her voice carried a yearning as she read this woman's passage.

"See here, she mentions an *east tunnel*. There's another one in here." She paged through the old book.

Just being near Billie, Jack felt something he didn't think he could ever feel again. He couldn't resist the urge to unclip Billie's long wavy tresses. Her soft silky hair fell loose, and Jack mindlessly ran his fingers through it.

She was so engrossed in the diary that Jack's touch only mildly distracted her as she flipped through its pages. "Okay, this one dated December 15th, 1928.

> Cliff wasn't there. I waited until I couldn't any longer. I'm scared. I don't know what happened to him. I'm tempted to go back in and check one of the other tunnels. I'm beginning to doubt myself. Was I in the wrong tunnel? Could he still be waiting for me?

Here she mentions *other* tunnels! What do you think?"

They were obviously mapping out the tunnels. He did not like the idea of Billie and Katie exploring the unknown under Burlington. He looked over to the map in front of them. He wondered how much they really knew.

Jack played it off like he was actually listening to what Sadie was telling, not just the key word, *tunnel*. "I'm not sure what to think, Billie. It sounds like this woman really loved Cliff, whoever he was." Jack caressed her cheek lightly with his thumb. Once again, Billie was so wrapped up in this diary passage, that he only momentarily distracted her.

"Haven't you been listening? I'm talking about the tunnels!"

"It is possible, I guess. I mean that was back during Prohibition. They had underground passageways out of speakeasies, so when one got raided, they could slip out undetected to keep from getting busted."

Billie started to rethink what she was about to tell him. She could not hold it in any longer. It was just too exciting and yet scary at the same time. She turned to look Jack in the eye, "Jack?"

Jack saw something in her eyes, the hesitation on her lips, "*Yes*, Billie?" He answered in a teasing manor.

She chewed her bottom lip, ready to burst. A spark of excitement flashed in her big beautiful blue eyes.

When she reached for the folder that contained the photographs she had taken and handed them to him. Jack was a bit taken a back, "I want you to take a look at these."

That wasn't at all what he thought she was working up to. Curious, he took the folder from her and then sat back.

Billie hopped up next to him, hugging her knees and rested her chin on them while he opened it.

He could not believe his eyes. The first picture was of brick and mortar intersecting vaulted arched ceilings. "Where did you take this?"

She leaned over Jack's lap to reach for the map on the table. She knew instantly where they found this and pointed it out to Jack. "Right under here. We found a way in through that hidden basement and followed this tunnel but it's collapsed, and then this one shoots off to the northeast and this one goes under Pine Street."

Jack took a closer look at the map she held. He asked, "The pink lines are the one's you've explored?"

"Yep!" She said proudly.

"How exactly did you find the entrance to get in here?" He calmly asked as he flipped to another photo. The idea of the girls exploring the Burlington underground was unsettling.

Billie proceeded to tell him everything; starting with the hidden door to the basement, which she had already told him. Then, how they noticed there was something suspicious with the way the one wine rack stuck out from the wall, and how Hondo led them right to the void that wasn't sealed up like the other doorways.

She was so eager to share with Jack what they had been doing she had to take a breath from talking so fast.

Jack knew these tunnels not only held secrets, but were also dangerous. He kept glancing between her photos and the map. While Billie revealed their discovery of the bowling alley, and that they suspected someone had been down there recently; because of the trash they found. Hearing that only made his gut tighten even more. His first thoughts were to Midas, and the Meth lab.

Time past quickly, and before Jack knew it the sun was coming up. He had the pictures spread out on the table with post-it notes stuck on them with some remarks he jotted down. Jack looked over to Billie, who had fallen asleep, content as a baby curled up at the end of the sofa.

He knew Midas was the key to stopping the bikers. They needed to know more about this man in the suit.

Jack lovingly picked Billie up off the couch, and put her to bed. Torre was delighted and immediately curled up next to Billie. Checking the time, it was not worth going home now. He looked back down admiring the sleeping beauty. An unmanageable curl lay across her face. He lightly brushed it aside, pausing to caress her lovely cheek. Jack was completely drawn to Billie. She stirred him in ways he never expected.

"Argh, Jack what are you doing?" he said to himself.

As Jack passed Billie's darkroom, he peered inside before returning to the living room. What he saw stopped him in his tracks. Upon entering the darkroom, he found more captured images of the girls exploits hanging on lines. The ones that caught his attention contained the images of military weapons boxes. *"Son of a bitch!"*

Jack had suspected the weapons were somewhere in the tunnel system, and here BJ had taken pictures of them. He didn't know if he should be angry or kiss her.

23

It disturbed Cal greatly to learn Kate and Billie were exploring tunnels under Burlington. His night had been long and restless thinking about the jeopardy the girls could have faced, with the added danger of the SSS using these tunnels under Burlington to hide their Meth lab. The best-kept secrets are always right under your nose.

Cal had been up since the crack of dawn. He wondered what else could be down there. Cal did not know anything about these tunnels. With everything Kate had been through; he could not shake the horrible thoughts of what could have happened to them down there.

Katie awoke to the wonderful aroma of coffee, Cal was brewing.

From downstairs, he heard the water in the pipes echoing in the ceiling, and knew Katie was now up and in the shower. "Come on, Hondo; let's go for your walk!" Cal hooked the leash to Hondo, and was a bit surprised to find Billie knocking on his door before 7 a.m. "I didn't expect you so early."

"I was up and decided to take a walk! Besides I'll do anything to help!"

"Kate's in the shower and coffee is on. I'll be back in a few minutes."

Cal returned to find the two women chatting over coffee. He kissed Kate before having to dash out. He turned back to them; trying not to sound too cross, Cal hesitated before he spoke, "For now, I need you both to stay here! You two need to stay clear of the tunnels and that building! And *please*, just try to stay out of trouble? When I return, I'll need to know exactly where you found those boxes!"

As Cal slid behind the wheel of his Crown Vic his cell phone rang. "Detective Chapman."

"Cal, its Jack, I need you to meet me at Sonny's...its important!"

Jack was already at the diner, confidently waiting for Cal in a booth facing the front door.

Cal looked haggard, showing signs of distress as he slid in behind the booth's table. He coolly looked around to those sitting at the other tables to see who could actually be listening before they began their conversation.

"Gee, Cal...you look like hell!"

Cal glared at Jack, annoyed that Jack could just casually sit there with an air about him matching that of Steve McQueen. There was only a hint of reservation before Cal unleashed some of his pent-up anger. "What would you say if I told you your girlfriend and my fiancé had discovered tunnels under Burlington, along with some pretty disturbing treasures down there?"

Jack straightened in his seat, as his cool demeanor quickly gave way. He didn't have to tell Cal about the stolen military weapons, he apparently, already knew.

"That's right, Jack – 'Nancy Drew times 2' have been snooping around in some tunnels!"

The expression on Jack's face told Cal he already knew about the tunnels. "You knew – and you didn't say anything?" Cal was furious.

"Actually, that's why *I* called, *you*! We've only known about the tunnels for a few days." Jack turned the questioning back on Cal, "Why don't you tell me *exactly* what the girls found?"

"You mean besides the Meth lab you've been looking for?"

The startled look in Jack's eyes told Cal he knew a lot more than Jack wanted him to know. "How about a cache of stolen military weapons?"

As uncomfortable as a whore in church, Jack shifted in his seat.

Cal carefully studied Jack as he would a suspect in interrogation. "You son-of-a-bitch!"

Jack let out a defeated sigh; there was no way to ease into this. They were already knee deep in it.

"When were you going to tell me – or weren't you?"

Jack and Cal studied each other in tentative silence.

Cal had read between the lines and knew Jack was not completely truthful when he said he was with MET. "Damn it, Jack, you're ATF?" Cal said in anger as he sat back heavily into his seat. His jaw tightened, holding back the anger he wanted to unleash. "You guys are like a roach motel, information goes in, but it doesn't come back out!"

Jack understood Cal's frustration, and rightfully so. If things had been reversed, he would be pissed-off, too. Now, because of what the girls found, he had to bring Cal in on what was really going on. The Meth lab was only part of Jack's assignment; up until now they did not know where the lab or weapons were. He allowed Cal to finish chastising him before he set the record straight.

Aware of Cal's past history with the Bureau, Jack took a gamble. "You finished? Now, you need to hear *me* out."

Cal gave Jack a respective nod.

"I was attached to the DEA Mobile Enforcement Team when one of theirs found the weapons. However, he got himself killed before we could make contact. I know how the LEOs feel about alphabet soup government agencies. None of you take the MET guys seriously, and I needed to be able to work under the radar, so...I told you I was with MET. I wanted to help you out but you have to understand my position."

Cal could have punched him right in the mouth; however, he restrained the urge.

Jack read his body language and snapped, "Don't be a dick – I wasn't in any position to tell you what was really going on!" Agitated, Jack shifted in his seat. His voice remained low and strong. "We know the guns were stolen from a National Guard weapon's depot. That's when Wyllie, the MET officer disappeared, he got word to us that the SSS was in possession of some stolen military weapons. I was put on the case - but it ran cold, and here I am - still sitting on it! The SSS haven't moved the guns, but now we've heard whispers about another arsenal shipment. Our contacts at the weapon's depot ID'd a Satan's Knights member, associated with the Gehring brothers. TJ has been working the drug angle, but this is a tight group. Cal – remember when I told you this organization had deep roots here? Look, I do trust you, but I couldn't take the chance that this would leak back to someone in the department."

Cal didn't like the sound of that. His eyes narrowed, as he quietly glared back at Jack.

"Yeah, Cal – it's true. You have a leak in the department." Jack clenched his jaw as he glared back at Cal. In a low even tone he said, "And, don't you *dare* think for one minute, I'd be reckless enough to put the girls in harms way! Until I saw the photos Billie had taken, we didn't know where they hid the guns!"

Cal's shoulder was throbbing. All the stress he had been under was starting to wear on him. "Tell me who?"

Jack did not have the answer, "I wish I knew."

Cal sat back in his seat, trying to get a handle on what Jack was telling him; going over in his mind who the leak could be. He glanced back to the now silent Jack. "I asked you, Jack...to help me, to come clean with everything. I can't help you or keep the girls safe if I don't have all the facts."

Jack needed Cal's help just as much as Cal needed his. Jack hesitated. The apprehension showed in his eyes, "Cal, I'm gonna need to ask you for a favor?"

Although it was unspoken, Cal understood Billie did not know Jack was working undercover. "That's up to you; it's not my place to tell her."

*

"What in the hell were we thinking?" Billie was expressing some regret.

"I'm not done down there, Billie. I want to go back."

"Katie – Cal will never let you go back down there, not now!"

"What else did the diary say about what was in the tunnels?"

Billie's big blue eyes stared back blankly at Katie. "Are you serious? *I'm* not going back down there!"

"I didn't say *we* were..."

"Hah!" She pointed to Katie, "I know you – you can't let anything go!"

"You and I both know there is more to those tunnels than what we found. Why else would Burlington keep the tunnels such a damn secret, when other towns are exploiting them? Did Sadie write anything that might tell us what the tunnels were used for? Or - maybe another way in?"

Billie was so wrapped up in the connection between the two lovers she had not really paid that much attention to the content about the tunnels, just that there *were* tunnels. She shrugged, "I'd have to reread it."

While it was still fresh in their minds, they did their best to show on the map the tunnels they took and an educated guess as to where they had crawled through the grate opening. And then where the Meth lab was from there.

Billie had a couple more roles of film to develop but would have to wait until later.

They heard the front door when Cal had returned with Jack.

Billie was happy to see Jack but was a little confused as to why he was there.

She flashed him a warm yet hesitant smile.

He only nodded in kind. Jack was rigid and vigilant, almost cold. He resembled the Jack the girls first met months back, not the Jack they have gotten to know.

Cal had his arm around Kate, as livid as he was, he was very glad not to have to be looking for her in the tunnels. Cal quickly directed the conversation, "Alright you two, let's sit down - you have a lot of explaining to do!"

Jack made a gesture with an open hand to have Billie sit on the couch opposite him. Between them, laid out on the table was the map of downtown Burlington, along with some photographs Billie had taken.

Katie shared a look with Billie before she confessed as to how they came to find the tunnels.

As if on cue, Hondo trotted in, stretched, and then sat beside Cal placing his head on Cal's thigh. Hondo switched his brows back and forth as if following their conversation. He even looked up at his master as if to say 'don't be mad'.

Cal reached out his left hand to pet Hondo while Katie told her story.

Every now and then Billie interjected. Mostly the girls told them about the diary, and how they found the entrance to the tunnels through the hidden basement.

Cal caught the subtle change in Jack's demeanor when the girls mentioned the rooms down in the tunnels. Jack was good, but every good poker-player has *a tell*, and Cal just read his. Whatever relationship Jack had with Cal was now being tested.

Billie curiously watched Jack as well.

Having seen the map last night, he looked back over it to what they had highlighted. Jack realized they had walked right through where Midas lived; however, neither one had said a thing about the homeless man.

Jack knew if the bikers were smart enough to keep their cookers hidden in the tunnels, then that's where the stolen weapons were, too. It would only make sense to use the concealment of these tunnels to their advantage. After all, that is what he would do. Most of these guys were paranoid to a fault, and would have had something rigged to let them know if their stash had been compromised. This worried Jack.

The stress was building inside Jack. How was he going to explain to SAC Cooper, that he found these tunnels without getting Billie or Katie involved – or Midas for that matter? The problem was he did not really think he could.

Once the girls were finished telling them about their discovery, Jack stood with a heightened agitation. He gave them a stern look as he spoke, in typical "Jack" fashion, low and slow. "You ladies aren't going to like what I'm going to say, but it needs to be said. Until we work this all out, neither one of you are to go back down there. You *and* your Scooby-Doo adventures are on hiatus for a while. You are welcome to continue your research of the building itself, but nothing – and I mean *nothing* in those tunnels."

Billie and Katie both expected this, but they still could not help but feel like they just got grounded.

Jack then addressed Cal. "I'd like to speak to you in private."

Katie was curious as to why Jack was now doing all the talking. She turned to Cal with a questioning glance.

The girls watched as Jack followed Cal out of the room.

"What in the *hell* is going on?" Katie asked out loud, to no one in particular.

In turn, Billie sat with a blank stare; she barely heard what Katie had said. "Why do you think Jack is acting all cop-like?"

Once in the foyer, Jack turned to Cal. "You have no idea the *cluster fuck* this just turned into!"

"Just tell me what you need?"

"I'm tired of these guys slipping through our fingers. I've got someone already in the tunnels setting up audio/visual feed. I'm hoping to get something tangible. You're going to have to really watch your step at the department, just keep your eyes and ears open. Let me know if something seems hinky. We still don't know who's protecting these bastards."

"And Billie?"

Jack shot Cal a dirty look, "What about her?"

"She may be blonde, but she's not dumb! She's going to ask."

Jack let out an exasperated sigh. He turned back to the doorway, "Hey Blondie – need a lift?"

Billie was happy to accept the ride home, but she was still trying to figure out why Jack was the one in control of that conversation.

*

The apprehension Jack was feeling, was becoming more difficult to keep under control. He deeply cared for Billie, but *this was over the top*. Jack knew he had to confess everything, but was concerned that once Billie learned the truth, she would not forgive him for keeping it from her. Trust was always a dealmaker or breaker. He would soon find out which one this was.

"Have you eaten?"

Billie shook her head, "No."

"Would you like me to pick something up?"

"How about delivery and *only* - if you're going to eat, too."

"Pizza?" Jack offered.

Billie stared out the truck's side window; "Sure", she shrugged her shoulders; still wondering about Jack's intense interest in their tunnel escapades.

Their conversation was minimal as Jack drove. Within minutes he was backing his black truck into a parking space just outside of Billie's apartment.

Billie opened the truck's door and slid out of the cab. She turned to Jack, realizing his hesitation to get out of the truck, "Aren't you coming up?"

Reluctantly Jack took the keys from the ignition. The echo from the slamming of their doors brought Torre to the window. Her silhouette was like a beacon for Billie's return.

Billie had all the delivery joints in town on speed dial, so she ordered a pizza before they even got inside.

Torre readily greeted Billie, but sassed at her - letting Billie know she was out of food.

Billie picked up the complaining feline and carried her into the kitchen so she could feed the demanding fur-ball.

As much as Jack wanted to spend time with Billie, he had too much on his mind. He was torn between his job and having any real relationship. In his line of work, Jack didn't think he could juggle both and give justice to either one.

Billie had sensed Jack's turmoil, and now watched him pace her tiny living room floor. She called out to him, "Can I bring you a beer?"

"No, thanks, but I'll take a soda if you have one?"

Billie brought Jack a can of Sprite and handed it to him. Casually seating herself on the sofa with her own can, she watched Jack in bewildering silence. "You want to talk about it?" she finally asked.

Jack popped the top as he came around to sit next to her. "I just got a lot going on right now."

"Are you working on something with Cal?"

Jack's eyes slanted sideways. "You could say that."

"Well, if it has anything to do with those bikers, just be careful."

Jack's sexy smile crept across his face, "I promise!"

24

Katie wore the little peach and cream-colored summer dress that she had worn on her first date with Cal, only adding a cream silk and linen blazer over it. She finished buckling her strappy high-heeled shoes, and checked her lipstick in the front hall mirror. Behind her, Cal came down the stairs, in need of a little help with his tie. She knew the cool dampness in the air bothered Cal's shoulder some mornings, but he would never complain.

She turned to greet this handsome man with a charming smile. "Here, let me help you with that."

He smiled recognizing the dress she wore. It hugged her curves perfectly, accentuating her beautiful plump ivory breasts, giving them just the right amount of cleavage.

Pulling Kate in tight, Cal nuzzled her neck, and breathed in her soft heavenly sent, as he whispered in her ear, "You are so beautiful." He was tempted to skip church all together, so he could stay home and make-out with this stunning woman tying his tie. If he did not need to go to work right afterwards, he would have tried harder to talk her into staying home with his kisses.

The mischievous gleam in his eye, told Kate he really did not want to go to church.

Cal's steely gray eyes held her deep emerald gaze; "We should get going if we're going to make mass on time. You know my mother will be waiting," he sighed.

Easter morning started out like most others. A cool breeze wrapped itself around the churchgoers as they cautiously stepped over rain puddles. The children were tempted to jump in each and every one along the way, but knew better. The rain had let up just long enough for everyone to attend church, and then the Heavens opened up again to wash away their sins.

Mrs. Chapman had saved seats for Katie and Cal in her usual pew. A few rows up Mary Reid was mournful and being received by several of the parishioners.

Constance flashed her son a scornful glance when they arrived, with but moments to spare.

Easter service was usually one of the longer ones, like Christmas. However, Katie was not really focusing on the priest's message today. Her mind had wandered back into the tunnels, and before she knew it everyone was rising to leave.

As the Easter service ended, the church bells tolled, and the sun poked through the grey skies. Cal kissed his mother and Katie good-bye before heading off to work.

Well aware of Katie's distractions in church, Constance invited Katie to join her for breakfast. Not only was she curious as to how far Katie had gotten on her research, but had real concern for how Katie was doing after her abduction.

Once Constance and Katie were seated at their table and their orders had been taken, Constance sat poised, taking a scrutinizing observation of Katie, sitting across from her.

In a concerned yet tender tone, Constance finally asked, "Katie, Dear, is everything all right?"

Katie looked up in surprise. "Yes...why?"

"I noticed you seemed to be elsewhere during the beautiful service?"

"It's nothing, really."

"You do realize what today, is all about?"

Katie raised a puzzled brow.

"It's about resurrection, Dear."

"I'm not sure I understand your meaning?"

"Today is about a miracle, and having a strong faith in that miracle."

Constance studied the confusion on Katie's face. "Not only is today a day to celebrate the miracle of Jesus rising from the dead, but of your own resurrection. Sweetheart, you have already been through so much in your young life, more than most could handle. But you are so very strong. You work hard to over come such pain."

Constance saw some recognition in Katie's eyes. "I feel you are still very guarded and not relishing in your own accomplishments. Know that I see it, Cal sees it and we are both proud of your strength to over come what you have."

Katie's eyes began to sting and water as a single tear rolled down her cheek.

Constance offered her a fancy handkerchief, "My Dear, I don't mean to sadden you. I only meant for you to see that today is a good day to celebrate *you*, as well."

*

Davey Holtz was forced into wearing a suit and tie, and hated it. Now that church was over, he was itching to get out of it. Luckily Davey was too old to participate in the egg hunt, or he would have to endure another hour or so of torture.

Expecting family over for dinner, his mother, Edna, had a Sunday roast to attend to back at home.

Davey's cousin, Lucas, could have been his twin. Both boys were constantly busy and had a knack for keeping their parents on their toes. Barred from the house Davey and Lucas were bummed about having to hang out with only grown-ups while they played cards.

Tom slammed a playing card onto the table. Pinochle was the family's game of choice and always a vicious yet lively game. Especially when Grandma Holtz played; she always cheated but no-body ever called her on it. Well, once – it was Davey, and he got dragged away from the table by his ear for calling G'ma a cheater.

His big brother, Brandon, did not have any time for him or anyone else in the family these days. And his sister, who was now away at college, hardly came home any more.

The women folk were in the kitchen cackling about their husbands and the price of groceries while fixing vegetables and potatoes for the Sunday meal.

Uncle John, Lucas's dad, was a cool guy. He saw how bored the boys were. "Hey, Tom, don't you have a small job or something for them to do?"

Tom looked to his brother, John, and then to Davey and Lucas. "You – sorry - sacks can't possibly be bored?"

"Yeah – I mean yes, sir." Lucas said.

Davey just nodded his head, with his thumbs hooked on his belt loops.

"Well, we've got some sick chickens out back. If you boys want to, go grab your .22 rifles - you can go kill 'em for me?"

The boys loved that idea. They were so hyped they hardly heard the instructions Tom was giving them.

They each took a rifle and carried out a metal case of ammo. More than what they really needed, but they were going to make sure they did a good job.

Behind the big barn were the chicken pens. Some were separated into the left pen and the majority of birds were in the right pen. The two boys looked at each other with dumbfounded expressions on their faces.

"Which ones are we supposed to shoot?" Lucas asked.

"Damned if I know. I thought you were listening."

"Well, he said something about on the left side and not to kill the healthy ones."

"So, the healthy ones are on the left?"

"Which side is left? Does he mean left of the barn or on our left?"

"Go back and ask!"

"I'm not going back to ask, you go back! They'll get pissed if we interrupt their game."

"Which ones should we shoot?"

"If it were only this dozen or so, why would he tell us to get our rifles?"

"That's true!"

The boys happily loaded their rifles. Then took aim as they randomly fired away. Bang, bang...bang, bang, bang! The shooting went on for over 30 minutes.

Tom slammed another card to the table. He looked over to his brother, "How damn long does it take to shoot a few birds?"

John laughed, "They're probably shooting at posts now or somethin'."

The boys continued to fire away.

With-in minutes Chapman pulled into the Holtz's long gravel driveway, followed by Sgt. Nelsen.

Tom watched them pull up and park. Tom and John met them as they got out of their squads. "What can I do for you, Officers?"

Cal pointed to his ear, "Don't you hear that?"

"What – the shooting?" Tom asked.

"Yes, sir. It is Easter Sunday, and we've gotten complaints that it has been continuous. What's going on?"

"I sent the boys out back to kill some sick chickens, that's all."

Sgt. Nelsen asked, "How long does it take to kill a few chickens?"

Tom and John shared a sudden look of concern. The four men walked at a quick pace to the back of the big barn, where two boys stood reloading their .22 rifles. Approximately 400 chickens lay dead and the 14 or so sick chickens just stood there, looked around, and watched the show all from one side of the pen.

Cal then shared a look with Jim.

Tom was furious. Profanity spewed from his lips.

Davey and Lucas looked back to where all the shouting was coming from dropped their guns and took off for the back 40.

John tried to grab his brother's arm to keep him from pursuing the boys.

"You stupid little bastards!"

"Sir." Cal tried to speak with Tom. "Sir!"

Sgt. Nelsen raised his voice. "TOM! You need to calm down!"

*

Back at the sub-station Jim chuckled to himself as he typed up the report, he just could not help himself. Cal came out of his office and found Sgt. Nelsen laughing like he had not seen him do in months.

Cal stood in front of Jim's desk, "Serge?"

Jim did not even look up, "All those dead chickens! *After* ol' man Holtz tans their hides, those boys are going to have to work all summer to pay for them damn birds they shot!" He laughed out loud. "I'm sorry, I know it's not funny...oh hell...yes, it is!"

A huge grin spread across Cal's face as well. He was glad to see Jim cheerful and laughing for a change. "Davey keeps things interesting, that's for sure. I wonder what he's going to do next."

25

Looking out the kitchen window toward the dark gloomy sky rolling in from the west, Cal poured himself a cup of coffee.

Katie came up from behind wrapping her arms around Cal, resting her cheek against him. "Off to work already?"

"Yes, but I'll try to come home early tonight." Cal took Kate by the hand drawing her around to give her a proper kiss. "I love you."

"Love you, too."

"Don't find anything else today! I don't think I can handle any more work."

"Ha ha – you're funny!" Katie chuckled as she threw a dish towel at Cal.

He flashed her a devilish grin as he ducked out.

Cal crossed paths with Billie in the driveway.

"You're here early?" Cal commented.

"I couldn't sleep so I thought as long as I'm up..." Billie shrugged her shoulders.

Cal's smile was warm and friendly, "Just do me a favor...can you two at least *try* to stay out of trouble today?"

She batted her eye lashes, "Oh, I suppose we could – *try*!"

Cal was in a jovial mood and just shook his head smiling as he climbed into the Crown Vic.

Billie knocked, but when Katie didn't answer she just let herself in. Greeted by Hondo, Billie called out, "Hello? Katie? Are you upstairs?"

Katie was making her way up the basement steps when she heard Billie. "I'm in the kitchen!"

Hondo happily followed Billie through the dining room to the kitchen. Seeing the basement door was wide open she had to ask, "What are you doing down in the basement?"

Katie took a sip of coffee before answering, "Making a project area for us!" Katie looked over Billie's shoulder to the table piled high with folders, notebooks, and photos.

Billie giggled, "Yeah, I suppose Cal would like to have the dining room table back! How's it going?"

"Well – since our tunnel escapades – you could say we've been grounded. We might as well make the best of it. I figured we needed a larger area to lay everything out, so I'm hanging up those dry-erase boards we bought the other day."

Billie took a look out the window behind Katie, "It sure is getting dark fast," as the rain drops hit the window.

"Nice, more rain."

Holding up the old red-leather diary Billie brought with her, "It's a good day to do some reading don't you think?"

Katie smiled with excitement.

They settled in the living room on one of the big leather sofas with their legs curled up underneath them.

Billie read aloud from the diary as Katie hugged a pillow, listening to her speak Sadie's words, words that had been stowed away for over 80 years. She turned to the beginning of the red leather book to reread the entry that got her hooked. Then read certain excerpts she had marked from each month.

June 18th 1928.

"Tonight, the gin-joint was full of bimbos and the lobby of the Plush Horse turned into another petting party. My dogs were tired and I had room 4.

My turnkey was a man named Cliff. He's no cake eater; he's sweet. I pray he comes back."

July 4th 1928.

"Today was perfect! Cliff took me down to the parade. He had packed a picnic basket for us and took me down to the lake. It was a lovely romantic spot. He said he did not care what anyone else thought about us. He told me that I made him happy! I am surely smitten."

August 29th 1928.

"I don't know what it is about Cliff. We have a strong connection. He trusts me and has started to confide in me. Tonight, Cliff told me he was a part of something that he cannot talk about."

September 17th 1928.

"I saw Cliff with some pretty powerful men downstairs. I don't think I want to know what he does. My heart tells me he's a good man. I want to believe a man who can be so tender in bed can't be a monster like those he is with."

October 5th 1928.

"I am very worried – Cliff never misses a date, but he did tonight. I pray he's all right. Is it wrong of me to hope for something good for myself? I have fallen in love with this man. I may not deserve him, but I can't imagine being without him."

With a loud clap of thunder, the lights went out, leaving the girls in the dark. Katie jumped up and grabbed the candles off the dining room table. Placing the candles on the coffee table – she lit them.

Billie slid off the couch to the floor next to Hondo, and continued to read.

October 9th 1928

"While everyone is talking about Babe Ruth hitting 3 homeruns in the World Series, I am privy to something much more important. Cliff says there are things the country isn't ready for. He wants to take me away from this place, but he has to do something first to keep anyone from using it. If it ever got into the wrong hands, he says millions could die. This talk frightens me...the sooner we can leave this place the better."

Billie was obsessed with the diary of this woman of ill-repute. This woman's love story intrigued, yet saddened Billie to know that in the end Sadie never knew what became of her lover. However, there was one entry that Billie was excited to share with Katie.

Before they delved back into the idea of exploring the tunnels further, Billie skipped ahead in Sadie's diary. "Listen to this; it's the very last entry:

December 29th, 1928.

"I never should have looked for Cliff. Our lives are now in danger. If they haven't found me yet, they soon will. I am so scared. What will happen to us? They have secrets hidden in the tunnels. What I saw in that room I never should have seen. I had to know if Cliff was one of them. They can't allow me to live after what I discovered. It's not just me anymore."

Billie wrinkled up her nose, "The ink is smeared, and it looks like her tears washed some of it away, so I can't read it, but down here it says: *Hopefully one day someone will find this and learn the truth."*

Katie was just as intrigued as Billie, but for other reasons than the sheer romance of it. "A room? She said she had to know if Cliff was 'one of them'. See there *is* more to these tunnels than what the bikers are using them for!"

Billie shrugged, "I don't know...but Sadie said 'our lives' and 'it's not just me anymore'... What in the hell is *that* supposed to mean?"

"I don't know about you, but I want to know *what* is under Burlington!"

Billie was hesitant, "You heard Jack and Cal...we are *forbidden* to go back down there!"

Billie's skin tingled with goose bumps just thinking of the possibilities of what they could find. She put an inattentive palm to her chest, with fingers searching to fiddle the charm she always wore. In recognition of what was no longer there, her heart sank. Wincing, she cried out, "Oh no!"

"What?"

Billie said almost in tears, "My Grandmother's Celtic cross – it's gone!"

"Check your shirt, maybe the clasp opened up and your bra caught it?"

Billie looked down her shirt.

It wasn't there. She quickly got up looking in the cushions. Nothing! A sad and almost horrified look came to Billie's face with a realization, "I bet it fell off when we climbed into that room!"

"What do you want to do?"

Billie chewed her bottom lip, "I have to find my necklace! That's all I have of hers!"

"You know I want to go back down there anyway? But we better wait a day or two...they'll be watching us like Hawks!"

"Alright, but Katie...I *need* that necklace back!"

"I know you do. We'll find it, okay?"

26

Davey was grounded – no dirt bike, no 4-wheeler, no tractors, and no guns. With nothing to do he took an angry walk, kicking at clods of earth as he stomped through mud-filled ruts.

The north tree line was traced with the faint remnants of snow all the way down the horizon. Davey made his way to the swamp. It was located on the furthest parcel of Holtz' land situated between the woods and Kirkman's land.

Soon the stench of decay caught Davey's attention. The smell of death and decay did not turn him away. Maybe he would find a deer carcass the coyotes had brought down, and he'd bring home its rack for a souvenir.

The closer he got the more potent the stench of decomposed flesh had become. He stumbled upon a muskrat den, and became distracted as he picked up a thick stick to poke at it. Davey quickly became bored with the lack of response from the muskrats and preceded to poke and stab at things in and around the swamp's edge.

Davey stopped in his tracks. Through a cluster of cattails, he spotted an unusual large blackened object.   This was no animal. Its appearance was bizarre in nature, and the stench was the strongest here. He leaned in closer to jab at the oddity. As it tipped and slightly rolled to its side, that's when he spotted a boot. This was no debris. To his surprise, these were human remains that still had the appearance of raw meat showing through the cracked shell of charred flesh. Davey was freaked out by the skull with its mouth gapped open in a silent scream.

He immediately pulled out his cell phone only to learn he had no service out there. He ran as fast as he could back to the barn, occasionally stumbling over last season's plowed clods of earth beneath his feet.

His father saw him running like hell itself was chasing him. "Davey – what's wrong?"

"I found a dead guy – call the cops!"

Tom Holtz had enough of his son's pranks and foolishness to last him a lifetime, but today was different. He believed Davey. The look of fear in his son's eyes told him he spoke the truth.

*

"Unit 125."

"125, go ahead."

"Unit 125 respond to a suspicious circumstance in the marsh where Kirkman's land meets Holtz's for a report of a possible dead body. Complainant will meet you at Holtz's barn and take you back."

"125, 10-4 en-route."

Once again, the Burlington police were called out to the Holtz farm. This time Randy O'Brien accompanied Cal with the evidence truck.

The officers followed Davey and Tom Holtz out to the marsh. The closer they got, the stronger the stench of decay had become.

Davey pointed to the blackened mass of the decaying corpse somewhat hidden in amongst the cattails.

Randy radioed to first confirm they had a body, and then to call Sgt. Nelsen out to the scene.

"Secure the scene. I'll send Gentry and Young out to assist. And I'll contact the ME for a possible homicide. What else do you need?" Sgt. Nelsen responded.

All Randy could think of was that he should have taken a piss before he got out there.

After they had secured the scene, Cal questioned Davey and Tom Holtz. Trying to keep the situation light for the boy, Cal joked about what Davey was going to do next to keep the B.P.D. on their toes.

Luckily the weather was good and time would be on their side. Randy took his time as he photographed and measured the location of the body using a GPS system.

It was not long before Sgt. Nelsen arrived, and conferred with Cal about what they had found.

When Mitch arrived on scene, he put on his waders and trudged out into the marsh. He took notes of his own, and took a closer look at the body.

Officer Young approached O'Brien and Mitch. The sickening sweet smell of burnt flesh mixed with decay hit him as he looked down at the badly burned body partially submersed in the water. His gag reflexes kicked in, as he tried not to vomit right then and there.

Randy shouted, "Get the hell out of here! Get away from the crime scene! If you gotta puke - do it somewhere else!"

Young held it until he was out of sight from the body. Then he let loose, retching until his gut hurt. A burned body is one of the most gruesome sights, and smells one can experience. Although Young had been a cop for 6-years, this was his first burn victim, and not one he would soon forget.

Randy looked up in the direction of Young's misery; he noted an obvious crumpled section of cattails in line with the body.

Young bent over, hands clutching his knees, spitting the bile from his mouth. He took deep breaths while he tried to keep from smelling the stench of decomposing flesh that permeated the air.

Sgt. Nelsen who never smoked, but always kept a pack of cigarettes on him, pulled two from the pack. He broke off the filters and handed them to Officer Young. "Here kid – stick these up your nose. It'll help."

That is when a blackened pattern not far from where they stood caught Nelsen's attention. There was an obvious irregular circle of charred marks - some spotted and then a larger more concentrated area. He gave a sharp whistle and then yelled, "Over here!"

Sgt. Nelsen stood looking at the burned corpse, he commented to Cal, "This just keeps getting better and better! Now we have 3-murders to solve! How much do you wanna bet that's Charlie Nix?"

Cal turned to Jim, "I'm not much of a betting man, but that would be my guess."

Jim placed his hands on his hips and shared a look with Cal, "Well – *if* we found our murderer, who do you suppose took care of him?"

Sgt. Nelsen spotted Dot parked along side the evidence truck.

Dotty had picked-up an order of sandwiches from Polly's Deli, and personally brought them out for the guys. She always looked out for her men. They had been out at Holtz's all afternoon, and now it was dinnertime.

Nelsen walked up to help her carry the highly treasured bags of food from Polly's. "God bless you, Dotty, you're a life saver!"

Dotty smiled wide. "I figured you boys would be pretty hungry about now."

"You know it!"

Randy finally took this opportunity to find a relatively private spot on the backside of the marsh behind some tall cattails to take a piss. He took a quick look over his shoulder, and then turned back. Randy happily relieved himself as he stared off to a noticeable beaten down patch of tall grasses that looked as if vehicles could have possibly been parked there. He shook it and put it away. Taking a better look around that area; he then spotted a shiny object embedded in the mud. "I've got something!" He yelled.

Chapman followed Nelsen over to where Randy stood, photographing some object in the mud along the edge of the marsh.

It was a lighter. Not just any lighter, it was a very specific lighter; an antique Zippo, circa WWII.

Nelsen's cantankerous mood lightened. "There ain't no way it's gonna be that easy!"

*

As Brandon sat quietly trying to drink his beer in peace, he could feel several pairs of eyes on him. Overall, he wasn't one to give-a-shit what people said or thought, just as long as they left him alone.

There had been a lot of gossip circulating around town as to what exactly was found out on Holtz's farm. Katie and Billie had befriended Brandon Holtz, and therefore had no problem approaching him to ask about all the chatter.

Brandon looked up to find Billie and Katie standing over him. Billie was not as bold as her friend, so she stood back and let Katie do all the talking. "Is everything okay out at your place?"

He smiled. After all, Katie was one of the few people Brandon had considered a friend. She never judged and was not one to gossip, starting it or spreading it. She genuinely cared if everything was okay with his family. He gestured for them to take a seat if they wished.

Both pulled out a chair and sat on either side of Brandon.

He knew others would be straining to hear what was being said. He set his beer down, leaned in close to the girls and spoke in a soft tone, barely audible. "They think Davey found Nix!"

Billie's eyes grew large with surprise.

Katie placed her hand over his on the table, "I bet that freaked your brother out, finding a body like that. Is he okay?"

"That crazy kid is always doing the damnedest things. Maybe this will teach the kid a lesson!"

Billie leaned in close to Brandon's ear, "Some of these dumb-asses think if it *is* Charlie Nix, that you're to blame. But *we* know you didn't have anything to do with killing Charlie."

Brandon just laughed. "Thanks for that...he certainly deserved what he got! But just to confirm... *NO*, I didn't have anything to do with killing that sick, fat son-of-a-bitch. If I had, I certainly wouldn't have dumped his roasted carcass on *our* land!!!"

"I'm glad you have a sense of humor about all this." Katie stood up and placed a hand on his shoulder, "If Davey ever needs to talk to someone about what he saw, don't hesitate to ask Cal for help. I'd suggest my shrink, but I doubt a 15-year-old boy is going to want to discuss his feelings with a woman."

"I'll keep that in mind – thanks!" Brandon said with an easy smile.

The Brick Yard had an unusual vibe tonight. It started with the whispers and curious glances toward Brandon Holtz. It wasn't until well into the night that most of the gawkers had moved on. Now, just past midnight, all that remained were the Thursday night drunks playing pool and getting rowdy.

Brandon was ignoring the general populous, sitting at one of the back tables just trying to mind his own business.

One of the regular losers, Josh thought himself to be a real ladies-man. Tonight, he and a group of friends found themselves downstairs scoping out the scenery. At first, he tried to hit on a couple of girls at the bar without much success. Then he saw Billie. Her long legs made her denim skirt seem even shorter. It was the black tank-top she wore with some rhinestone encrusted design on her chest matching the large sparkly earrings dangling from her ears and peeking through her long wavy locks of blond hair, that lured Josh and his ill intentions to her.

As Billie bent over a table to wipe it off, Josh decided to move in on her.

Jack might not have been able to see what was happening from the bar but Brandon could.

Taking inappropriate liberties, Josh roughly grabbed Billie's hips from behind as he pressed himself into her and delivered sloppy kisses to the side of her face.

In an instant, Brandon pushed out of his chair and had his heavily tattooed arm around Josh's neck, as he jerked him off Billie.

It happened so fast Billie was not sure what the hell took place.

"Get the fuck off me!" Josh hollered, as he clutched at Brandon's arm around his neck. "Mind your own damn business!"

"You just made it my business!" Brandon growled in Josh's ear.

Quickly, two of Josh's friends pounced on Brandon, although he never released his hold from Josh's neck. The men punched and hit Brandon trying to force him to release Josh. This only made Brandon tighten his grip. The jocks might have enjoyed a good bar fight, but Brandon was not a fighter for the sake of fighting He always stood up for what he believed. Right now, he was protecting Billie.

Katie quickly jumped in to grab Billie out of the way of the brawl. Moving to the bottom of the stairs Katie hollered up for help, "Erik! We need you now!"

These jocks always have to jump in, and save that one asshole that strayed from the pack from getting his ass beat, even if they truly deserved it.

Erik swiftly flew down the steps jumping right in. He grabbed one of the two, plucking him off Brandon's back before they knew what hit them.

TJ stepped out of the back room and quickly made his way across the bar to break it up. The second guy hastily stepped aside, not wanting to tangle with this muscle-bound heavily tattooed beast.

Jack had called the police and was now helping TJ with Brandon and Josh.

Sgt. Nelsen and Officer Young arrived to break it up, but the two bouncers and Jack had already restored order in the bar before they got there. A few busted lips, and black eyes, but no one was seriously injured, except for maybe their prides.

After the melee, everyone had cooled down enough to work it all out with the police. Although Brandon had gotten the worst of it - he did not want to press charges. That is all Brandon needed, one more run-in with the Burlington PD.

As a cocktail waitress you expect to deal with a certain amount of crap from the patrons; it is just part of the job. Billie was not letting Josh off the hook. Although she was not going to file a complaint, Billie did have Jack ban Josh from coming back to the Brick Yard for a while.

Jack was feeling very protective of Billie right now, and his adrenalin was running high. He wanted to do more than just ban Josh. This was the second time she had been grabbed by some asshole in the bar. He was thankful Brandon was there to stop it.

Katie and Billie continued working the floor like nothing had happened. Jack kept a close eye on Billie as she consumed his thoughts.

At closing Billie hauled up the remainder of the glasses and empties to the bar. Jack gave Billie a little wink with that sexy, crooked grin of his, making her turn a bright shade of fuchsia.

Billie stirred Jack's blood. The more he fought it, the more he wanted her. She left him feeling disoriented and not in control; two things that were not in Jack's nature. "Can I give you a lift home?" escaped from Jack's lips before he could stop himself.

Billie was not about to refuse a ride home from Jack. "Absolutely!" she said with a happy twinkle in her eye, tucking a long wavy blond truss behind her left ear as she flashed him a sultry look with those big, blue eyes of hers.

She happily climbed up into the cab of Jack's truck but sensed there was something more. His usual cool demeanor was replaced with an unfamiliar tension. Jack surprised her when he offered his hand as he drove.

Billie's heart raced. She suddenly became very aware that her hand had turned cold and clammy. He made her nervous, but in a good way.

By the time she took a deep breath, trying to calculate what was happening; Jack had already backed into his usual spot behind her apartment building.

She turned to thank him for the ride home, and locked onto his mysterious gaze.

He let out a huge sigh as he squeezed her hand, which let her know she meant *something* to him. By nature, Jack was a liberator, a protector. Tonight, he felt he had failed Billie. "I'm glad Brandon was there tonight."

"Me, too!"

There was more he wanted to say; he just could not find the words. She was intoxicating, and he longed for her. He had to look away from her angelic face, or he would not be able to leave; however, he still held her hand.

Jack had been acting somewhat out of character tonight and Billie sensed it. "Okay, well...thanks for the lift." She said with a confused tone.

Jack turned back to meet Billie's captivating, blue eyes, lifted the hand he still held, and gently kissed it. "Good night, Billie."

The mere brush of his lips upon her hand sent an electric current through her. Dizzied, she slid out of his truck. Everything seemed to slow down; her long walk to the door was surreal.

Jack waited for her to open the door to her apartment before he pulled away. Normally he would have walked Billie to her door, but he needed to see someone tonight. He knew that if he did walk Billie to her door, he would be staying.

How she even made it in the door was beyond her. She was dazed with a tingly warm over-whelming feeling of love. Locking the door behind her, she dropped her hand-bag to the floor, and sank into her pillowed sofa. Billie could not help thinking about the hold Jack's gaze had on her. *"When in the hell did that happen?"* She thought to herself.

27

Jim awoke having a heavy heart, with the realization that Alison Chamber's funeral was today. He had made arrangements to escort her mother, Rebecca, to the grave site.

Lying in bed next to her husband, Kristine felt his sadness. She rolled over to place a comforting arm around him as she kissed his cheek. "You want to talk about it?"

"No one should have to bury their child. It's just not right."

Kristine lay in Jim's arms, giving silent comfort. She knew today was going to be especially difficult for her husband. They had known Alison and Rebecca for many years. Alison and their daughter had grown up together. One couldn't help but think 'what if'.

*

Special Agent in Charge, Wesley Cooper was a former Marine, whose experience as a task force Executive Officer landed him a job with ATF & E. Although he was a hard man, who had a no-nonsense, cut through the bullshit attitude, which kept his men in line; Cooper never asked anyone to do anything he would not do himself, and for that, he had earned everyone's respect.

Cooper loved the Corps, and the men he served with. It was the bureaucracy he despised. Taking the job with ATF, he replaced his silver oak-leaf for a gold shield, and exchanged one kind of bureaucracy for another. He did not know which was worse, the military or federal bureaucracy. To him, they were nothing more than bean counters - which did nothing, but hinder operations.

Tom Jeeters (TJ) and Jack Carter both had outstanding military records, with only a few minor infractions peppered in along the way. Their integrity, diversity and commitment were the values that attracted SAC Cooper to bring them on his team. These were the kind of men you could trust with confidence, to do whatever was needed to get the job done. Cooper knew what he was dealing with, and knew exactly how to make it work.

Jack and TJ were now personally vested to this case and hoped Cooper would not find holes in their discovery.

Cooper had been doing computer work, which he did not like to do, and it always put him in such a pleasant mood.

"Good morning, Cooper!" TJ was the more jovial and vocal of the two.

Cooper's mood was already disgruntled and could shift either way, quickly. He grumbled under his breath, "Take a seat." A few more strokes of the keys, and he hit "send".

SAC Cooper sat back in his leather desk chair, quietly observing the two sad sacks in front of him. "Well?"

Jack handed over the folder containing a map of the tunnels, along with the photos Billie had taken of the weapon boxes.

Cooper's brow creased as he scrutinized over the information handed to him. After what seemed like an eternity, he looked back to Jack and then TJ. "What don't I know about this?"

TJ for once did not have an answer.

Turning his attentions to Jack, Cooper studied him.

Jack knew this was coming. They liked Cooper; he worked with them not over them. Hoping he'd understand the situation with which they were dealing, Jack presented it. "Two good citizens stumbled upon it. But found the entrance to the tunnels they're using with the help of a homeless man."

"You've been compromised? Two local-yokels and now a homeless man?"

Jack sat forward, "Information was shared, and we know this homeless man." Jack looked to TJ.

TJ gave a slight nod.

"He's a fellow Marine, Sir. We were in the same unit. We trust this man with our lives."

Cooper sat back, taking a long hard look at his two agents. "The whole idea of an undercover operation is to have as few people in the know as possible!" He hung his head and sighed. "I need this all to come together. How is this going to play out in court? You understand that?"

"There's more."

Cooper gave Jack a look, "Of course there is! You two are determined to give me ulcers, aren't you?"

"The man's name is Kelly Green, and he's a genius with electronics. He lives in these tunnels and knows them well. We couldn't have gotten what information we have without him."

"This is what I need you to do, draw up a contract for your friend. We need to officially make him a confidential informant and subject to the CI files. Make sure he understands what this means. He is to report directly to you two on all occurrences involving the gang's movements." Cooper glanced to TJ, "Do I make myself clear?"

"Yes, Sir."

"Now, Jack, these two 'good citizens'...they won't be in any danger, will they?"

"No, the two LEOs we're dealing with handled that."

"Cooper gave Jack a squinty eyed glare, "Indeed."

*

Jim Nelsen blew out a breath, getting himself together before he knocked on Rebecca Chamber's door.

She was sitting in her wheelchair staring out the window, solemnly waiting for his arrival. Rebecca's brown shoulder-length hair was neatly combed. She wore a black pantsuit with a vibrant blue top, which enhanced the blue of her eyes. She smiled when Jim entered, but started to cry all over again.

Jim stepped up to console her.

Rebecca gladly accepted his hand, and forced herself to speak, "Thank you...for doing this."

Jim patted the hand he held, "Rebecca, I can't tell you how sorry I am."

She smiled at Jim, and then to the photo of her and Alice on the bookcase.

Jim turned to see the 8 X 10 of the two the of them from a happier time, smiling back. As he retrieved the framed photo for Rebecca to hold, he noticed there was an accounting ledger next to it. "Rebecca, do you recognize this?"

Her eyes trained on the book Jim held up, and shook her head 'no'.

"May I?" Jim politely asked.

Rebecca nodded giving permission.

Upon opening the ledger, Jim realized the significance of what he just found. "I will need to hold on to this, Rebecca. I believe Alison left this here for safe keeping."

Before Rebecca could ask anything, the nurse entered the room. "Are we ready to go?"

Jim handed Rebecca the framed photo of her and Alice.

Rebecca nodded, holding the picture tight to her chest, as the nurse wheeled her out.

Kristine waited for her husband and Rebecca to arrive at the cemetery. She flashed him a sad yet warm encouraging smile as he wheeled Rebecca down to Alison's grave site.

There was a small gathering around a white casket, covered in a blanket of yellow roses. Among those in attendance were Cal Chapman and Randy O'Brien.

Keeping his distance, although everyone was well aware of his presence was Richie Collins. Strangely, he was alone and stood back lurking from under a large oak.

As angry as that made Jim, he knew this was neither the time nor the place. Kristine placed a supportive hand on her husband's shoulder, reassuring him to behave.

Today was about Alison Chambers and her mother who was now left all alone in this world. The Pastor spoke beautiful words, about the life that was taken all too soon. The happy, smiling picture of Alice and her mother stood looking out from the podium.

Rebecca said 'good bye' to her daughter with a quiet solace that she was now in a better place. She laid a single long-stem white rose on the top of Alison's casket.

As Jim wheeled Rebecca away from the casket, he placed a calming hand on Rebecca's shoulder, and she just cried.

When Jim looked back to the oak Richie had been standing under, he was already gone.

28

After the funeral, Jim was pensive, more so than usual. Cal was concerned, but gave Jim some space to workout whatever it was that weighed heavily on his mind.

When Jim carried his silence over into work the next day, Cal knew there was a problem.

However, Chapman would have to wait to speak to the sergeant. He would be tied up for awhile with another one of the Chief's priority details.

Of all days Sgt. Nelsen got involved in a troubled tenant complaint, the landlord of Shady Hills Apartment complex filed a FOI (freedom of information) request, wanting to evict the tenant due to all the complaints. Jim spent the better part of the morning returning phone calls, going through e-mails, and going through over 20 – complaints. All of which turned out to be legitimate reports.

Even Lucy Meyers, the troubled tenant in question, called Sgt. Nelsen to try to work things out, asking him for copies of those reports. The last thing she wanted was to be evicted because of her no-good ex-boyfriend's issues.

Now that the loser ex-boyfriend was gone, and Lucy promised to keep the trash away from her doorstep, Sgt. Nelsen told her he would put in a good word to the landlord for her.

For the most part, Jim liked the job and the men he worked with, but hated the office politics, all the paper work, and the basic "babysitting" duties that go along with being a sergeant. He would much rather be out on the road, and today was no different. The stress of the daily grind was suffocating; Nelsen had to get out of the office.

Chapman returned to the substation to find Nelsen gone. He tried Jim by radio, but had no response. Cal had a feeling he knew where to find him.

Sure enough, as Chapman pulled into the gravel lot surrounded by woods, there he found Sgt. Nelsen's Crown Vic. By the rapid *thump, thump, thump* echoing back, Cal knew he was right, something *was* bothering Jim.

Cal took his range ears from his duffle bag, and strolled out to where Nelsen fired away.

The rapid firing stopped as Jim released the empty 15-round magazine, and placed the unloaded Smith & Wesson M&P.40 on the table. He sensed Cal's approach as he started to reload the magazines, "So you found me?"

"I took a guess."

Jim filled one magazine, tapped it hard in the palm of his hand and grabbed another to load.

Cal reached for the third mag to load for Jim. "You want to talk about it?"

He was not ready to share.

Cal handed Jim the loaded magazine.

Jim slapped the mag into the grip.

As Jim engaged his weapon, Cal put on his ears.

Cal joined him, and pulled his side arm left-handed in an attempt to hit his target.

Left-handed, Cal was no marksman, but he did manage to hit it a few times. However, Jim was working through some built-up frustration and blew the shit out of his targets.

*

Billie anxiously waited outside the 480 building, for Katie. She had a bad feeling about going back down in the tunnels. Not just because they were told to stay out, but apparently the biker's guns and drug lab were not the only things down there. Sadie's written words gave Billie the chills.

When Katie pulled in along side Billie, she instantly felt better.

They let themselves in through the front door like they had so many times before. Only today their tension ran high; doing things they knew they should not be doing.

Katie opened the hidden door to the cellar. As it swung open, its hinges cried out loudly and echoed down to the dark empty space below them.

Billie swallowed hard as she shared a look with Katie.

Their flashlights lit their path, and the weight of their decent on the old wooden staircase sent a subtle warning announcing the girls' presence.

Cautiously they slipped through the open passage way and into the first tunnel. Neither one spoke as they took their time taking in their surroundings, every sound, every smell.

Billie almost felt naked without her camera around her neck. This time her experience in the tunnels was all too real. She could not hide behind her camera now.

Although Katie wanted to be back exploring these tunnels, looking for hidden rooms and places from the past that were mentioned in Sadie's diary, she felt uneasy about this. Something just did not feel right. Maybe it was because they were told to stay out, or maybe because she knew how close they were going to be to the biker's stash of weapons. Cal never said anything more to her about what the police were going to do. She kept playing different scenarios in her mind of things that could happen. The last thing she wanted was to get caught, either by the bikers or Cal.

Once they made their way into the tunnel which branched off toward the room with the weapons, Katie sensed they were being watched. Possibly her imagination was working overtime, even on the verge of paranoia, but she could not shake the feeling someone else was in the tunnel with them.

Katie's jaw clenched tight.   Becoming over heated, she suddenly felt ill. Katie placed her hand in her pocket, wrapping her fingers firmly around the grip of her pistol.

Billie quietly and cautiously followed behind. Even she was feeling a bit more jittery than usual.

When they arrived at their destination, the step-stool they had left behind was still there. They never even returned the iron grate they had removed.

They shined their lights around the area, making sure they did not miss the necklace lying on the ground, cautious not to shine their lights too far ahead.

Billie turned to Katie, "What if it's in the sublevel with the guns?"

"Then we will get it."

"We really shouldn't be back down here. I don't feel so good about this."

"I know, but we're here now. Billie, nothing has really changed. We've done this before without knowing what we know now."

"Yeah, well ignorance is bliss!"

Katie softly chuckled, "If only that were true!"

Katie stepped up onto the step-stool and peered inside the cold dark empty room. "So, how do you want to do this? I think one of us should go in to search for your necklace, and the other should stay here to pull them out."

"What?"

"I'm just thinking; we have to leave the same way we go in, because we don't know what we're going to run into out that door. We were lucky once..."

"No, you're right. I'll go in; I'm a little taller than you and can jump up to the window."

Katie stepped down, allowing Billie to crawl through. She dropped down and carefully searched for her necklace. It was not there.

Watching from the window, Katie whispered, "Look over by the hatch in the floor."

Billie's chest hurt, realizing she had been holding her breath. Her heart pounded in her ears as she carefully raised the lid to the sublevel, and there stuck in the crevasse of the dirty wooded floor was a broken silver chain. She put her flashlight in her mouth and held the hatch lid up with her head while she maneuvered to retrieve the necklace. Billie was overjoyed when the Celtic cross was still attached.

As quietly as possible, she closed the hatch, even sweeping a little dirt back over it. Quickly she pocketed the necklace, and handed up her flashlight to Katie before making her way back up through the opening.

Billie's pulse was racing a mile a minute, she was scared yet it felt invigorating all at the same time.

The girls put the iron grate back up, and Katie folded up the stool to take with them.

Katie was beginning to feel better about their little excursion. Now they just needed to get back.

Knowing they had to keep quiet, neither one spoke. Billie still felt a little jittery and kept looking over her shoulder.

When they got to the fork in the tunnel system, Katie continued the way they came in; however, Billie was busy looking over her shoulder, and had even stopped. She missed which way her friend had gone.

Billie thought she heard something, switched off her light standing poised and attentive. After a few seconds she whispered, "It's nothing", as she turned back to Katie.

But Katie was not there.

Billie's heart leaped into her throat. "Katie?" she called out in a hushed whisper. "Kate! Where did you go? Kate?"

It was within but a heartbeat, that a knit gloved-hand grabbed Billie from behind, covering her mouth to muffle the scream that was to come.

Billie's hands grabbed for the hand which covered her mouth. When she could not budge it, she elbowed him and kicked while she desperately tried biting his hand.

He wrapped his arms around her in a forceful bear hug, as he growled in her ear, trying to quiet her down. *"Shh! Stop – just stop it! Shh!"*

His hand clamped down a little harder on her mouth.

Something told Billie he wasn't trying to hurt her, but he urgently needed her to be quiet.

Katie hadn't realized Billie wasn't following her until long after the footsteps that she should have heard, were no longer there.

In a hushed whisper she called out to her friend, "BJ! BJ? Where the *hell* are you?"

Katie shined her light down the tunnel, in the direction she just came from. No sign of Billie. Katie started to panic. "Damn it, Billie! This isn't funny!" She waited, listening for any kind of response. Again, she called out, "BJ?"

Once Billie calmed herself, she nodded her head "ok".

In a gruff whisper he spoke in her ear, "Just listen, forget about me, and just listen! What do you hear?"

Voices, echoed down one of the tunnels. Loud, angry voices! Billie could not make out what was being said, but this man, who ever he was, just saved her from walking up on the men arguing.

Again, the man who still held her mouth spoke quietly in her ear. "I'm gonna get you out of here...*do not* make a sound. Do you understand me?"

Billie nodded her head 'yes'.

Although she let him know she understood, he still did not trust that she could keep quiet. He had been following the girls and watched them many times. He did not want them to get hurt. He pulled a roll of duct tape from his jacket, and then told her "You're going to have to trust me, Blondie." As he carefully ripped a piece of tape off with his teeth and placed it over Billie's mouth.

She was not happy about it, but she still, did not really feel threatened by him, until he zip-tied her hands behind her back.

"This is for your own good, Sweetheart." Then he covered her head with something so she could not see where they were going.

Billie jerked her head in protest, but it was not any use. She was not sure if she should show how afraid she was. All she could do was hope Katie would come back for her.

"I know you're not very happy about this, but don't fight me. I am trying to help you." He took her forcefully by the arm to lead her down the corridor.

Billie paid close attention to the sounds she heard, even when they changed direction. However, she lost track as to what direction they were really heading when this man stopped to spin her around a few times before continuing.

*

Katie knew going back too far could possibly get them both lost. She needed to get back to the building where there was cellular service and call Cal for help.

Cal's cell rang, but he had never heard it over the gunfire at the range.

When Cal did not answer, she called the only other person she knew she could call, Jack.

"Jack Carter!" He answered.

"Jack? It's Katie...Billie needs your help, *now*!"

"What happened?"

"We went back down into the tunnels and somehow got separated, and now I can't find her!"

He was beyond upset. Jack and TJ were already on the road on their way up to meet with SAC Cooper. Bad timing for sure, but they knew the danger Billie could be in. "I'm on my way!"

At the next exit, TJ got off I-94 breaking speed limits to return to Burlington.

*

Billie was seated and then tied to a chair before the covering was removed from her head. She blinked a few times adjusting to the dimly lit space. Cautiously she glanced around the room. Behind her she felt the presence of the man who had escorted her there.

He asked, "Can I trust that you won't scream if I remove the tape?"

She nodded, 'yes'.

He reached from behind and ripped off the tape.

Billie mashed her lips together and exercised her mouth a bit, trying to squelch the stinging pain from the tape being pulled off. "Do I know you?"

He hesitated before he answered, "I don't think so!"

"Are you going to stay behind me or in the shadows the whole time so I can't see you?"

"Does it make a difference?"

"I'm not sure. Something tells me you don't want to hurt me, but you have a funny way of showing it."

"I *don't* want to hurt you."

"Then why do you have me tied to this chair?"

"It's for your own good."

"So - you keep saying."

"You shouldn't be down here. This isn't a good place."

"The tunnels? Are you kidding - they're incredible! But...I guess you already know about the bikers?"

He did not respond.

"Oh – my - Gosh! You're not one of the bikers, are you?"

"No!"

"Is that who was arguing, a couple of the bikers?"

He did not respond.

Now that her eyes were more adjusted, she took a better look at her surroundings. "Do you live here?"

He still did not respond.

She crossed her legs and sighed. She heard him tinkering with something behind her. "So - whatchya doin'?"

He did not respond.

"How long are you going to keep me here? Cuz - I'm pretty sure my friend will come looking for me. And by the way, her fiancé is a detective with the Burlington Police Department!"

He finally came around to get in her face.

Her eyes grew large with the sudden movement from her captor.

He barked in annoyance, "Stop, just stop already! Why do you ask so many questions? Just sit still and *shut up*!" To his surprise she had no reaction to is war scarred face.

She took a good look at the man before her. "Hey – I do know you!" She remembered how she thought he had kind eyes.

"No – you don't!"

"Uh - huh! I've seen you at the Sci-Fi! You have breakfast there…you always order Brad's biscuits and gravy! I'm sure of it!"

"Please, just shut up! Don't make me regret removing the tape." He gave his captive a stern look, "I'm warning you, if you don't stop talking – I *will* put tape over your mouth again!"

Her mouth gaped, but shut it thinking better of the comment she wanted to make. In a huff she flippantly kicked the leg she crossed, repeatedly in agitation.

It took Jack and TJ less than 20-minutes to make their way back to Burlington. They wasted no time getting to Midas for his help.

When they emerged from the concrete shaft leading to Midas's lair, in full tactical gear and donning their ATF jackets, Midas greeted them with, "I was wondering when you'd show up?"

Jack was relieved when he saw Billie.

Billie was surprisingly calm. Her vibrant, ocean-blue eyes transfixed on Jack as she just observed him interacting with the man who brought her here.

"I see you saved us the trouble of looking for her!"

"Jack, I was starting to regret bringing her back here! That one *never* stops talking!"

"Did you have to tie her up?"

Midas turned to look at the blonde, "Yeah, well...I didn't want her doing anything stupid."

TJ just smiled wide, "Hey, Billie!"

She gave a nonchalant nod to him, "TJ." Her tone was low and somewhat cool.

Jack finally approached the perplexed blonde. "Are you alright?"

With a smug grin on her face, "Oh sure...I'm just hanging out here with my new friend."

Knowing now that Billie was safe, Jack was not sure if he should laugh at the situation or be angry with her for disobeying his request. "Is there something you'd like to say, Billie?"

"Actually, is there something *you* need to tell me, *Jack*?"

A smirk spread across his face, "Yeah, you didn't use very good judgment, did you?"

She couldn't be mad at him, not with that damn sexy grin of his, and the impish spark in his eyes. "You knew I'd be a handful!"

TJ chuckled loudly from behind Jack.

"You're not helping!" Jack tossed over his shoulder to his partner. He bent down to get right in Billie's lovely face. Smoothing out her disheveled blonde locks, "What am I going to do with you?" His smile was warm, and tender.

"You could start by untying me!"

"Actually, I think you're fine right where you are."

Midas quickly interjected, "Oh, Hell no! You need to take her off my hands!"

Jack laughed, "I see you've made quite an impression, and in such a short time too! I'd say that's got to be a record."

Billie was not about to have a battle of wits with Jack right now. "I surrender, Jack. Apparently, the tunnels aren't the only secret in Burlington. When you're ready to tell me, I promise, I'll keep yours."

Within the hour, Billie called Katie. She was so relieved to hear from Billie. Their day did not go exactly as planned, but all in all, no one got hurt, and they did get Billie's necklace back.

She did not need to worry about what she was going to tell Cal; Jack had already filled him in on the girls' misguided excursion. Needless to say, he wasn't very happy about it. After the lecture she received, Katie welcomed a night working at the Brick Yard.

*

At Jim's insistence, Randy met him at Chapman's Victorian for a late-night meeting.

Jim held a brown paper bag. "What I have here I believe holds the answers we've been looking for. And Cal, before you give me a lecture on protocol...let's review the position Perry has put us in!"

Cal furrowed his brow, "Show us what you have, Jim!"

Nelsen produced the ledger found in Rebecca's room.

Randy shared a look with Cal. "Is *this,* what Alison was murdered for?"

Jim set the ledger on the coffee table in front of them, "She told me she had something to show me. This was hidden in her mother's room. I can only speculate, but if we can figure some of this out..."

Cal opened the book's cover and started to page through it.

Randy pointed to some initials on a page, "P.D. - is that possibly for police department?"

Cal looked to Jim, "Or Patrick Dunn!" He looked back to the ledger. "You're right, Jim. We can't turn this in to evidence, just yet."

Cal retrieved a legal pad and pen, handing them to Randy. "Take some notes, Hollywood! I think it's going to be another long night."

Starting from the beginning they noted the dates. One in particular caught Jim's attention. "That's the night of the big fire at Green's farm."

"By the date is a number, could be a dollar amount?" Randy pointed out.

There was scribbling next to numbers and only a few descriptions written out. The initials, P.D. kept coming up. Jim had great recall, and remembered some of the events that correlated with some of the dates: a robbery and a couple of major fires, very suspicious circumstances, of course.

They could not possibly figure out what any of this meant in one night.

Jim spoke with an air of caution, "Okay – If someone on the department is on the take, we're gonna have to be careful, watch what we say and to whom."

O'Brien asked, "With this book, our suspicions about the Chief and all the reports he had us change - couldn't we just turn this all over to the feds?"

Cal leaned back, "Guys, when it comes to the FBI, there has to be a quid pro quo!"

Jim smiled with a Cheshire cat grin, "Exactly, and *now* we have Richie's journal! We don't know who this book implicates! I've already made copies of every page. I'll check this in, and put a copy in our files, but we're also keeping a copy. I'm sure the State's Attorney will be interested! We just let *her* take it to the Feds."

Once Katie came home, they called it quits. Cal walked Jim and Randy out, "Let's pick this up again tomorrow if we can?"

Jim left with the ledger and went home to his wife.

Randy left with dates, numbers, and initials curiously playing over in his head. He always did enjoy a good puzzle, and this was a big one.

29

Cal did not like the tension that was building between him and Kate. He felt guilty for spending so much time away from her, while focusing on the issues with the chief and his investigations. He wanted to make it up to her by a night out, in the city.

He was lost in thought about the romantic surprise he had for her, when out of no where, two members of the 7 Sons of Sin riding side by side rode straight for Cal, almost forcing him off the road. He recognized them as Marty and Dean Gehring.

He swerved to miss them, "Son-of-a-bitch!" Quickly swung a U-turn, hit the lights, and went after them. Now he was annoyed. He was finished working for the day, and didn't want to make his day any longer. However, these drunken ass holes were in danger of making that happen.

Although the Gehrings had been suspected of gun running, somehow, they always seemed to escape the long arm of the law. Today, they were feeling invincible! Out celebrating another large weapons deal they just put together.

Seeing the lights race up behind them, only made them laugh even harder for almost forcing a stupid cop off the road. Marty got the bright idea to have a little fun with this cop. They were going to scare the crap out of "Barney Fife". Rustic Road was full of hills and curves; so, when they got far enough ahead, they pulled over, parked their bikes, and waited for the officer to catch up to them.

The bikers stood with their pistols drawn as Cal crested the hill, ready to fire away.

Detective Chapman did not have time to assess the situation. His innate instinct to survive went into over-drive.

He reacted without any consideration for his shoulder; the adrenaline kicked in and superseded the pain as he drew his .45 with his right hand, firing through his windshield. The deafening percussion dulled the immediate pain in his ears.

Shooting at the inebriated bikers not only took them by surprise, but pissed them off as well. Cal sped past them, getting some distance. He slammed on the brakes as he parked his car at an angle and quickly bailed out to tactically engage them.

Marty was furious, shouting insults, along with threats, "I'm gonna kill you, *pig* – you're a dead man!"

They thought it was going to be easy to fuck with a lone officer. That would prove to be a big mistake on their part. They expected him to be a stereotypical lazy hick cop who would not bother, and just let them go, except he came after them.

Dean was angry as hell and aggressively advanced toward the squad car in rage as he riddled it full of .44's.

Safety glass rained down in little marbles and bounced off the pavement. Cal shocked the hell out of Dean when he shot him in the foot from underneath the car.

Quickly sobering up, Dean yelped in pain as he hit the ground.

Marty was going to take this filthy pig out, himself. "Chapman, I hope you said good bye to that pretty little redhead of yours, 'cuz when I'm through with you, I'm gonna pay her a visit! I bet she's a firecracker in bed!"

Cal saw all the glass on the pavement and had to move in the opposite direction to keep them from hearing him. He deliberately moved laterally across the front of his car as Marty made his assault to behind the Crown Vic.

It was too late; by the time Marty realized Chapman was on the move, he turned to meet the advancing cop and hit the ground dead.

Dean who still had some fight left in him hollered, "You're a fuckin' dead man!", as he concentrated his Smith and Wesson .44 on Chapman, but Cal was too fast for him, putting two .45 slugs in him. Luckily for Cal, Dean's shot went wide and missed.

Even with the incessant loud ringing in Cal's ears caused by shooting from inside his car, he heard the sirens closing in fast. He took a deep breath, giving himself a moment before all the chaos began.

Cal knew the Chief was going to have a field day with this incident. He also knew he did what he had to do. Somebody was going to die today, but it was not going to be him.

Sgt. Nelsen had seen Cal was shaken and breathing hard, but otherwise all right. "I just told County; it was *all* theirs!" He said, with a facetious grin.

Cal just gave Jim the 'look'.

"Hey – I had to before Deputy Dog screwed this up some how."

Cal just smiled and shook his head at Jim's tenacity for agitating their Chief and his carbon copy.

The second ambulance had brought Cal to the hospital just to get checked out. Other than a few minor cuts and bruises and an unrelenting ringing in his ears, he was fine.

Debbie Daniels was the head nurse on call when Cal came in, and she immediately took over. She had been seeing Katie's best friend Pete, for several months now. Cal got to know her fairly well in that time. One thing was for sure, she was a great nurse and as tough as nails. Nothing seemed to faze her.

"How are ya doin', Debbie?"

"Cal, I do believe *I'm* supposed to be asking *you* the questions!"

They shared a friendly smile as she checked his blood pressure. "Your blood pressure is elevated."

Cal sarcastically raised his brow, "Gee, you think? I *was* just in a shoot out!"

"Hey, don't get smart with me! I've got Katie on speed dial!"

Cal let out a surrendered sigh. "Telling Kate about this isn't going to be easy."

"She hasn't been called?"

Cal shot Debbie a sideways glance. "She doesn't need anything else dumped on her right now."

"That isn't up to you! You know damn well you better call her over here!"

Cal could not argue with that.

The curtain quickly slid open. Cal looked up to find Kate with worry in her eyes, staring back at him.

Randy had picked her up on his way to the hospital.

"Hey, Kate!" Cal said, flashing her one of his devilish grins.

"Don't 'hey Kate' me! Are you okay?"

"I'm fine."

Katie looked to Debbie for verification as she rushed to Cal and held him tight. "I'm so glad you weren't hurt!"

Cal cringed with the slight pain her hug caused his already overly sensitive shoulder. He looked over to Randy as if to ask a silent question.

Randy shook his head, "Dean didn't make it. He bled out in the ambulance."

*

Sgt. Nelsen answered his desk phone. With a satisfied grin on his face, he listened to Deputy Chief Dan Dogget chastise him for allowing the County police to handle the investigation.

"Are you finished?" Jim waited for Dan to shut up. "I didn't allow anything, it was one of *our* officers involved in the shooting, so of course County is going to investigate; or does Perry want a dark cloud hanging over our department? We already have enough publicity! You know people just love conspiracies and cover-ups involving the police, what's one more?"

The Deputy Chief grumbled something under his breath and then ordered Sgt. Nelsen to give him a full report by the end of the day, before he hung up.

*

Katie could not bear losing Cal. It had been a very stressful day, for both of them.

Snuggling with Cal in bed, she leaned in to kiss his lips. He timidly kissed her back.

"I need you..." she whispered.

Cal studied Kate's lovely face. The insatiable spark in her eyes told him - it was time.

She playfully nipped at Cal's lower lip.

He hungered for her kisses and eagerly responded to them. Cal's strong hands slid over her smooth bare shoulders and down to the curve of her hips before wrapping his muscular arms around her, drawing her in close.

Lost in his kisses, Kate forced Cal back into the pillows and took control. She broke their lip-lock to get a better look at this incredible man who had saved her life and almost just lost his, again. The man she loved and the man who wanted *her* to be his wife. She gathered up her nightie to make it easier to straddle him. She lovingly traced her fingertips across his forehead, around his steely eyes, down his nose and over his lips. Kate then brought her attention to his bare chest, and abdomen, lightly tracing along every muscled ridge. She enjoyed watching the way his muscles flinch with her every touch. She could feel his growing hard-on pushing up through the soft fabric of his pajama pants.

Cal closed his eyes, enchanted with her soft fresh sent. Everything about her drove him to the edge. How he longed for her, enjoying the sensation of her touch, until Kate raked her nails down his chest and along his rib cage. He couldn't take much more. Cal opened his eyes, catching the pleasured look on Kate's face. He reached up for her, running his fingers through her long dark wavy tresses and gently grabbed hold, pulling her towards his lips. The intense passion burning between them was not to be denied.

His lip service was quite enjoyable. He pierced her lips with his tongue, deepening their kiss.

Cal gave a slight recoil in response to his surprise as Kate reached down between her legs to find his rigid member, releasing it from the constraints of his pants. She was most definitely in the driver's seat.

Still locked into passionate kisses, Kate teased Cal by stroking the head of his thick rod against her hot damp sex.

He ached to be inside of her, to feel the heat of her slick walls swallow him. Kate read Cal's body; she knew what he wanted. It was the same thing she wanted. It is what she needed. Giving in to their passion, she slid onto his erect member, seating herself down to the hilt.

Their kissing paused as she did this.

Slightly parting his lips, he let out a soft subtle moan of long desired pleasure. Kate rhythmically rocked, slowly back and forth, tightening around his member as it throbbed deep inside of her.

They laced their fingers together; holding hands only intensified their love making. The sight of her enjoying this pleasure was beautiful. She was absolutely stunning. There were times he had to ask himself, 'How could he be so lucky?'

Attracted to the swells of her breasts and her taught nipples bursting through the silky fabric of her gown, Cal enjoyed the sight of her mounted-on top of him. She rode him, rocking in perfect tempo. She ground her hips, bearing down on him driving his hard throbbing member deeper inside her. Her movements mixed with the moist heat between them only intensified the pleasure of his growing orgasm. He felt her climax, as she tightened her grip on his rod. She took a sultry breath, locking her gaze onto his loving smoky eyes as they climaxed together.

All the frustration, worry and questions they both had, had disappeared with their release. Kate had been stronger than most would have thought. But she was still a woman - *all* woman.

She collapsed on to Cal's heaving chest, and he embraced her, lightly stroking Kate's arms thinking about the intense passionate sex they just experienced. It had been the first time they had made love since her kidnapping. After the shoot-out today, he needed her, and it was quite obvious, she needed him as well.

30

Cal was put on administrative leave until the shooting could be investigated fully. Of course, the chief needed to sign off on it. With the way Perry was handling things and the tensions between Chapman and his chief, he fully expected his leave to be a lot longer.

Now that he was not burdened with the daily bull shit the chief handed him, he could concentrate on his investigations without interruption. He was not to be anywhere near it, but that wasn't going to stop him, he was determined to see this through.

*

Once again, Randy tailed Chief Perry. Tonight, when he followed Dennis and his wife back to their neighborhood, Chief Perry dropped his wife off at the house and then quickly left again.

O'Brien's cell rang, "Cal, let me call you back."

Randy waited for his chief to gain some distance before he followed after him. He was surprised to see Chief Perry had pulled into the old grainery along the train tracks. Randy continued on, driving past, and then made a quick left to round the next block. He turned his lights off and quietly parked across the street so he could observe.

It was not long before Mayor Dunn turned in, pulling along side the Chief. The moonlight was just bright enough to make out their faces through the long shadows that were cast across the empty gravel lot.

Randy let down the passenger window on his Charger trying to hear what was being said.

A cold eerie numbness ran through Randy's veins. That same feeling from long ago, of dread and deceit washed over him.

After Chief Perry pealed out in a huff, Randy called Cal back to meet him and Jim at the Victorian.

Randy was adamant, "Well, if the Chief is secretly meeting the mayor late at night, I'd say it's obvious! I think with the folder full of reports that Perry made us rewrite, our suspicions, and that ledger - you will see they're involved with the 7 Sons of Sin! Can't we bring the feds in? I'm sure the feds would be very interested in what the connection the chief of police has to this biker gang. And then there's the mayor! Obviously, the chief is suggestible to the mayor's schemes, whatever that might be."

Cal knew even if *they* felt their Chief and the Mayor were connected, they needed concrete proof. "Jim, when you turn that ledger into evidence, make sure you report right to Chief Perry. Make sure you cross your T's and dot your I's. One of them knows the significance of what's in that ledger!"

*

Sgt. Nelsen was surprised at how easy it was to get Richie Collins to come in for an interview, but that did not mean a thing. Richie had been through the system a few times and was well versed in the due process. No, Richie was no fool; he knew how to play the game. The first thing a guy like Richie learns from being incarcerated is to keep your mouth shut.

Detective Cal Chapman was well versed, and had finesse for interviewing. Jim was not as skilled or polished as Chapman, but with Cal put on leave, Jim would have to handle this without his detective's expertise. Sgt. Nelsen was aware of the one-man balancing act he would have to perform. Jim knew he had to take a different approach, one that he had a talent for; getting inside their heads. He could not get in

Richie's face backing him into a corner. Any hint of accusation and he would lawyer up.

Officer O'Brien had escorted Richie to the small conference room. Sgt. Nelsen purposely made Richie wait a little while before gracing him with his presence. Jim was well aware of Richie's hatred for cops, but he wasn't intimidated. In his arrogance combined with the false sense that he was smarter than the cops, Richie would eventually condemn himself. Giving Collins the impression that he had some control of their interview, Sgt. Nelsen could get a better feel for his target's mind set while watching and listening to his words.

"Thank you for coming in today; this is just a routine inquiry." Jim made eye contact with Richie as he proceeded. "I'm investigating a homicide, and I think you may be able to help me out."

Richie sat forward, resting his forearms on the conference table, folding his hands. "Oh, is that right?"

"Well, Richie, this is a relatively small town and there isn't much that happens here that sooner or later everyone knows about. I'm sure you've heard we recovered a body out on Holtz's farm?"

Richie smirked, "I did."

"You wanna take a guess as to who it is or do you know that, too?"

"I'm not positive, but if the rumors are correct...someone toasted Charlie."

Sgt. Nelsen attentively watched Richie's body language as well as his facial expressions. He had to play it straight with Richie, or he would get up and leave for wasting his time. "No, the rumors are true. That's why I've asked you here. We know he frequented your establishment and you'd been seen with him on numerous occasions."

"Yeah – so what?"

"Could you tell me what your relationship with Charlie Nix was?"

Richie cooperated, to a point, only to avoid suspicion. "Charlie came in to Puss 'n Boots all the time. You know that. Hell, that fat fuck tried to date every one of my girls. Look, he had a reputation for being rough with them and after he'd smack one or two of them around, they wouldn't go out with him. So, what exactly are you asking, Sgt. Nelsen?"

"I'm asking what your relationship to Nix was. Were you friendly, did you conduct business with him or was he just an acquaintance?"

A faint smirk crossed Richie's lips, "Friendly? No. I tolerated him, and on occasion we had a few minor business opportunities that crossed our paths."

"What can you tell me about him? Did he have any enemies?"

Richie belted out a hearty laugh. "You are shitting me, right? Of course, the guy had enemies!" Richie confidently sat back, crossing his ankle to his knee. His black leather motorcycle boot showed many miles of wear. Including that he walked on the outsides of his feet. "Look man, you probably know more about the guy than I do. He was a chef for Pioneer's Inn, the ladies stayed clear of him 'cuz he liked to rough them up, and the guy was a drug dealer. Did I leave anything out? Oh, yeah...no body liked the guy. He was even sweet on Chapman's girl from the Brick Yard. Maybe Chapman got tired of him sniffing around his piece of tail and took matters into his own hands? I'm just sayin'?"

Sgt. Nelsen returned a grin. "Alright, fair enough. What do you know about Charlie's connection to Courtney Roberts?"

"You mean besides that fact he's the one who probably killed her? Yeah, that's right, we know the score, but you're barking up the *wrong* tree! You think because he killed Courtney, we'd return the favor?"

Jim sat forward, staring Richie right in the eye, "Well, did ya? Did you kill Nix?"

Mirroring Sgt. Nelsen's posture, he let out a snort. "Didn't lay a hand on him, Serge!" Richie cocked his head with a confident smile, "Ya know - we were all wondering why you guys never arrested Charlie for Courtney's death. Maybe if you had, he'd be someone's bitch right now instead of a crispy critter?"

Sitting back in his chair, Jim shook his head and smiled. "Know what's funny...you *not* taking credit for Nix's death. The sick and twisted way he was killed, that alone would instill fear in the hearts and minds of anyone associated with you. I would have bet my last dollar that you disposed of this shit-stain for taking what wasn't his."

The glare Richie gave Jim, spoke volumes. Sgt. Nelsen knew he pushed a button.

"After all, he didn't just kill Courtney and Alison; he did some pretty horrendous things to Alison." It was hard for Jim to speak without emotion, when it came to Alison, but that is exactly how he had to approach this, devoid of emotion.

Jim watched as Richie's eyes narrowed.

"Wasn't Alison your girl? I know you, Richie."

In an angry tone Richie ground out, "You don't know shit!"

"Well, there ain't no way in hell – the 'old' Richie Collins would have allowed that piece-of-shit to take something from him without repercussions. But, maybe I'm wrong; maybe someone else had it in for Nix and took care of him for you. You slipping, Richie?"

Richie adamantly stood, "Serge, I think we're done here."

Jim stood, "Yep – you're free to go. Just don't leave the area; I might have a few more questions."

The disgruntled Collins flung the conference door open and marched out. That was the only response Sgt. Nelsen was going to get. But that was okay, Jim was satisfied for now.

*

Richie was explosive. Sgt. Nelsen seemed to have all the answers, and he wanted revenge for Chapman killing his men, his heightened agitation made him even more dangerous.

Brock was tired of all of Richie's crap. Richie's impulsive and erratic behavior mixed with delusional paranoia was a volatile mix. War with the cops was just plain stupid. Brock needed to distance himself; he was through with all of this. What he really wanted was to get the hell out, disappear and settle down. Make a life with the new family he was starting. Richie tainted everything; he was a cancer. Keeping Richie away from anything that meant something to him was almost impossible. When the time was right, Brock would do what he had to do.

He did not dare tell Richie he was wrong. He could; however; hope the police would take care of Collins the same way they did the Gehring brothers. Brock did his best to keep Richie focused on their business deal.

"It's your deal, Richie; we've got 3-days! We can do this without the Gehrings. They might have set this up – but now you're going to have to close the deal!"

Richie absently reached for his Zippo lighter; patting himself down when the realization that he did not have it on him came to light. He glared in Brock's direction. "Where the fuck is my lighter? Didn't you pick it up?"

Brock had always been careful. He remembered retrieving the lighter before the two clowns he was left with, tried to move Nix's body.

He returned a blank stare, with a sudden sinking feeling that swallowed him.

"Well?"

Brock kept his cool, "I did – but I don't have it now. I don't know what happened to it."

Richie pulled his gun in anger, engaged a round into the chamber, aimed it in Brock's direction and squeezed off the round. "Aaaah!"

The .45 whizzed just past Brock's head. Brock refrained from pulling his own and firing back. He knew if Richie wanted to kill him, he would have.

For the first time, Richie revealed a crack in his armor, and Brock recognized it.

Richie Collins just made Brock's decision easy. It was now survival of the fittest.

*

Midas had taken Jack and TJ back to the entrance used by the cookers through the grainery. They observed how after each batch the lab was sanitized. Richie Collins was so paranoid, he went to extremes having everything wiped clean, leaving no prints.

With the camera Midas managed to install just outside of the entrance to City Hall's records room, they were able to capture Mayor Dunn in all his haughty glory leaving the records room through a false wall, just as Stella claimed he did.

As they review the surveillance tapes, Jack had not realized how much danger Billie had really been in, until now. The day Midas grabbed Billie; she was about to interrupt Dunn arguing with Collins.

They also caught him on tape meeting with Collins in another tunnel along the river just under the grainery. The beauty of this was there was no way he could deny taking a large sum of money from Collins. Once he was handed the manila envelope, the untrusting bastard had to open it to check it.

TJ was enjoying every second of tape, "What a dumb ass!"

Jack snapped, "Well, thanks to Chapman, the two idgits we were after are now dead! He could have blown this whole thing!"

TJ frowned, flashing Jack a look, "Hey, man — you would have done the same thing if you were in Chapman's shoes! I don't believe they were the *only* two assholes who knew about the guns? Richie is too controlling for that! Midas rigged up audio/visual to that room where the guns are too. We'll finally have some evidence on these shitheads!"

Jack's cell rang, it was Cooper. "Carter!" He listened for a couple minutes, and asked, "Are you sure? How reliable is he?"

TJ could not tell if it was good news or bad. Jack did not show much emotion.

"Yes, we're on our way." Jack snapped his phone shut. "Cooper just got us an informant. I guess the son-of-a-bitch checks out, too. The deal goes down in 2-days."

"Let's go meet our informant!"

"I don't know how I feel about trusting this guy. Besides, without the Gehring's - Richie is going to be extra cautious. How much is this informant really going to help us? I know we'll just be wasting our time. He's going to come up with some excuse not to deal with these guys."

"Aren't you Mr. Negative?"

"No — this just isn't my first rodeo! It might take a couple tries before it actually goes down."

TJ glared at his partner. "You're probably right! One dirt-bag is gonna think the other dirt-bag is setting them up, and it could get tricky!"

"Richie is a paranoid douche, but he's greedy. He'll do this deal. And when he does, we're going to let it play out until the end."

"That almost never works out. Don't you watch TV?"

"That's a made for TV version of how cops play these things out. We're not actors playing a role for some special effects or political agenda. This is just like any other assignment. We'll observe them, see who all the players are, and let the deal go down; however, that may play out, and then when they're feeling pretty confident ...one team will take down Richie's group. The other will take down the Milwaukee players."

Shaking his head in disbelief, TJ let out a hardy laugh. "O-yeah? Is that how you see this going down?"

Jack's confident grin told him that is exactly how he saw this scenario playing out. "I guess we'll soon find out!"

31

Today was the day. Their informant, for all intents and purposes, Jack nicknamed *Judas*; was miked and ready, but he still could not nail down a time for the exchange. In a way Jack respected what *Judas* was doing. It took guts, courage. He could almost understand the choices this man made in life. He really did not have many other options, but kept true to his convictions until he was forced to make a stand. For that, he earned an ounce of respect from Jack.

TJ was with Midas watching the monitors. Something had stirred the hive. He recognized most of the cookers, they all had arrest records. Not only were they scrubbing their lab, they were also disassembling it.

Jack came in, business as usual. Glancing between the monitors, "What's happening?"

"I think they're moving out!"

"Have we heard from Judas?"

"Nothing, yet. Hey – what's going on here?"

They watched Richie Collins hammer a note to the door of the records room and then spit.

"I wonder what the love note says." TJ commented.

"Where did he go? Can you follow him?"

"I've got most of the tunnels wired – but he's not coming up." Midas switched to different cameras. "There!"

Richie was seen arguing with Brock.

"He's pissed about something! Did we catch any audio on this?"

"But, of course!" TJ grinned.

Jack's work phone vibrated. He looked at the caller ID, "Its Judas." He answered, "Whatch-ya got?"

"It's on - today at 3 – the Wal-Mart in Franklin – you don't have much time." The voice on the other end said.

Jack snapped his phone shut. "Call the team – it's a go."

*

Chief Perry barged into Mayor Dunn's office. Stella sensed the urgency with the way the chief stormed through. He shut the door rather hard and quickly loud muffled voices erupted.

Stella tried to hear what was being said.

"Sgt. Nelsen just turned into evidence a ledger supposedly belonging to Richie Collins! And then called him in for an interview! What the fuck have you gotten me involved with?" Chief Perry's face was beet red.

"If they turned it in – make it disappear."

"Look, I'm all for promoting the town for the greater good, but I'm *not* tampering with evidence!"

"Don't give me that crap, Dennis! You're as moral as a fox in a hen house! You think you're above reproach? Think again! I hired you to be my lap dog. Stop pretending you're innocent in all this! You took money under-the-table directly from me, not through the village! You knew that wasn't on the up-and-up!"

"I can't do what you're asking! Sgt. Nelsen and Chapman already don't trust me!"

"Chapman is on leave! He won't be a problem. You'll figure it out!"

Dennis turned on his heels, flung open the door and stormed out, angrier than when he came in.

Stella had Dotty on the phone, "He's as mad as a rabid dog, I tell ya!"

Dotty hung up with Stella to pass the information along to Chapman. She called Cal's cell phone, knowing he'd pick-up, where ever he was. "The only thing she could hear clearly was the mayor ordering Chief Perry to remove something from evidence."

"Thanks, Dot!" Cal suspected their chief, and now they knew Mayor Dunn was the other party. Cal was kept in the loop with Jack and TJ; it was all beginning to come together.

Richie Collins was not willing to give up his strong hold on this town. Until Alison betrayed him by stealing his ledger, he had the mayor where he needed him. Now, that the police had his ledger, all bets were off as far as he was concerned.

32

Tact team one was set up in the Wal-Mart parking lot. Jack sat in a cramped hot van on the east end of the lot. Team two held their positions across the street in a strip mall. Both teams had an unobstructed view of the given location.

Not only was their informant miked, but they had an undercover agent in with Satan's Knights. The same agent who brokered the initial deal with the Gehring brothers.

They watched as a blue late-model pick-up truck with a white cap slowly drove up and down each isle until they parked not far from Jack's van, of all places.

IDs were made on all three individuals in the truck; the driver - Brock Miller, Luke Michaels, and Richie Collins.

Soon a gray sedan pulled in, and parked. No one got out. They waited, and then moved on to another parking space making their way over to the pick-up truck. They flashed their lights.

The pick-up flashed their lights and then pulled up along side the gray sedan; but it did not stop. It slowed, rolled up its passenger side widow and continued out of the parking lot.

After the truck drove off, the sedan flashed its lights, and they drove off as well.

TJ was in with team two. He used his cell phone instead of the radio, "What just happened?"

Jack answered, "Looks like Richie called it off - something wasn't acceptable. Keep your eyes open, there's a third vehicle here, somewhere! We need eyes on that third vehicle, that's the one with the guns!"

There were too many possibilities for transport of the weapons. Team one and two could not just randomly stop them. Frustrated they packed it in and returned to Cooper, empty handed.

SAC Cooper was not happy, but when dealing with 2-gangs you can't expect the marriage to work on the first try. Satan's Knights were moving up fast in the Milwaukee area. They wanted what the 7 Sons of Sin could offer. With the Gehring brothers gone, there were trust issues. That alone kept the two on edge. Richie called it off this time, something either spooked him, or he just wanted to pull out to prove something to the other gang.

Brock did not have any answers. This little song and dance would have to commence at another time and place. Richie certainly was not making Brock's job any easier.

*

The mayor was agitated with his chief of police, and finding Richie's little note on the door to his records room made him furious. He called Richie to the tunnel under the grainery.

"You think you're going to black mail *me* – you stupid piece of shit!"

"Watch yourself, Mayor!" Richie's tone was calm yet cool.

"How dare you threaten me! If it were not for me, you'd be cooking that shit out in a trailer somewhere in the woods and the cops would have already had your ass back behind bars!"

Richie glared at Patrick, "No, Mayor, if it weren't for *me,* you'd still be pushing foreclosed real-estate. You greedy bastard! You take my money easy enough – for what? Rent on a few of your wife's vacant properties?"

"You arrogant, ass! That ledger you keep threatening me with...the police just checked it into evidence! I can't protect you any more. And IF they figure out what's in there, you're going down with me!"

Richie laughed, "Protect me? Good one, Mayor!" From what? The cops – you own the chief of police, don't you? Besides, I'm not going back to jail. You on the other hand...you wouldn't fare so well in prison!"

"Don't threaten me, Collins! Who do you think they are going to believe, you - a convicted felon or me – the good Mayor of Burlington?"

Richie continued to glare at the pompous ass before him.

The mayor would not drop it, "You did this – you kept records, Richie! In your wake you've left two dead whores, and I'm sure you're the one who burned Charlie alive! Jesus – I told you not to mess up my town. You're leaving a very messy trail. Now – I suggest you clean this mess up!"

Richie's jaw clenched tight; the mayor made a grave error calling Alison a whore.

In the Mayor's haughtiness he waited for an answer.

Unzipping his jeans, Collins pulled out his dick and relieved himself on the mayor's fancy leather shoes.

Shocked at the heathen's disgusting display, the mayor declared, "It's time you leave town, Collins!"

Richie merely shook and zipped back up. "I'm not going anywhere – but you – you're done here.

With that, Richie left the mayor standing in a puddle of urine.

This time Mayor Dunn was not only captured on tape, but his meeting with Richie could be heard loud and clear.

Cal and Midas had been standing right beside Jack and TJ watching the entire thing. Cal was utterly stunned.

TJ could not hold in his laughter. Seeing the Mayor getting pissed on struck his funny bone.

Cal was angered with the depth of deceit stemming from the mayor's office, and determined to end this. "Jack, you were right, it goes much deeper than the department. Let's do this right, the States Attorney is going the have a hay day with this."

*

It was late when Jack's work cell vibrated. "Tell me what happened?"

The voice on the other end of the phone was agitated. "The paranoid bastard doesn't trust anyone anymore! He feels everyone's out to get him. I don't know if I can let you know when the next meet is. He's keeping it to himself and making shit up as he goes!"

"Look – you understand your role in this – you need to find a way!"

"I can tell you this – he's not going away quietly!"

"What the hell is that supposed to mean?"

"He has a list, and Chapman isn't the only one on it!"

"Good to know – who else is on it? Do you know his plans?"

"I don't know – he's not in the sharing mood since you *wired* me! But I know it's *not* good! He did say he was going to send a message that would make history. If you weren't listening, I just wanted to give you the heads up."

*

Cal held the sleeping Kate in his arms. She was finally sleeping peacefully, no nightmares, no crying out; just restful slumber. His cell vibrated on the nightstand jarring him from his thoughts. The ID told him it was Jack. "What's up?" Cal answered in a hushed tone.

"Richie has declared war; I think you and Kate better leave town."

"I'm sending the girls to Kate's parents' in the morning. But, I'm not going anywhere."

"Suit yourself! Wait – Billie is going, too?"

"I thought that would be best."

"Cal, thank you."

"She's here if you want to talk to her?"

"I don't want to wake her."

"I'm sure she's worried and would like to hear from you."

"Tell them to be careful."

"Will do." He snapped his phone shut. Looking down at the beautiful woman sleeping in his arms, he held her close, kissed her lovely cheek and closed his eyes.

*

Jack hung up. He sat heavily on his couch and looked at the picture Billie gave him hanging on the wall. He could not fight it; he had to hear her voice.

Billie could not sleep. To calm her nerves, she tried reading a few pages from Sadie's diary, when the ringing from her cell startled her. Setting the book aside, she answered it.

"Billie? It's Jack. I didn't wake you, did I?"

She could not contain the joy she felt hearing his voice. Her smile came through in her tone, "Not at all. Actually, I'm having some trouble sleeping tonight."

"I'm sorry to hear that. I just wanted to check on you...you, okay?"

"I'll be fine - when this is all over. Just do what you have to."

"I will, now that I know you'll be safe."

"Jack, when this is over…?"

"I know…we'll talk, okay?"

"Just be safe."

"You too, Blondie!" He smiled.

He could not see the large smile he brought to Billie's face, but he could feel it.

*

Friday morning, Jack and TJ found Midas sitting at his usual table in the back of the Sci-Fi café.

Brad was making his famous biscuits and gravy.

They seated themselves on either side of Midas.

Suspicious, of the two characters who just came in, Brad came around to greet them. "Can I get you gents anything?"

TJ answered, "Sure, 2-coffees, black!"

Brad looked to Midas, "Everything good here?"

Midas nodded a 'yes'.

Brad was also a Vet, and as a rule Vets stuck together. He kept a close eye on them. In all the times Midas frequented the café, not once did he have company. He always kept to himself. Today, two men sat with him.

"Richie broke into the basement of City Hall early this morning." Midas said.

"Who was with him?"

"No one- he was alone."

TJ asked, "Did he take anything?"

"Not that I could tell. I didn't see him leave with anything."

"Any clue what he's up to?" Jack questioned.

"Your guess is as good as mine."

"I'll have Cal talk to Stella. I doubt the mayor will report whatever Richie did, but she should know."

33

"Hey – gotta go! Just got a text from Judas, they're going to the movies this afternoon!"

"Nothing like very public places in broad daylight to play 'Let's make a deal'!" TJ's sarcasm put a smile on Jack's face.

Richie's greed was driving him. He was forced to play the hand that he was dealt.

Once again two tact teams, coordinating DEA and ATF waited. The element of surprise was in their favor. Hoping they would throw them off guard by out numbering them so they could not react. No one wanted a shooting. The more tactical officers the more control.

Jack spotted a blue minivan. Sure, enough he recognized the two inside. "Brock Miller is the driver, looks like Luke Michaels with him."

"So, where's Collins?"

"Anyone got eyes on Richie Collins?"

TJ, keeping the radio clear, used his cell to call Jack. "Our friend is parked 3-rows over from you, Buddy!"

"Which vehicle?"

"Black SUV on your left."

"I got him. Looks like he's watching the same thing we are."

"I've got another blue minivan!"

"Can anyone ID the passengers?" Jack kept his eyes on Collins.

"I've got that gray sedan! Yep, they're here for the game not the movie."

Jack responded, "Let it play out. Let's see if it's a shell game or bait and switch."

Collins waited for the second van to park. Slowly driving out of his spot, he moved towards the second van.

Then a Hertz truck pulled in and blocked Jack's view. "What the hell?"

TJ called Jack back. "Hold up – we've ID'd the driver from that truck. He's a Satan's Knight."

As the first blue minivan moved closer to the Hertz truck, Collins flashed his lights.

The Hertz truck flashed their lights and switched parking spaces.

Brock and Luke got out of the van.

Two members of Satan's Knights got out of the Hertz truck.

Brock sent Luke to the truck, while he showed the two Satan's Knights members the contents of his van.

Luke gave a nod with approval from what he was shown.

Walking towards each other they tossed keys, switching vehicles.

Brock and Luke got in the moving truck, and were then escorted by Richie Collins in the black SUV.

Then the two minivans drove off following the gray sedan.

"Team one?"

"We're on 'em!"

Just as Richie and the truck turned off the strip and headed towards the highway, team one made the stop, preventing them from getting on the freeway.

Team two made a clean stop on the Satan's Knights.

*

Suddenly, back in Burlington, a horrible loud explosion cracked the streets and buckled sidewalks around City Hall. An implosion took the historic City Hall building and dropped it. Its windows blew out raining glass on the pavement. The police station, along with the bars and restaurants along Pine Street all rumbled.

Everyone was in shock.

First responders were sent out.

Jack's cell went off amid making arrests. He handed the cuffed Brock Miller over to another agent. Seeing it was Chapman, he answered. "Hello!"

The grievous expression on Jack's face told TJ something bad just went down.

He hung up with Chapman, and glared in Richie's direction. The smirk on Richie's smug face made Jack suspicious. "I think that fucking prick just blew up City Hall!"

TJ gave Jack a sideway glance. "He - what? He's right here."

"Midas saw him break-in to City Hall early this morning, remember? We can only guess what he was doing."

"How many injured?"

Jack shook his head, "We won't know the extent for awhile."

*

Long after ATF and the DEA processed everyone and all the evidence, Burlington was still reeling from all the chaos.

Burlington Memorial Hospital was working overtime, treating patients.

Police and Fire departments worked tirelessly looking for survivors, and helping as many as they could. The explosion left a huge crater, collapsing most of the tunnels that ran near its subbasement.

Bob Donnelly closed the Brick Yard for business. His employees and even a few of their patrons jumped in to help. The Brick Yard was not the only business to do so. At times like these, people come together to help strangers as well as their neighbors.

Returning to Burlington, Jack and TJ found themselves in a twisted reality, more fiction than real. They were happy to find Midas, alive and well, giving a helping hand.

Detective Chapmen flagged Jack and TJ over.

Jack asked, "What the hell happened?"

"We won't know for sure until they investigate, but they're speculating someone tampered with the hot water heaters."

"That would certainly create one hell of an explosion." TJ commented. "How many dead?"

"Well, luckily most leave work early on Fridays, or there would be a lot more casualties. We have two so far; a maintenance worker and a secretary. We have not found the mayor yet."

Jack filled Cal in, "Collins, Brock Miller, Luke Michaels, and Adam Knox are behind bars. You would not believe how much Meth they packed into that truck, and we caught them with the stolen military weapons. They won't be seeing the light of day for a long time."

Midas joined them, "Did you get him?"

"We sure did!" TJ placed a supportive hand on Midas's shoulder, "You, okay?"

"I'm fine, but the tunnels have collapsed. I won't know how bad they're damaged until I can get back in."

"Shit! All our recordings are probably lost now!" Jack spit out in anger.

Midas proudly said "I've got it covered", as he handed Jack a thumb drive.

A genuine happy smile came across Jack's face, and a huge weight was lifted in that instant.

"You're the man!" TJ proudly announced.

Midas looked out at the devastation all around. "Jack, I've changed my mind. I will testify, if you still want me to?"

24-Hours Later

Seated around the conference table at the Substation, SAC Wesley Cooper, Special Agents Jack Carter, and Tom Jeeter (TJ), Detective Cal Chapman, Sgt. Jim Nelsen, and Officer Randy O'Brien reviewed all of Midas's recordings.

Realizing Richie Collins was not the one who blew up City Hall, everyone in the room was stunned.

Up until now, they believed the mayor to be dead. When in fact, Stella had seen Mayor Dunn leave a couple hours before the explosion. He also had kicked everyone loose at 3 o'clock that day. Last night, Mrs. Dunn was distraught thinking her husband had perished in the explosion. Until this morning, when the bank opened; she realized their accounts had significantly decreased. Being the disgruntled wife, Mrs. Dunn was now willing to throw her husband under the proverbial bus.

Cooper looked around the table, "I've already contacted the Bureau, and the State Police are looking for him now. Racketeering is the least of Patrick Dunn's worries. We're going after him for murder, arson, criminal damage to property and anything else we can find!"

*

The explosion did more than take lives and implode a historic building. Some of the newly discovered tunnels have been lost forever; however, that same explosion opened a Pandora of historic secrets that had been sealed in the deep, dark crevices of the Burlington underground.

While everyone tried to make sense of the chaos above ground, the dust was settling in those tunnels still intact, now revealing a large fracture in its foundation walls, waiting to be discovered.

34

Mitch Carter was just settling into his easy chair with a Scotch in hand to watch the evening news when the sound of someone knocking on his door disrupted him.

"I'm comin', I'm comin'!" He said making his way to the front door. He found his son, Jack, standing behind it, and then opened the door further letting Jack inside. "Is everything alright?" Mitch asked cautiously closing the door behind him.

Jack's heavy silence told Mitch his son needed to talk. Father and son made their way into the kitchen. Mitch grabbed a rocks glass, put in a few ice cubes, and poured a Scotch for his son. "Here – now why don't you tell me what's on that mind of yours?"

They sat in tentative silence at the kitchen table as Jack stared into his glass.

Jack lifted the golden liquid to his lips. It warmed him as he swallowed some of the 12-year-old liquor. "Tell me about Mom...how did you *know*?"

An all-knowing smirk spread across Mitch's face. He in turn, took a sip of Scotch. "Jack, your mother was the most *infuriating* woman I've ever met...yet I loved the hell out of her!" He studied his son's regal face. "So, this is about a woman?"

Jack's eyes met his father's.

"Son, if you are ever lucky enough to find someone who stirs your blood, and makes you absolutely crazy at the same time...you take that leap! Most of us never find that...I did - and I thank God everyday for that moment of happiness, even as short as it was."

Mitch saw some recognition on Jack's face. "If you have that once in a life time opportunity to be happy, you take it, son, and hold on to it. Sometimes - you get hurt, but if you don't put your heart out there from time to time, you'll never know how deep and intense a love can be."

Jack took another sip of liquid courage. "She doesn't know who I am...or the things I've done."

"But she does know you?"

"Yes..."

"Have you shown her anyone other than the Jack sitting here?"

"If you mean, have I played a role with her, the answer is *no*."

"Then she sees you for you. It does not matter what you've done in the past, Jack."

"She thought I was a bartender! I doubt she'd understand!"

"Why not? You're still Jack Carter. Does she want the bartender or the man?"

Jack liked the relationship he had with his old man. From early years he could always come to his father to work out a problem, even if he didn't know what it was, he needed to find. The darkness Jack felt hanging over his head would always be there, but it helped to talk aloud. He did not feel he deserved the ray of sunshine Billie brought to his life.

*

It had been the first real warm sunny day of spring. Jack took Billie out for a long leisurely ride on his bike; they were not going anywhere in particular just enjoying the open road.

Billie loved cruising on the back of Jack's Harley. The vibration between her legs, the wind in her hair, and her arms wrapped around this man who made her heart skip a few beats, was all she needed.

She was thrilled Jack had finally owned up to the relationship. Billie had wanted to be with Jack for close to a year now. Katie was right; if she really wanted it, she would have to be patient for it.

Lost in thought about the wonderful day she just spent with Jack; it took her a moment to register the fact that it was now beginning to rain. They were too far from home, and a long way out from a diner or other stop. Behind them the dark and lowering sky moved in quickly. The wind picked up whipping the trees around them. A roll of thunder and a clap of lightning sparked a bombardment of large rain drops.

Jack spotted an old barn half a mile up. He raced to escape the rain that was threatening to dump on them. As a blanket of dark ominous clouds hovered overhead, he pulled into the quiet little farm. No vehicles were present. The house looked gloomy and abandoned. Noticing the barn's doors were not closed all the way; he rode over to seek refuge there. They were already wet but, moved the bike and themselves into a dry shelter until the rain passed.

Jack walked his bike into the shadowy cavern of the old barn. He found a level surface to park it. He knew it was not going to be easy to control himself with her. When he glanced over to Billie leaning in the doorway with her damp t-shirt clung tightly to her slender curvy body; he knew he was going to fail miserably. Her nipples stood at attention, poking through her lacey bra, beckoning for him to come warm her. Certain thoughts immediately came to his mind.

Jack stood beside Billie as they peered out through the open barn door into the now pouring rain. A large smile spread across his face; she smelled like sun with a hint of wild flowers.

To her surprise, Jack boldly wrapped his arms around her as he nuzzled her neck, affectionate and sweet. His tender touch was an electric current that instantly warmed her.

Enjoying Jack's advances, Billie relaxed into him and pressed her firm round butt against his already growing arousal in his jeans.

Although eager to mash his lips to hers giving into the lust, he resisted, only to softly kiss her cheek. Now that Jack knew what he wanted, he wanted to do this right.

His touch sent tingles across her skin with the tense anticipation of what this could mean. Billie's pulse quickened, feeling nervous and a bit awkward. Her hand instinctively moved from the door to Jack's thigh. She felt him shift his footing with her touch.

Being so close to Billie like this only heated his blood, driving his passion to eagerly have her.

He confidently turned her to face him, and then slowly backed her into the door. Taking her lovely face in his hands he searched deep into her big blue eyes, and gently moved a long wavy truss of blonde hair that hung in her face before kissing her hard on the mouth. It was fiery and intense.

In his arms, her knees buckled. They kissed with unbridled abandonment. With each stroke of his tongue on hers, she felt a heated desire to have him building inside her, and deepened their kiss. This is what she had been waiting for.

Jack had been fighting the sexual tension for months. He struggled with his feelings, but now realized there was no denying it. He had never felt so intensely for anyone like he did for Billie. A hunger filled him. Being so close to her, smelling her, touching her, tasting her lips, it was more than he could take. Jack's *desire* to know this woman intimately quickly became a *need*.

Sporadic flashes of light bounced through the darkness. He took her by the hand and led her to the loft.

At the bottom of the ladder Jack found an old lantern that still had some kerosene in it. He let go of Billie's hand to light it. He put the glass dome down, and then upped the wick for more light. Billie climbed up the ladder first, while Jack followed close behind. He noticed there were still some bails of hay stacked neatly to one side of the loft.

He spoke with a tender yet raspy voice, "Stay put, I'll be right back", then kissed her before cautiously stepping across the loft's floor making his way to the loading door. He slid it open to the storm that brewed outside. The wind was a combination of warmth mixed with cool. With one of his crooked seductive smiles, he made his way back to Billie.

He had been alone far too long, and now he was ready to give love another chance. Although Jack had been struggling with his feelings for Billie, he knew what he wanted. It was not just about the sex; it was getting close to this exhilarating woman with whom he fell in love.

He roughly cleared a spot with his motorcycle boot to set down the lantern. He regarded Billie, and removed his leather jacket, laying it out on a bed of hay.

Holding out his hand, which Billie graciously accepted, Jack pulled her in close, nose to nose.

Her sweet lips parted, wanting to say something, but she chose to be silent and just let things happen. Realizing they were about to cross a line from which neither could return; she just followed Jack's lead. Her heart raced. Her nervousness began to show, as her body started to shiver in anticipation.

They deepened their kiss, holding each other tight in a hypnotic lovers' dance as the storm played their song.

He guided Billie to sit down in the hay, and he got down on his knees. Not having to speak they read each other's movements.

Jack kicked off his boots as Billie did the same.

They hungrily kissed as they explored each other's bodies, and hastily shed some clothes.

Jack drew off Billie's tee exposing her small perfect breasts. He pulled Billie onto his lap, and she gracefully wrapped her long legs around him, holding him tight. She was aroused and wanting.

Jack brought his lips to her chest, kissing the top of her breasts while he stripped away her sheer lacey bra. Holding her securely to him, he was like a hungry beast that had not been fed.

His hot breath hovered over one of her nipples; and when he flicked it with his tongue, a wave of heated anticipation swept through Billie as a soft moan escaped her lips.

She bore down on him, seating herself tightly into his lap as she attentively squeezed her thighs drawing his erection to her.

His cock ached to be inside her. Jack's strong hands gripped a fist full of Billie's long hair in response as he hungrily kissed her.

The thunder rumbled outside, and the rain pelted the roof.

She felt his growing anticipation, and pushed Jack down into the hay as she worked diligently on his jeans. They awkwardly maneuvered in a first-time lovers' haste to be naked. Flesh on flesh.

Billie's eyes flashed an insatiable spark, the only warning he got before she lightly raked her nails down his muscular toned chest, and then bent down to playfully nip at his bottom lip.

In a smooth yet forceful move, Jack rolled her onto her back, mesmerized by her eyes, "You are so beautiful."

Billie had never heard those words. She could not believe she heard them now. Not quite sure if she should say something back, she only smiled.

"I want you, Billie!" He watched her facial expressions in the soft light as he traced her nakedness with his fingers and ran his semi-rough hand over her soft curves.

He loved the way she responded to his every touch, letting him know she took pleasure in him.

Billie's soft full lips could not get enough of him. She kissed him deeper, slipping him her tongue. Her fingertips discovered razed marks as her touch explored his back and shoulders in the dark. She presumed they were scars from having been injured during the war.

Jack explored her soft, smooth, nearly flawless body; intimately getting to know every inch of this sexy young woman who entrusted him with her naked body.

As he found her swollen clit, he gently worked it until she was damp with anticipation. She spread her long legs out before him, and arched her back pushing her bare breast out to him as he slipped a finger inside her. His rigid cock ached to be inside her, but he took his time with Billie.

She allowed him full access as she lay back trusting him with such intimacy. His lips pressed into her with each kiss, working his way south. Jack's scruffy chin brushed against her smooth belly as he caressed her firm breasts. Her flesh tingled with his every touch. Jack settled in between her thighs, teasing her with kisses and gentle nibbles before bringing his attentions to her sweet spot. His tongue expertly stroked her clitoris.

When he slipped a finger inside her, Billie gasped, realizing she had been holding her breath. She moaned with an intense desire to have him inside her.

The escalating storm outside was almost forgotten as he went down on her. It had been so long since she had been with a man in this way, she almost lost control. She ran her fingers through his soft hair and firmly grabbed hold, letting him know she was very pleased with him.

Billie arched her back, the pleasured look on her face and the quiver of her thighs as she pulled his head forward letting him know she was ready for him. She wanted him desperately. Her fingertips roamed over Jack's shoulders and down his heavily scared back to his firm buttocks.

The sensation of her touch stirred Jack's blood. He kissed her with a heated passion...a longing to ravage her body. He lightly bit her pert nipple sending another wave of pleasure; the sounds that escaped her - were ecstasy to his ears.

He took a tender moment to gaze deep into her blue eyes, before pushing inside her. Her slick heat engulfed him as he eased his way into her. It frightened him how much he desired Billie.

He groaned as he pushed inside her. The hot moist folds of her sex tightened around him. It felt so good to be inside her.

The storm raged outside, and the wind whipped up cooling their hot bodies as it blew over them through the open doors.

Moving with Jack's rhythm Billie tilted her hips allowing him greater access. As he plunged deeper inside her, she contracted her muscles around his hard member with a craving to feel all of him.

Holding back from releasing his own pleasure, Jack's body shivered. He pushed up and away from her kisses to see her lovely face.

As they made love, he wanted to *really* see her. They enjoyed each other for quite some time, when the throbbing between her legs intensified, reaching a fevered pitch which matched that of the storm outside. With a burning desire her breathing hitched, and she bucked under him. He felt her tremor. He himself let out a groan needing a release.

He spilled his seed, filling her, and watched in amazement as her orgasm shattered her.

At that moment she was the most beautiful thing he'd ever seen.

He collapsed on top of her, catching his breath. He rolled onto his side, and pulled her into his arms as he held her close.

She rested her head on his heaving chest and listened to the beating of his heart.

The storm's fury had slowly died down. The two lovers just held on to each other, comforted with the sound of the steady rain tapping on the roof of that old barn.

Epilogue

The morning light filtered in through the open loft doors of the old barn. Song birds chirped, and sang just outside.

Jack had been awake for a while, just watching Billie sleep. She had awakened something deep down inside of him that he was sure he would never have again.

Billie suddenly became very aware of him. A slight smile slowly spread across her face, along with a blush. "Good morning," she said as she peeked at Jack.

Jack leaned in to pluck a piece of straw from Billie's mussy blonde mane. "Good morning, Darling!" Cracking that sexy grin of his, placing his fingers under her chin to draw her lips to his, he kissed her sweetly. "Thank you."

Billie flashed Jack a puzzled looked, "For what?"

"For last night, silly."

They smiled affectionately at each other.

Billie propped herself up on her elbows. Her smile grew, kind of a cross between embarrassment and happiness. She did not know what to say. Her heart and mind were racing. Being this intimate with Jack had been intense. All she could do was smile widely and lose herself in his eyes.

"Are ya hungry, Sweetheart? There's a diner up the road, I'll buy you breakfast."

They pushed the motorcycle out of the barn and noticed the farm was void of anyone's presence other than their own.

Billie turned to Jack, "Let's check it out? It looks abandoned."

"Sure, why - not!" He parked the bike, and held out his hand.

Billie enjoyed the feel of Jack's rough, strong hand holding hers. He made her feel safe.

Some of the porch boards creaked under protest to their trespassing; as they peered through the windows of the little white farm house. It was locked up, but definitely empty. The house looked like it had been well kept.

Moving on, they strolled over to the garage. Through the back door they could see a car, but it was covered.

They checked out the other buildings on the property before going to breakfast.

*

As a rule, Billie could eat a large breakfast and think about having dessert and tea, too. But this morning she had trouble concentrating.

She felt Jack's eyes upon her. When she'd look up to meet his gaze, Billie quickly lost herself in his smoldering expression, getting herself, all worked up again. Not sure if she was reading more into last night or not. She hardly touched her food.

After breakfast, Billie raced over to the Victorian; she could not wait to share her exciting experience with her best friend.

Katie opened the door to find her friend, almost vibrating, and ready to burst. "Wow – what's with you?"

Billie stepped inside, but was speechless.

"Okay, well, I was working in the basement this morning, come on down and we'll talk."

Billie was surprised with the progress Katie had made, giving the basement a complete make-over. Katie had really worked hard to make the space workable for her needs.

Photos of the tunnels in correlation to their location under Burlington were posted on boards. "That looks like a 3-D map!"

"That's kind of what I'm shooting for. After the explosion, all I know is the tunnels have collapsed! I hope I get another chance to explore the ones that haven't. I'd like to find the tunnel Sadie mentioned in her diary."

Katie, watched Billie, although she was physically there, mentally Billie was elsewhere. "You didn't hear a word I just said – did you?"

Billie's busy mind finally slowed enough to engage in the initial conversation she had needed to have. She took a breath, blew the blonde tendril out of her eyes, and then proceeded to fill Katie in on the incredible night she had with Jack.

Made in the USA
Monee, IL
18 March 2024

55137594R00154